# ENGAGING THE EARL

## AN ACCIDENTAL PEERS NOVEL

OTHER BOOKS BY DIANA QUINCY

THE ACCIDENTAL PEERS SERIES

Seducing Charlotte
Tempting Bella
Compromising Willa

# Engaging the Earl

An Accidental Peers Novel

## Diana Quincy

This book is a work of fiction. Names, characters, places, and incidents are the product of the author's imagination or are used fictitiously. Any resemblance to actual events, locales, or persons, living or dead, is coincidental.

Copyright © 2014 by Dora Mekouar. All rights reserved, including the right to reproduce, distribute, or transmit in any form or by any means. For information regarding subsidiary rights, please contact the Publisher.

Entangled Publishing, LLC
2614 South Timberline Road
Suite 109
Fort Collins, CO 80525
Visit our website at www.entangledpublishing.com.

Edited by Alethea Spiridon Hopson and Kate Fall
Cover design by Heidi Stryker

Manufactured in the United States of America

First Edition June 2014

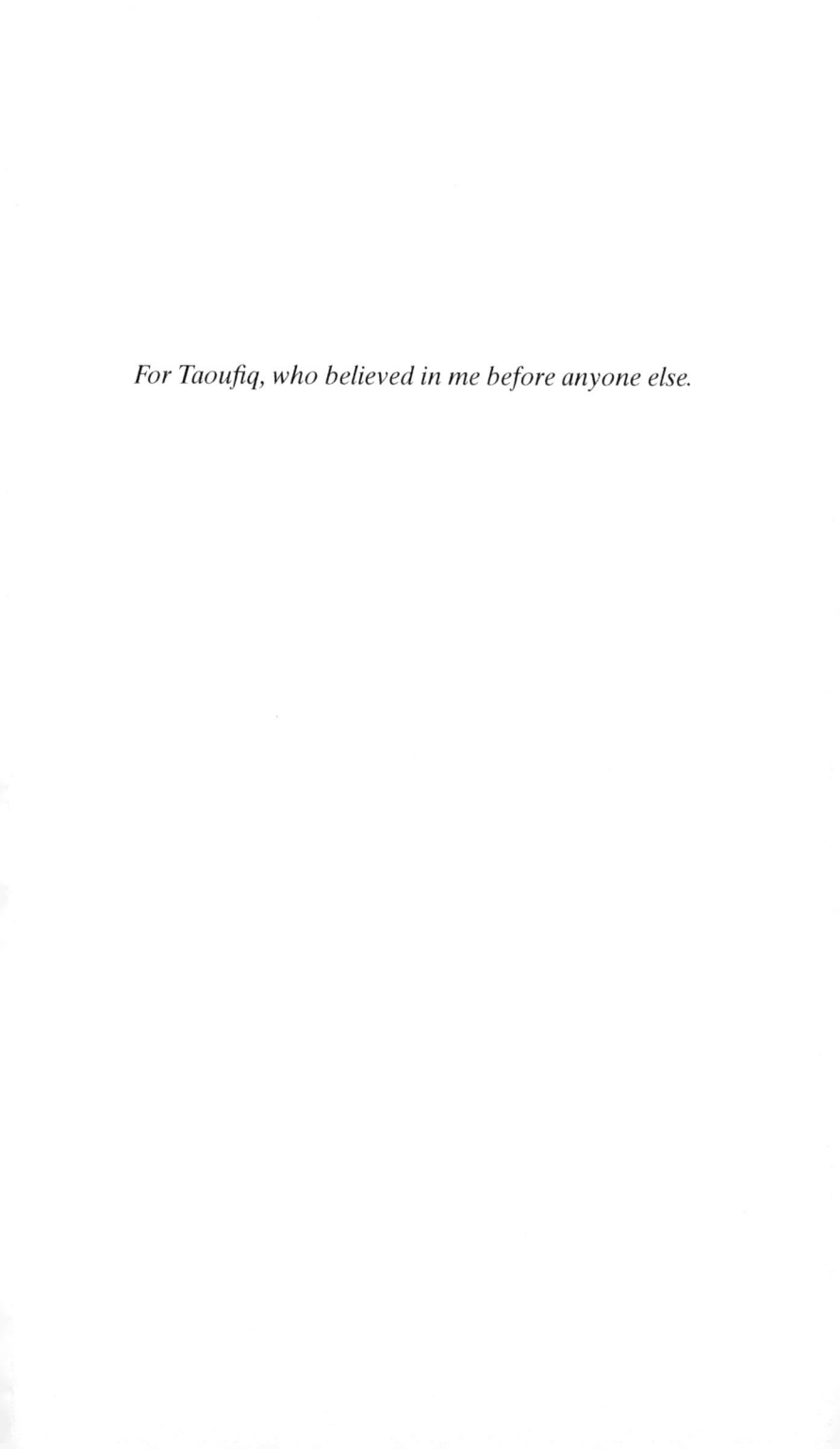

*For Taoufiq, who believed in me before anyone else.*

# Prologue

If she let him leave, he would be lost to her forever.

"You must ruin me." Lady Katherine Granville's clumsy fingers struggled to unlace the satin ribbons holding her snug bodice together. "It's the only way."

"Stop talking nonsense, Kitty." Edward Stanhope's large hands closed over hers, preventing Kat from exposing herself. His long musician's fingers inadvertently brushed the tender swell of white flesh above her bodice and the sensation burned its way through her blood. With a sharp intake of breath, he snatched his hand away and gently urged Kat toward the doors leading from the music room to the terrace.

"Your maid awaits." His tender hand brushed a tendril from her face. "You must return home before your father discovers you are not abed."

Panic welled. If she left now, untouched, Edward would be lost to her forever. She looked into the face of the only man she could ever imagine loving, into the slant of his velvet green eyes topped by dark amber curls. His rounded cheeks were still full in the way of a boy who'd not yet matured into the man he would become.

"No." She almost screamed the word. Grabbing Edward's arm before he could ease her away from him, she gulped air into her deflated lungs. "Let us go to Gretna Green. Now, before we are discovered."

Edward closed his eyes. When he opened them, pain shone in those clouded depths. "We cannot. There is no honor in that. Hush now, Kitty. You will wake the household."

They were all asleep above stairs, Edward's parents and brothers. She'd found Edward alone in his favorite place, the music room just off the terrace, where he'd returned after meeting with her father.

"It's the only path for us now that Father has rejected your suit. Surely you see that." She blinked against the pressure of tears building behind her eyes. "I hate him. He had no right."

"He has every right." His tone was firm. "The daughter of an earl should set her sights higher than a mere mister."

"You are the nephew of a marquess. Soon to be the brother of one."

"With no fortune to speak of."

"You are an artist." She thought of his passionate music compositions. "The most talented musician in all of England."

"Hardly that. I am a second son who dabbles in music. Your father is quite right to say I have no prospects."

"Don't speak of yourself that way." Fear squeezed her chest. "It isn't true."

"Of course it is. My brother will be a marquess, but what of me? I am one-and-twenty with no prospects beyond amusing myself with music."

"Those are my father's words, not yours."

"You are young, Kitty, just ten-and-six. You'll be a diamond of the first when you make your come-out. Titled gentleman will vie for your affection."

"Stop! Why are you talking like this?" He was like a wave pulling away from the beach and she was helpless to stop it. Her father's words from earlier in the evening reverberated in her head. *You will thank me one day, Katherine, once you've realized I stopped you from ruining your life.* Now, standing at the glass terrace doors, feeling the chill coming through them, she raised her voice. "I don't care if we awaken the entire household. I hope I do. Then I shall be compromised and we will have to marry."

The grim set of his features sent fear arrowing down her back. "You should know," he said evenly, "that I have purchased a commission. I leave in a fortnight."

"What?" Her pulse blasted in her ears. She couldn't possibly have heard him correctly. "You can't *leave*."

Firm hands gripped her shoulders. "I'm joining the fight on the Continent."

A horse stomping on her chest could not have been more painful. "You would give up on us?" she asked in a voice edged with growing hysteria. "You are leaving me?"

"I do this for us." His determined gaze bored into her. "I shall serve valiantly. Once I make something of myself, I'll come back for you."

She shook her head, disbelief crowding out all cogent thought. "What if you die?" Fear blanketed her. "What will become of me then?"

"I will not die." He cradled her face with his tapered artist's fingers, brushing away her tears with his thumb. "I have far too much to live for."

"No. Marry me now." She would lose him forever if he went off to war. Snatching his hand from her cheek, she pulled it to her breast with both hands. The tender little mound swelled under his touch, its peak straining upward. "Why would you go to war when we can go to Gretna Green?"

His breathing arrested and he recoiled as though he'd touched a venomous snake. But Kat held tight to his hand with both of hers. "You want this as much as I," she pleaded, tears flowing down her cheeks.

He cursed. Something she had never heard him do. His large hand closed over her breast and she almost sobbed in triumph. "Devil take it. You tempt me so." Groaning, he pulled her close, burying his face in her hair. She'd left it long and loose on purpose, knowing how much he appreciated the shiny, wheat-colored strands. He cupped her breast through her clothing, kneading it, his thumb running over the pearl tip with increasing urgency.

Elation and relief poured through her. She'd won. He'd not abandon her after all. She rubbed herself against his body, savoring the comforting angles of his form and the way his clean soap scent poured over her. The firm pressure of his arousal against the swell of her belly caused a thousand nerve endings to dance with anticipation.

"I'll always be with you, Kitty, always." His hand slipped inside her bodice to fondle her bare breast and her skin purred with delight. No one else could make her body feel these strange, wondrous sensations. She arched into him, her mouth seeking his, and he obliged, his warm soft lips coming down to rub against hers with gentle insistence. She floated into the pleasure of it, her legs feeling like ribbons streaming in a warm breeze.

Then his tongue was pushing into her willing mouth, stroking against hers in urgent motions. He'd never kissed her like this before: hot, wet and open mouthed. He tasted like life and breath. She would die without him. Her terror at his leaving gave way to the physical need ratcheting up in her body.

His warm lips trailed down her neck, pulling her bodice open, baring her to him. He licked the top swell of her breast before taking the point fully into his mouth. Her insides swelled with sensation and she trembled, feeling close to bursting.

"Promise me," he said as he mouthed her tender flesh.

"Mmmm, anything." She strained against him, her head thrown back, eyes closed. "I shall promise you anything."

"I couldn't bear for any other man to see you thus." His humid breath swept across the moist tip of her breast. "Promise you'll wait for me until I return."

*What?* Disbelief surged, followed by anger so intense it swamped her senses. Slamming her palms against his shoulders, she shoved him away with the full force of her fury.

The suddenness of the movement stunned him, knocking him from his kneeling position at her breast to flat on his arse, his hands braced behind him. His eyes widened. "What was that for?"

Glaring at him, she pulled her top closed to cover her

exposed flesh. "You still intend to go?"

"I thought you understood." He frowned, appearing genuinely befuddled. "I do this for us, for our future. Once I make something of myself, we shall marry."

"Why? I've told you I love you as you are." Tears stung her eyes again. Her body still hummed from his caresses. How could he even think of leaving her? "I don't have a care for what my father thinks."

His eyes changed—the green in them darkened, draining them almost of all color. He pushed up from the floor, his lanky legs moving in a swift motion. "But I do care," he said in a hard voice. "The earl's esteem is of importance to me. You will want your husband to have your father's respect."

"I can't believe you're deserting me." The answering surge of pain and fury almost incapacitated her. "How could you do this? How could you?" Trembling with anger, she stumbled toward the glass terrace door and pulled it open. A rush of icy winter air pelted her face. His pleading voice followed her into the frigid night.

"Promise me that you will wait for me. *Promise it.*"

She turned to take one last look at him. Her eyes moved over the dark amber curls, the turn of his boyish cheeks, the tall full body whose soft warmth she craved. Dread raked her skin. Her gentle Edward was no soldier. He would die on the battlefield.

"No." Her voice shook with feeling. "Mark me, Edward Stanhope. If you go, I will not wait for you. I swear to hate you until my dying day."

Color leached from his face. "You mustn't speak that way."

"If you leave, don't come back. I mean it." She stumbled

out the door and along the terrace to where Fanny, her maid, waited for her.

Fanny stepped out from the shadows with concern etched in her face. "We must hurry, my lady. His lordship will have my head if he finds you gone."

Numb with grief, she allowed Fanny to usher her away. A shattering noise pierced the air. Kat froze, listening to the crashing sounds of splintering wood coming from the music room she'd just left.

Fanny's eyes narrowed at the expression she saw on her mistress's face. "Come along, my lady. We must return."

Ignoring her, Kat pivoted and flew back to the windowed wall of the music room that ran along the terrace. She peered in from the shadows to see Edward holding his violin high above his head with both hands, bringing it down with all of his force, smashing it against the wall, pieces of the fine wood splintering everywhere. Shock paralyzed her. Nothing was dearer to Edward than his music. The violin, one of his most prized possessions, had come from Italy.

The look on his face caused her stomach to contract with alarm. Edward's countenance, always so kind and expressive, now beheld a storm of darkness, his eyes nothing more than hollow shadows.

Sucking in a shuddering breath, she forced herself to turn away.

# Chapter One

SIX YEARS LATER

"You'll make such a beautiful bride." Kat's mother dabbed a handkerchief at her eyes. "We thought this day would never come."

Kat swallowed hard to tap down the nerves fluttering in her stomach. This evening, after five glittering Seasons as the toast of the *ton*, she would finally become betrothed. She studied her reflection in the looking glass, smoothing her hands over the low-cut, pale yellow silk bodice that showcased her modest breasts and slender form to full advantage.

She smiled, pleased with what she saw, knowing many young debutantes would flock to their modiste for a dress similar to her betrothal gown. She'd been an incomparable all these years on the marriage mart, turning down numerous offers before agreeing at last to a match that made her father proud.

Her mother clasped her hands to her chest while looking over Kat's shoulder in the looking glass. "You look ravishing. Lord Sinclair will no doubt think so as well."

Her betrothed, Viscount Lawrence Sinclair—Laurie—would appreciate her in this gown. His warm blue eyes always gazed upon her with sincere affection and admiration. He loved her, Kat knew that for certain, and she returned his affection, although not in the same gut-wrenching way she had loved Edward. She shivered. Never that.

She closed her eyes as the unbidden memories stole over her. With a shuddering breath, she recalled the feel and taste of him, the sensation of his mouth on her skin that final night. A familiar sharp pain, almost paralyzing in its intensity, spiked up through her belly and into her chest. Forcing herself to breathe through the discomfort, she shoved thoughts of Edward out of her mind. She must not think of him. Especially not tonight of all evenings.

She'd been right to hate him for leaving her. He never returned after abandoning her six years ago. All he'd left her with was the pain. It slithered up on her, unbidden, at the most inopportune times, whether it was while calling on friends or walking in the park. The smallest things—listening to someone play the violin or the pianoforte, any mention of the war—triggered thoughts of him. No, she didn't love Laurie with that kind of painful intensity and was glad for it. She'd barely survived loving Edward. Losing him had scorched her soul. She would never love another person that way again.

"Come dear," said her mother. "Lord Sinclair will be waiting."

She focused on her image in the looking glass. Chin up.

Shoulders back. Smile in place. The woman in the looking glass didn't appear to have a care in the world. It was time to put Edward Stanhope in the past and move on to her future.

"As always, you are a vision." Laurie's warm smile floated up to greet her as she descended the grand staircase.

Reaching the bottom, Kat curtseyed, forcing gaiety into her countenance. "I have outdone myself, don't you think?" She twirled, showing off her gown.

He grinned. "It is perfection. All of the other girls will burst into tears and throw themselves to the ground when they see you in that gown."

She smiled, feeling a comforting surge of affection for Laurie. "Oh, that would be too much." She fluttered her lashes. "Perhaps just bursting into tears without swooning would suffice."

He laughed, his striking blue eyes glittering with approval. "I will certainly have my hands full with you, my future viscountess."

"No doubt," she said, taking his arm to join their families. Instead, Laurie pulled her into the nearest door, an empty salon that had not been opened for this evening's guests. "Laurie, what are you doing?" she asked as he shut the door and edged her up against it.

Sliding his hands around her waist, he drew her close. "I mean to have my arms full of you post haste."

She giggled and turned her face up to welcome his kiss. It was soft and gentle, with the respect and consideration a gentleman shows his intended, in a way that prompted a warm sensation to flutter down her body.

He broke the kiss, resting his forehead against hers. "I vow I will make you happy, Kat. On my honor, I will."

She smiled. "I know you will." She put a hand to his cheek. "You are such a dear."

He blew out a breath. "I would be more than that to you."

Feeling hedged in, she gave an uncomfortable laugh. "Of course, silly, you are to be my husband and we shall be deliriously happy."

His searching gaze prompted nerves to flutter in her belly. She slipped her hand behind his head and brought his lips to hers once more. She kissed with deliberate enthusiasm, determined to show Laurie how much she appreciated him. And to distract him from that probing gaze that sometimes seemed to see too much.

He held himself aloof at first so Kat parted her lips, allowing him a taste. He made a muffled sound and then his tongue swept inside her, stroking along her cheeks, touching her tongue. Not an unpleasant sensation. She focused her attention on the exploration, allowing it so he would be reassured how much she cared for him.

She tried to ignore the growing din beyond the door of the little parlor, the opening doors, footsteps against the marble floors, and chatter out in the public rooms. She indulged him a few more warm kisses—enough to convince him of her devotion—before pulling away.

"Our guests are here," she said in a gentle reminder that they should greet the arrivals.

His breaths came short and sharp. "I vow the wedding cannot come soon enough."

Disengaging from him, she gave a teasing smile. "But the anticipation is what makes a betrothal so amusing."

He tugged his waistcoat straight and offered his arm. "I would not describe it as amusing. More like tortuous." She took his arm, recognizing his frustration, but not really comprehending it.

Her father's Mayfair townhome had begun to fill. An invitation to the betrothal ball of Lady Katherine Granville, daughter of the Earl of Nugent, to the handsome and well-regarded Lawrence Sinclair, the fourth Viscount Sinclair, was the most coveted event of the Season. Despite her advanced age, Kat had remained the *ton*'s reigning beauty for several Seasons. And, in addition to his title, looks, and considerable purse, Laurie possessed an innate kindness and effortless charm that attracted people's regard. Both were shining lights in the *ton* and, to all outward appearances, an ideal couple.

She threw herself into enjoying the party. As usual, her dance card was full, but she'd taken care to reserve a waltz and the supper dance for her intended. When she wasn't on the dance floor, Kat held court with a group of merry friends, which included her cousin and best friend, Beatrice. Kat never took her popularity seriously, but she did enjoy it. It was certainly preferable to being a wallflower. During a break in the dancing, she wandered off to fetch lemonade with Bea, anxious for something to cool her since the air in the crowded ballroom had grown stiff and humid. Sipping her drink, Bea watched Laurie dance with Alexis Campbell, one of the girls from their set.

"He is very fine," Bea said. "You are most fortunate."

Kat sipped her lemonade, following Bea's gaze. Laurie

was well formed and uncommonly handsome with those flashing blue eyes and firm jaw. His hair, like hers, was a golden blond. The idea of being joined to him for all eternity made it difficult to breathe; her ribs felt as though a tight band was wrapped around them. Taking a deep inhale, she fought the suffocating sensation, and changed the subject. "Tell me, is your brother coming?"

A shadow crossed Bea's face. "Toby assured me he would attend, but he still finds crowds difficult."

She put a hand on Bea's arm. "Does he continue to be unwell?"

"That awful war has ruined him." Tears welled in Bea's eyes. "You know how he was before, so charming and amusing. Now he's touched in the head." She swiped a tear away. "Sometimes he is all that is agreeable, but then he experiences one of his episodes."

Kat's throat squeezed. Dear Toby had always brought a certain liveliness to any party, and hostesses had clamored to have him grace their tables. Yet, since returning from the war, he'd avoided most large gatherings. She squeezed her cousin's hand, feeling protective of both Bea and Toby. "Hush, Toby just needs time. You mustn't let anyone hear you suggest he has windmills in his head."

"You have the right of it, of course." Bea braved a shaky smile. "Toby is bringing a friend with him tonight, his commanding officer, I think he said."

A heavy weight compressed Kat's chest. Talk of the war always reminded her of Edward. It had affected Toby's mind, but at least her cousin had returned home at the end of the fighting. Edward hadn't bothered. She'd heard he'd gone off to India instead. He'd not only abandoned her, but he'd clearly forgotten she even existed. Kat forced her thoughts away from him, but the tiny shadow of pain in her gut, which had lingered since their final evening together, remained.

When the music came to an end, Kat watched Laurie approach with Lexie Campbell on his arm. She favored her intended with an incandescent smile.

Laurie's eyes lit with appreciation and he sketched a bow. "Lady Katherine, Miss Hobart, Miss Campbell. I am surrounded by all that is beautiful." He addressed them all, but his gaze remained fastened on Kat. "I am the most fortunate of men."

Lexie eyed Kat. "That is the most delightful gown I have ever seen. You sicken me, Kat. Do you never look poorly?"

Kat uttered a delighted laugh and smoothed a hand down her bodice. "Nonsense, your gown is lovely as well."

Lexie shot her a disbelieving look before casting her gaze around the crowded room. "They say the Earl of Randolph is in attendance. Have any of you seen him?"

Kat drew a blank. "Who is the Earl of Randolph?"

"Some war hero." Ever solicitous, Laurie took the empty lemonade glass from Kat to hand off to a footman. His manicured masculine fingers brushed hers, lingering far longer than necessary.

Kat's cheeks warmed when her gaze met Laurie's flirtatious one. "An earl who is a war hero?" she asked, looking away.

Beatrice's face lit up. "That must be the friend who is accompanying my brother this evening. Toby said the gentleman was granted an earldom for his brilliant service in the war."

"Is he a gentleman?" Kat's curiosity sparked. "I've never

heard of him."

"It is a new title," Laurie said. "I believe he recently arrived home from abroad to receive it."

"New or old, a title is a title." Lexie scanned the room. "His wife will be a countess. Perhaps I should set my sights on Randolph now that Kat has brought Laurie up to scratch."

Intrigued, Kat wanted to know more about the mysterious Lord Randolph, but Willis, the butler, alerted her that it was time for the announcement. She took the arm Laurie offered and sought out her father.

Her father, the Earl of Nugent, signaled for the orchestra to stop playing. The loud chattering came to a stop as the crowd directed its attention to where Kat's father stood on the elevated landing. With his shock of gray hair and trim form, Kat's father remained an attractive man in his forty-ninth year.

"Thank you for joining us on this auspicious occasion," he said. "It is with profound pleasure that we host this event this evening."

Kat and Laurie joined him on the landing. When she looked out into the sea of people, Kat's nerves erupted again and the insides of her hands started to itch. Suffocating heat pressed against her skin; the warmth of all these human bodies in the ballroom made the June evening air all the more stifling. As the thumping in her ears grew louder, Kat pasted a smile on her face and tried to focus, reminding herself to keep her chin up, her shoulders back.

Seeming to sense her distress, Laurie placed a comforting hand over hers where it rested on his arm and gave it a reassuring squeeze. She forced herself to breathe evenly. This was supposed to be a moment of triumph, of celebration. She looked into Laurie's smiling countenance and the robust warmth and love she saw in his expression buoyed her, quieting her nerves. She drew a deep breath, her smile becoming genuine, and focused on her father's words.

"This evening I announce the betrothal of my daughter, Lady Katherine Granville, to Viscount Lawrence Sinclair of Wiltshire." Footmen appeared with champagne flutes on trays. Laurie took two, handing one to Kat. There were murmurs of approval and sounds of clinking crystal as the guests received their champagne. Her father raised his glass. "To Sinclair and his future viscountess."

The guests raised their flutes, and calls of "here, here" and "well done" rang out. Kat smiled and raised her champagne to her lips. Looking over the crowd, her eye caught on a tall guest with dark amber hair standing near the back wall. Rivulets of awareness trickled through her.

She sipped the champagne, the bubbles fizzing in her mouth, the warmth sliding down her throat and heating her skin all over. She tilted her head to get a better glimpse of the man, but the guests crowding in front of him impeded her view. He moved toward the door. When he reached it, his back to her, the man stood quite alone. He was impossibly lean, his movements both precise and concise, as though he brooked no nonsense. When he paused at the door, a shiver tingled through Kat despite the warm June heat.

Then he turned around and their gazes met. And locked.

She recognized him at once, even at a distance — the sharp cut of his cheeks and the dark intensity of his eyes. He'd shorn his hair short, very close to his head and tremendously out of fashion. The amber curls were gone. He appeared much changed and yet achingly familiar.

*Edward.*

Her Edward.

The floor beneath her slippers wobbled, and somewhere a glass shattered. She realized she'd dropped her champagne. The crowd murmured and the heat in the room pressed in on her slick skin as she reeled into darkness, falling deeper and faster until strong arms surrounded her. Someone spoke to her, but she heard echoes that made no sense.

Blackness crept in and she gladly went to it.

# Chapter Two

"Are you certain you're well enough for a ride through the park?" A crease appeared between Laurie's brows. "You have not been yourself since the ball."

Avoiding his gaze, Kat forced a light tone. "Pish posh, it was just a touch of ague." She directed her horse onto Rotten Row, maneuvering through the crowd of riders on the trail.

Laurie's gelding inched up alongside her mare. He peered over at her. "But you fainted. That is not a sign of ague."

"You make me swoon, my lord." She tossed her head and flashed a flirtatious smile. "Most gentlemen would be delighted to have that effect on their lady."

Laurie's eyes twinkled and he laughed aloud, allowing the compliment to distract him, just as she intended. Desperate for an excuse to cut off the conversation, she shook the ribbons, commanding her mare into a trot. She fell into the rhythm of the horse's movements, the passing riders a blur of color.

It had been three days since she'd seen him. Edward. Agonizing hours full of uncertainty and turmoil that had left her physically ill. She'd taken to bed with a pounding headache and no appetite. When she tried to force food down, it tasted like foolscap and her stomach rebelled, threatening to expel the meal.

Her reaction mortified her. How could Edward still have this kind of effect on her? She'd reacted as though he'd abandoned her just yesterday instead of six endless years ago. She hadn't seen him since that glimpse at her betrothal ball. After her embarrassing collapse, Kat had insisted upon returning to the party. Shaken and out of sorts, she'd nonetheless been determined not to let Edward ruin her big night. Yet she couldn't help scanning the crowd for his face, desperate to look into those dark emerald eyes once more. Even now, she didn't dare ask anyone about him, fearing the questions her inquiry might raise in Laurie's mind. But what had Edward been doing there? Perhaps he'd come for her at last.

"Why, if it isn't Lady Incomparable." The familiar voice pulled Kat from her thoughts. She tugged on the ribbons, slowing and turning to see Tobias Hobart, Bea's brother, approaching. Toby's brown eyes moved to Laurie who had come to a stop next to Kat. "Sin, good to see you as always. I'm glad to have spotted you."

Laurie eyed Toby's attire with raised eyebrows. "With those breeches, we wouldn't have been able to miss you, Hobart."

Toby laughed, sweeping his top hat off while affecting a bow from atop his mount. A navy linen riding coat adorned with pewter buttons was Toby's only concession to the latest style of subdued colors for gentlemen. Beneath it, Kat's cousin wore a yellow-and-red striped waistcoat with yellow breeches tucked into gleaming black Hessians. A slight man, Toby had brushed his thinning reddish brown hair upwards to create an illusion of height.

He inclined his head, flashing a grin. "Lady Katherine, I do declare my cousin becomes more lovely each time my eyes behold her."

Delighted to see him, Kat smiled, taking in the pallor of his skin, so white that it looked almost transparent in the sun. Still, he seemed to be having a good day. She saw no evidence of the dark episodes his sister referred to. "Flatterer. I must take you to task for failing to attend my betrothal ball."

Toby's eyes widened. "But I did attend. A little tardy perhaps, but still in plenty of time to behold your rather dramatic swoon." He winked at Kat. "Very well done, my dear. It was in all of the broadsheets."

Her gut panged, but she forced a playful tone. "Never let it be said that I don't have a flair for the dramatic. I'm sorry I did not see you there."

"I attended with Lord Randolph." He looked past her. "Here he is now."

Kat's scalp tingled. She heard the snort of his stallion before she saw the man who rode him. The animal was huge and powerful, with substantial muscles and a shiny coat so black it glistened almost blue in the sun. The rider's black-clad thighs flexed as they hugged the animal. A trill of anticipation shooting down her spine, her perusal wandered further upward until she found herself gazing into Edward Stanhope's dark emerald eyes.

Their gazes caught, held, and the air left her lungs. Cool, distant eyes looked back into hers, containing nothing of the humanity and warmth that had once radiated from them. His eyes were full of vibrant green color, but empty of any spark. A burst of cold air gushed through her and she shivered.

"Ah, here is Rand now." Toby's words sounded very far away even though he was right beside to her. "Edward Stanhope, Earl of Randolph, may I present my cousin, the lovely Lady Katherine? And her betrothed, Viscount Lawrence Sinclair."

No trace of recognition penetrated Edward's impartial expression. "My lady." His eyes slid to Laurie. "Sinclair."

Laurie tipped his hat. "Hobart here speaks very highly of you," he said amiably. "Please call me Sin. All of my friends do."

A hollowed gauntness had replaced Edward's once-full face, his skin stretched taut across high cheekbones. "And I am Rand to my friends." He spoke in the sparse, gravelly voice of someone whose journey to this moment had been an arduous one. *Rand*. A name free of all embellishment fit this new version of Edward.

Laurie smiled. "May I offer my congratulations, Rand, on your newly bestowed title. Toby says you were his commanding officer."

"Indeed." Edward's frosty gaze was polite to the point of indifference. "Hobart served most honorably."

Toby waved away the compliment. "Yes, one does as one must, but conflict is so unpleasant." He wrinkled his nose. "Rand here is a genius in the art of war. An unparalleled strategist, in Wellie's words."

Interest sparked in Laurie's eyes. "You were with

Wellington, then?" he asked Edward.

"Indeed."

Edward had not spared Kat a glance beyond that first acknowledgement, but she could not tear her eyes away from him. This stranger bore little resemblance to the Edward she knew. He had no softness to him at all, he was all cut bone and sharp angles, taut muscle over long lean lines. He sat ramrod straight in the saddle, stiff and commanding.

Laurie leaned forward. "Were you at Waterloo?"

She barely registered Edward's answer—something about the Pyrenees—over the thudding in her ears.

"Don't you think so, Kat?"

She turned to find Laurie looking expectantly at her. "Don't you think so?" he repeated.

She twisted her mouth into the dazzling smile she often lobbed at Laurie when she didn't want him to guess her true thoughts. "Of course I do, my lord."

Laurie's smile broadened. "It is settled then. You and Hobart must join us for supper tomorrow evening, Randolph."

Fleeting surprise sparked in the impassive depths of Edward's eyes. Heat suffused Kat's face. Had she just encouraged Laurie to invite the earl to dinner?

Not knowing how she would bear it, she turned away, urging her mare back onto the path. "That would be lovely," she said with a flip of her head. "If it is all settled, let us not waste this glorious day, Laurie. You promised me a ride."

She heard the smile in Laurie's answer. "Excuse me, gentlemen. When a beauty such as Lady Kat beckons, how can I not answer? I am but a mere man."

• • •

Rand's shoulder ached like the devil.

He slid down in the bath, hoping the heat of the water would ease the persistent pain, as two footmen appeared with more steaming water.

Burgess, his valet, took the buckets and dismissed the footmen. "This should help ease your discomfort, my lord." He added one bucket full to the bath. The steam swirled around Rand's face and he inhaled deeply, savoring the humid heat.

"For God's sake, stop calling me that."

"Pardon, my lord?" Burgess went to retrieve the second bucket.

"Stop calling me 'my lord'. You know it grates on me."

Burgess poured the contents of the second bucket into Rand's bath. "Nonetheless, you are an earl now and it is my pleasure to serve you." He placed the empty buckets by the door. "The regent bestowed the title upon you. He also gifted you with this enormous town home. It would be an insult not to use the title allotted to you by God and king, or regent, as it were."

Rand made a disparaging sound and sank lower in the water. Burgess had faithfully followed him to hell and back. Through the battlefield, the chaos at Talavera, and then to India, back when Rand was merely the nephew of a marquess with no hope of acquiring a title. "No doubt it is your own elevation that thrills you."

"I don't deny it." Burgess moved to the dressing room and returned with Rand's evening wear for Sinclair's dinner.

"I am overjoyed to find myself in service to an earl who is a celebrated war hero. Although my wages have yet to reflect that."

Rand barked a laugh. "Grasping sot. We both know you've been overly compensated for years. I could employ two of Mayfair's finest valets for the same coin I give you."

Burgess pressed his lips together. "If you say so, my lord."

"I do." Eyeing the clothes his valet laid out for him, Rand felt the beginnings of a headache twitch behind his left eye. Why the devil had he agreed to attend? "Damnation. I should send my regrets. The last thing I am in the mood for is to spend the evening with Sinclair and his ilk."

"But that is your ilk now." Burgess brushed the deep green tailcoat. "And Viscount Sinclair is top *ton*. They say his lady is the incomparable of the decade."

Savage emotion clawed his insides at the mention of Kitty. "The decade? That is overdoing it, even for you, Burgess."

"She has reigned for many years, long past when others would be considered on the shelf."

He gritted his teeth against the turmoil of feeling that rose in his chest. Kitty the Incomparable. It wasn't hard to believe. If anything, she'd grown even more winsome since he'd last seen her. She'd lost the coltish awkwardness of youth, developing into a true beauty with vivid sapphire eyes that were difficult to look away from. Her betrothal gown had left little to the imagination, showcasing her lithe, petite form, creamy shoulders, and the tender little globes he'd once had the pleasure of tasting. The thought of Sinclair doing the same, of having Kitty in his bed, made his head pound. His hand slammed down into the water, sloshing the liquid out of the tub.

"What was that for?"

Rand looked at his valet. "Pardon?"

"Is there a reason you are making a mess of the floor?"

"Damn your impudence, man." He eyed the dark green tailcoat. "Is that what I'm wearing?"

Burgess stopped folding cravats and cocked an eyebrow at Rand, a glimmer of hope shone in his eyes. Rand didn't give a whit about clothes. Never had. "You are interested in your clothing this evening?"

"Hardly."

Burgess resumed his task. "I would be overjoyed if you were finally to take an interest in your attire. After all, an earl should dress with certain—" A wet washing cloth sailed through the air, landing with a slapping thud near Burgess' feet, splashing water on his immaculately shined shoes.

"Shut up with all of this earl talk. Get out so I can take my bath in peace."

Burgess pressed his lips together, affecting an offended expression as he quit the chamber, closing the door behind him.

Rand rubbed his shoulder and thought of the lady who would never belong to him again. He'd fully intended to come back for Kitty once he'd made something of himself, and he had been well on his way until Talavera destroyed his well-laid plans. Ironically, the battle that had made his reputation had also obliterated his chance at happiness. Now, he was barely fit to be in society, much less to be Kitty's husband.

His desire to protect her was the reason he'd absented

himself from England all of these years. If they'd been on the same continent, nothing could have stopped him from claiming her. He'd have stayed in India forever had the regent not essentially commanded his return to England by bestowing this wretched title upon him. Now the responsibilities of the earldom demanded his continued presence, not only in the House of Lords, but there were vast properties and tenants to look after.

There was no escape.

. . .

Kat arrived at Laurie's Curzon street townhome a little later than the appointed time. She'd been abed all day with a pounding migraine that was no doubt brought on by the thought of seeing Edward again. She despised herself for being so weak.

Greeting her at the door, Laurie took her wrap and handed it off to the hovering footman. "Late as usual, I see. Just in time to make a grand entrance."

She summoned a lustrous smile. "You know me so well."

"Sometimes I wonder about that," he said in that casual way of his. She darted him a look, but let the comment pass since she was too busy fixating on the prospect of being in close quarters with Edward. "You look marvelous as usual. That color suits you."

"Do you approve?" She gazed down at her pale gold silk gown with delicate ruffles across her bosom and tassels of the same shade adorning the hem. "It was just delivered this afternoon."

"I suspect all will clamor to their modistes on the

morrow to imitate you."

They entered the parlor where guests had gathered before supper. It was a small group, a dozen or so from their usual set, young Corinthians and the beauties, ladies, and heiresses they'd recently taken to wife. He guided her toward Bea, who stood with Toby and Lexie.

She felt a surge of relief to see no sign of Edward. "Has Lord Randolph sent his regrets?"

"No, in fact he asked to bring a friend."

"A friend?"

"Elena, the Maid of Malagon," Toby answered when they reached him. "She's in London to receive a commendation from the prince regent for her valor during the war."

"A recognition for valor?" Jealousy twisted in her chest at the thought of Edward escorting a lady. "For a female?"

"Not just any female," Toby said. "Elena is most remarkable. She fought off the French and single-handedly saved her village."

"Single-handedly?" Laurie asked. "How so?"

"The Spanish suffered heavy casualties and abandoned their posts. Elena loaded a cannon and lit the fuse herself."

"No!" Disbelief etched Bea's face.

"She shredded a wave of attackers just as they descended upon her."

Kat felt lightheaded. "Goodness."

"Hobart." Laurie spoke in a warning tone. "I'll remind you there are ladies present."

Bea's eyes lit up. "It's quite all right, Laurie. How splendid she is! What happened after that, Toby?"

With an apologetic glance at Laurie, Toby continued. "The sight of a lone woman manning the cannons on the rooftop inspired the fleeing Spanish troops to return. They held off the French and lived to fight another day."

"What a brave creature." Bea's face glowed with admiration. "She's quite the hero."

"I hardly think behaving like a man is heroic." Laurie frowned. "Unspeakable things could have happened had the French captured her."

The light in Toby's eyes dimmed. "Unspeakable things happen all the time in war."

The sound of the butler's voice announcing the new arrivals interrupted their discussion. "The Earl of Randolph and Miss Elena Márquez-Navarro."

"Goodness." Lexie stared at the couple. "She's an Amazon."

The statuesque woman on Edward's arm *was* stunningly tall for a female. Wearing a scarlet gown that showcased an overabundance of feminine curves, she surveyed the room with somnolent dark eyes set against a smooth café au lait complexion. Kat's stomach curled.

"What a handsome woman. Don't you think?" Bea nudged her arm. "Are you well? You look pale."

"Of course, I'm supremely well." She darted a glance at Laurie to make certain he hadn't noticed her discomposure. She needn't have worried. Her betrothed's eyes were fixed on Edward's Amazon. "Laurie," she said, irritation edging her voice. "Perhaps we should greet them."

The sound of her voice startled his attention away from the Maid of Malagon. "Indeed we should." He offered her his arm.

As they stepped away, a smirk appeared on Lexie's face. "It looks like you aren't the only sensation here this evening, Kat." Her voice trailed after them. "You'll have to share some of the glory with the Spanish senorita." Kat ignored Lexi because her attention remained fixed on the Amazon and Edward, who turned his attention to them on their approach.

"Well met, Rand," Laurie said in greeting.

Edward's distant gaze brushed over her before landing squarely on Laurie. "Sinclair. Lady Katherine. Allow me to make known Senorita Márquez-Navarro."

Laurie bowed. "Ma'am, it is a pleasure to welcome you to London."

Dark, glistening eyes fastened on Laurie. "Thank you, my lord." A Spanish lilt coated her husky voice. "I am anxious to become more intimately acquainted with my English friends."

From the familiar manner in which her arm rested on Edward's, as well as the close proximity of their bodies, Kat surmised the Amazon was already very well acquainted with at least one newly invested English earl.

Elena turned her attention to Kat. "Your viscountess is ravishing, Lord Sinclair." The unexpected compliment took Kat by surprise.

"Lady Katherine is my affianced bride." Laurie brought Kat's hand to his lips. "She cannot become my viscountess soon enough for my taste."

"Do you live here with Lord Sinclair?" she asked Kat.

She inhaled sharply at the suggested indecency. "Most assuredly not."

Laurie's jaw braced. "It is not the English way."

Edward turned to the Amazon. "Elena, shall I bring you a drink?" He was certainly on familiar terms with the senorita, addressing her by her given name.

"I think perhaps Lord Sinclair should accompany me and explain the ways of the English to a Spanish peasant such as I."

"Of course." Ever the gentleman, Laurie would not refuse, even though Kat detected his distaste for the task. Cloaking his curtness in polite tones, he offered his arm. "It would be my pleasure."

As he led the Maid of Malagon away, Kat asked, "Is she truly a peasant?" It was unheard of for a peasant to grace noble homes—unless as a servant who used the back entrance.

Edward turned a sharp gaze on her. "Her family is minor gentry. However, whatever her rank, she is as valiant and brave a woman as I have ever had the honor of knowing."

Jealously coiling deep in her belly, she turned to pluck a single flower from a nearby arrangement to hide her reaction. "She is quite handsome."

"Yes. Elena is as beautiful on the inside as she is on the outside," he said. "My felicitations, by the way, on your recent betrothal."

The sudden change in topic took her off guard. "Um... thank you."

"You and Sinclair seem eminently suited."

He thought she and Laurie suited? She trembled with outrage and hurt at his cold treatment of her, as though they were long-ago acquaintances and nothing more. "Yes, we are very well suited. I am devoted to him as I have been to no other man."

"I am glad to hear it," he said, his tone serious. "That is as it should be."

It was all she could do not to upend the entire vase of flowers over his head. He acted as if there had never been anything of consequence between them. "Yes, well, if you will excuse me, I should like to go and find my betrothed. He doesn't care to be without me for any length of time." Without waiting for his response, she turned and marched away, her fingers clutching her skirt as she passed the ornate arrangement of flowers.

...

She looked like a goddess.

Kitty wore a pale gold gown that spun around her delicate frame, a confection of gossamer fabric that made her appear angelic. She sat playing the pianoforte with a group gathered around her, like moths drawn to an irresistible source of light. When she hit the wrong key, sending an awkward note screeching through the air, she just laughed and made a light comment, the blue in her eyes sparkling. Sinclair sat by her side, clearly besotted, his gaze rarely leaving the angel beside him.

"She's a vision, is she not?" Toby broke into Rand's thoughts.

"Indeed." His shoulder throbbed. London's damp heat infiltrated the once-shattered bones that had somehow managed to fuse haphazardly back together.

Toby took a drink from a passing footman. "They call them the golden couple, on account of their coloring." Rand grunted some noncommittal response. They were similar in appearance, Kitty and her intended. Perfectly matched with blue eyes and hair the color of sunlight, one could mistake them for brother and sister. He reached for a drink from the footman, throwing it back in one large swallow.

Still seated at the pianoforte, Kitty turned to Sinclair with a radiant smile. The force of it left the man looking love struck as he stood to offer her his arm. She rose and took it, saying something in a laughing manner to the friends gathered around her. Rand watched the golden couple circulate, Sinclair's hand settled possessively at Kitty's waist.

He made an effort to keep a bland tone. "Why has she not married before now?"

Toby bottomed out his glass. "She's had many offers. I can assure you of that." He gestured toward Kitty. "Look at her. She enjoys her perch at the top. Perhaps she was loath to relinquish it too soon. Who could blame her?"

Watching Kitty stroll among the guests, still engrossed in laughing conversation with Sinclair, made a dark heat rise in his chest. "How did he win her?"

"He is considered quite eligible. Amiable, titled, and wealthy." They watched as Sinclair steered Kitty in their direction. "The women flock to him."

"It's a love match, then?"

Toby shrugged. "So it is said. Here they come, you can ask them yourself."

"I say, Rand," Sinclair said as they approached, "the word is that you're quite the accomplished musician. Would you care to take a turn at the pianoforte? I daresay we'd all enjoy hearing you."

Rand stiffened. "I fear you've been misinformed. I do not play." Ignoring Kitty's stunned expression, he set his empty glass on a nearby surface. "If you will excuse me."

He turned away, eager to escape her and Sinclair,

the growing crowd, and old memories that were best left unexhumed.

...

Kat stole out onto the terrace, and forced the summer air in and out of her lungs. Why had he come? She'd felt his dark eyes tracking her all evening and she'd obliged him with the performance of her life—laughing gaily with her friends, engrossing herself in conversation with Laurie, pretending Edward didn't exist. Acting as though her insides weren't being ripped apart.

Blast him for showing up and ruining everything, for destroying what little happiness she'd pieced together for herself after his abandonment. And now he was back and it certainly wasn't for the purpose of claiming her. He acted as if he barely remembered her.

"Are you escaping the crowd as well?" She recognized the voice right away. It was the same, yet distinctly different—the roughened voice of the stranger who'd returned, not the boy who'd left her. He stood a few feet away from her, lean hips resting against the balustrade, his arms and legs crossed.

"Why did you lie in there? Why did you tell Laurie you don't play the pianoforte?" No one played more beautifully—more soulfully—than Edward. It was an integral part of who he was as a man.

"It was no lie. I haven't played in years."

"How can that be?" She sucked in a shocked breath. She couldn't imagine him not playing. Edward without his music was unfathomable. "Music is part of your soul."

"I suppose I left that part of my soul on the battlefield."

The torchlight danced across the stony set of his features. His nose had changed. No longer well molded and straight, it now had a subtle bend to it, which contributed to his new, harsher appearance.

"What happened to your nose?"

Surprise flitted across his dark eyes. He ran a long finger over the bridge of his nose. "It met with the back end of a bayonet."

Dear God. Someone had broken his nose. "Did it hurt?"

"It was the least of my problems. I hardly noted it at the time."

"Why not?" Even as she asked, Kat wondered how they could be having this conversation. As though six weeks had passed since they'd last met, rather than six years.

"I was preoccupied with trying to stay alive."

Alarm filtered through her. "You were badly injured?"

Shadows dropped along the length of his face, making it hard for Kat to see his reaction. "I was shot in the shoulder and the leg, although I didn't know it at the time."

Regret clawed her insides. He'd been hurt, perhaps very badly, and she hadn't known. Over the years, desperate for news of him, she'd secretly followed Edward's war exploits as closely as possible. But with her limited resources, gleaning what little she could from newspapers and general chatter at parties, she'd never heard he'd suffered an injury. Had she been dancing in a ballroom while he'd lain wounded and alone somewhere on a faraway battlefield?

Tears filled her eyes. His stern brows drew together and he pushed away from the balustrade to come and stand before her. He smelled of shaving soap and brandy. Kat raked his face, hungrily taking in all of the details. He was only eight-and-twenty, but looked much older. Deep lines creased his forehead and his hairline was higher than it had been six years ago. Dark shadows emphasized the hollows in his cheeks. "What is this, Kitty?"

*Kitty.* No one else had ever called her that. A single tear ran down her cheek. He used a callused thumb to sweep it away in a gentle motion, leaving a trail of delicious agony in its wake. "You left me. I thought you'd never come back."

"You told me not to." His finger traced the edge of her face.

"You never wrote."

"As an unrelated male, I could hardly correspond with an unwed gentlewoman."

"You could have found a way." She swallowed around the lump in her throat. "If you had cared enough."

"Perhaps I could have," he agreed. "But it was for the better that I did not."

Her chest ached. "For the better? How can you say that?"

"I'm told Sinclair is the best of men. You've done very well for yourself."

"That's it?" Anger overtook the yawning pain in her chest. "After all these years, that's all you have to say?"

"There is nothing else left to remark upon. I'm happy for you, Kitty." The words were quiet. "Truly I am."

"There you are, Kat!" Lexie stood just outside the open terrace doors, her thin frame silhouetted by the glittering ballroom backdrop. "I see I am not the only person in need of some air." Her gaze moved to Edward. "Oh, you are not alone." She gave a coquettish tilt of her head. "My lord, I did not see you there. Won't you introduce us, Kat?"

Kat cleared her throat. "Allow me to make known Miss Alexis Campbell. Lexie, this is Ed…uh…the Earl of Randolph."

Edward bowed. "Miss Campbell, a pleasure."

Lexie curtseyed prettily. "My lord, what an honor it is to meet a great war hero." She cut a gaze to Kat and then back again to Edward. "I wasn't aware that you two knew each other."

They both responded at the same time.

"We don't," Kat said.

"We are old friends," he answered.

"What an intriguing puzzle." Lexie's gray eyes lit with interest. "Which is it? Old friends or strangers?"

"It is both." He favored Lexie with a charming smile, one that brightened his face, unleashing a deliberate potent flash of magnetism that made Kat's heart lurch. "We knew each other as children and are just now renewing our acquaintance."

Clearly impacted by Edward's show of charm, Lexie fluttered her lashes at him. "Oh, I see."

Laurie appeared in the doorway behind her. "There you are, my dear." He caught sight of Edward. "Oh, hullo Randolph."

"Sinclair."

Laurie moved to Kat's side and offered his arm. "Sorry to steal my betrothed away, but this is my dance."

"Not at all." Edward turned to Lexie. "Miss Campbell, perhaps you would honor me with a turn."

Lexie preened. "I seem to have room on my dance card."

Something heated and unpleasant simmered in Kat's belly. "I thought you said your card was full."

Lexie shot her a look of surprise. She pulled at the dance card attached to her wrist and crossed out one of the names written there. "No longer." She took Edward's arm. "Shall we go, my lord?"

# Chapter Three

Elena closed her eyes and took a deep inhale on the cheroot, clearly relishing the taste. "Your Lord Sinclair," she mused on her exhale. "I think he would not approve of a lady smoking, *verdad*?"

"*Verdad*." Rand sat with an arm slung over the side of the sofa, a glass of brandy dangling from his fingertips. They were ensconced in the cozy upstairs sitting room of the house she'd rented during her brief stay in town to receive her commendation from the prince regent. "You, *carida*, are going to shock all of the English before your visit here is over."

Next to him, she smiled and tucked her long legs beneath her, adjusting so that she sat facing him.

Handing over the cheroot, Elena studied him. "What is it, *carido*?"

"Nothing. *Nada*." He took a deep drag. "It is just strange to be back home after all of these years."

"I think it is your senorita."

"She is not my lady. Kitty is betrothed to Sinclair."

"And you do not like it, no?"

His gut twisted, but he forced a shrug. "He seems a decent sort."

She reached for the cheroot. "You should pursue her. She is not yet married."

"Are you that anxious to be rid of me?"

"I think you grow bored with me."

He ran a light hand over her shoulder. "You could never bore me."

"Me, perhaps not." Puffing on the cheroot, she gestured in the general direction of her bed chamber. "But we are finished with each other in that way."

Rand sighed, unwilling to refute the truth of it. He and Elena never lied to each other. Although she was a beautiful woman who he admired, the thought of bedding Elena no longer appealed as it once had. His diminished interest followed a familiar pattern; he never stayed with any woman for long. "Do I owe you an apology, my love?"

"No, we were always *compadres* first, *verdad*? Lying together was just a pleasurable pastime for both of us."

"Very pleasurable," he said gently.

She shooed aside the platitude. "You must pursue your lady."

"It is too late." He placed his emptied glass on the side table, grimacing at the pain that shot through his shoulder. "I have nothing to offer her."

She made a dismissive sound. "Ridiculous."

"It's true. The boy who left her no longer exists." He rubbed his shoulder. "And the man who returned is…

complicated."

"Have you experienced more bouts?"

He shook his head. "No, but one never knows when I will experience another." He looked at her with stark eyes, feeling dead inside. "It's been that way since Talavera."

Compassion etched her face. He knew she understood his demons; Elena had faced them herself. "We can never forget, *mi amor*, not really. But that is not an excuse to stop living. We must create the future we desire."

Shaking off the melancholy, he asked, "What is it that you want, Elena?"

She shrugged. "To do as I please. After my visit here, once your prince has bestowed my award, I shall return home to my people and live as I choose."

"Coming close to death certainly does change how one sees life," he mused. "Society's dictates no longer seem so important." He rose to go. "I cannot imagine you living any other way."

She watched as he reached for his coat. "If you prefer not to be alone, you are welcome to stay in my guest chamber."

"I don't think so." Pulling on his coat, he bent to brush a kiss atop her head. "If these past few weeks aren't proof of my malady, then I don't know what is. No sane man would reject the pleasures offered by the most beautiful woman in Spain."

"You most assuredly have a malady, but it has nothing to do with me," she said. "It has to do with a certain senorita who looks like an angel and has promised herself to another."

"Balderdash."

"And when you decide to rejoin the living," she continued as though he hadn't spoken, "I suspect she will be yours for the taking."

"She was never meant to be mine," he said gruffly against the weight pressing on his chest. "It was my mistake to have ever thought otherwise."

...

"The last straggler arrives." Rand and his eldest brother, Arthur, the Marquess of Camryn, watched their younger brother make his way across the grass toward them.

"You're late," Cam said when Will reached them.

Rand took amused note of Will's rumpled appearance and unruly short golden curls. "I see you didn't bother to dress for the occasion."

A slight frown marred Will's forehead. "We're unlikely to encounter anyone here."

True enough. Perhaps mindful of Rand's preference for avoiding crowds, Cam had tactfully suggested they walk in Kensington Gardens. Unlike Hyde Park, the gardens rarely drew the hordes—and certainly not the fashionable set.

"Sorry for the delay. I was observing a dissection with Doctor Drummond," Will explained as though it were the most natural thing in the world.

Cam shook his head. "Rather morbid, don't you think, even for you?"

"It's not a hobby as you well know." Will focused on his fingers, peeling away the dried paint. "The greater my understanding of the anatomy and musculature of the human body, the more realistically I can capture it on canvas."

"*Human* anatomy?" Rand grimaced. "Good Lord. What happened to horses?"

"I've recently progressed to the human form." They set off walking. "I think you would find Drummond interesting, Rand."

"I have no desire to examine the innards of human cadavers."

"He's very interested in injuries suffered by returning soldiers."

The war not being a subject Rand cared to discuss, he picked up the pace, pulling a fresh surge of air into his lungs. "I assure you, I am not interested in discussing my injury with anyone. And certainly not with this Drummond fellow. Besides, I thought corpses were more to his taste."

"I doubt he would be interested in your shoulder," Will said. "He's enthralled with nostalgia in general and wind contusions in particular."

A chill rocketed down Rand's spine. There was no way Will, or any of his brothers, could know about his malady, a condition battlefield surgeons had taken to calling nostalgia after witnessing odd behavior in soldiers. "And why would that be of interest to me?"

Will plucked a satisfyingly large chip of paint off the back of his hand and held it up for his own inspection. "As a commander in the field, I assumed you would have witnessed these conditions in your soldiers and would naturally have an interest in them."

The tension in Rand's shoulders eased. "Indeed. But let us leave that discussion for another time, shall we? Catch me up on your news."

Fortunately, Will was happy to converse about his work. The trio walked the gardens at a brisk pace until Will took his leave to keep an appointment.

After his departure, Rand turned to Cam. "Have you had any word from Sebastian?" Their brother, Sebastian, had been ensconced in the country with his wife, the Duchess of Traherne, following the birth of their third child.

"They returned to Town yesterday," Cam said. "But he had other matters to attend to today."

Rand pushed a branch out of their way as they traversed a rocky patch of hill. "Three children in three years. Our brother isn't one to waste time."

"What about you?" Cam asked. "A newly minted earl will have all of the marriage-minded mamas in raptures."

"My ever-present scowl has kept me safe from them thus far."

"Charlotte and I saw you at Lady Katherine's betrothal party, but you departed before greeting us."

"I didn't care for the crush."

"Was it difficult seeing her again?" Cam spoke in careful tones. He alone of the brothers knew the full extent of Rand's early involvement with Kitty.

He continued looking straight ahead as they walked. "I'm told Sinclair is honorable."

"He is."

"Then it is settled. The past is the past."

"True," said Cam in an idle tone. "Unless it isn't."

"I do not care to speak of it."

"You almost got yourself killed in that bloody war in order to prove yourself worthy of her. You're an earl now, higher even than her betrothed. If you want her, go and claim her."

"It isn't that simple."

"You put yourself through hell and back for that

female." Cam ran a hand over his head, ruffling his amber mane, which never appeared tidy. "Do you now intend to let her marry another?"

"It was a boyish infatuation that I have long since grown out of." It was a blatant lie, but he could never subject Kitty to a life with him; he'd never allow her to know the darkness that possessed him now. "If I still wanted the lady, do you think I would have gone to India after I resigned my commission?"

Cam shook his head. "I've never understood your decision to be away from England for so long."

"It isn't so very complicated. There was a fortune to be made in India and being the second son behooved me to seek it. That's quite enough about me. How is Charlotte?"

"Exceedingly well." Cam's choice of a wife had surprised him. His brother's tastes had always run to voluptuous beauties. Rand had met Charlotte for the first time a few weeks ago. With her willowy form and even features, the marchioness was nothing like Cam's former paramours, yet his brother had never seemed happier. "She seems to suit you."

Cam's eyes shined. "She does indeed. In every way."

Cam allowed him to direct the conversation away from Kitty and they spent the rest of the time discussing other matters as normal people might. Although Rand rarely felt completely normal anymore. When they neared Round Pond, Cam took his leave to join his wife and children for luncheon. Declining an invitation to join him, Rand continued on. Trotting down a slight slope, he inhaled the outdoor air and fragrant flowers, grateful they'd come upon so few people on their walk. Although he could manage crowds most of the time, they still made him uneasy.

A flutter of birds exploded in front of him, bursting out of a low tree so suddenly that his heart jumped and his shoulders tightened. His chest seized and a kernel of panic sprouted deep within him. Struggling to keep it at bay, he attempted to regulate his breaths, deep inhales that came far too quickly.

Lightheaded, he staggered toward the nearest tree and bent over, bracing his palms on his knees. He struggled to slow the fast, sharp pounding in his chest as perspiration blurred his vision. He blinked repeatedly, determined to drive away the blackness hovering at the edges of his mind. Standing upright again, he leaned against the tree and slid to a sitting position, the solid trunk protecting his back. Looking outward, the pond was a blue-brown blur while the green of the trees were indistinguishable dots of color.

Memories that were best left forgotten pulled at his mind. Pain ripped through his shoulder and a volley of gunshots ricocheted in his head. Drowning in despair and terror, he tried to shove them away, to rein his thoughts back into control. *This isn't real. This isn't happening. You are no longer on the battlefield.* The acrid scent of blood and decaying bodies filled his nostrils, making him wretch. Grief tunneled through him, plunging him into darkness and he gave into it, knowing once again that his battle for sanity was lost.

Something furry, wet, and foul-smelling assaulted him, followed by an enthusiastic yelp. Rand blinked at the brown blob, trying to remember where he was. He became aware of the grass, soft and moist beneath him, and realized he was curled up on the ground. As he struggled into a seated position against the tree, the brown blob began to take the shape of a very mangy-looking—and obviously very poorly trained—canine. The creature lapped at his face with such enthusiasm, it likely hadn't eaten in a while. And from the way it smelled, it hadn't bathed in at least twice as long.

He tilted his face upward to avoid all of that slobbering, but the creature licked his chin just as heartily. He took several deep breaths to try to calm his jittery body as the grim realization washed over him. Devil take it. He'd had another episode, and there was no telling how long this one had lasted. Thank God no one had been around to witness it other than this mangy whelp.

The odd-looking creature had the square jaw and drooped jowls of a pointer, but was as fluffy as a Pomeranian. Rand ran a hand down its matted fur, his heart rate and inhalations easing to a more settled pattern as he worked his hands through the animal's damp coat, massaging its body. The creature's presence proved surprisingly calming. They sat under the tree together for several minutes until Rand began to feel in control of himself once again.

"And who might you be?" he asked the dog after a while, running both hands up and down the animal's neck. The wiggly canine emitted a cheerful little bark, nudging into Rand's hands. "You like that, do you?" He smiled, treating the dog to a more vigorous, playful petting.

"Vera, you naughty creature." A strident female voice called out from across the way. "Come away from there. Assaulting strangers in the park, whatever will I do with you?"

*No. It couldn't be.* But it was. There was no mistaking that melodious voice with an underlying note of strength. As she came up on him at a determined stride, Rand looked up into breathtakingly familiar blue eyes.

...

Edward Stanhope was just about the last person Kat expected to encounter beside Round Pond, sitting under a tree petting her animal.

Far from his usual stiff-spined stance, he appeared relaxed—the lines of his shoulders and lean body falling into an easy posture—as he vigorously petted the creature. He looked a little pale, almost haggard, but the stern countenance that belonged to this new version of Edward eased as he murmured something to the dog.

He looked up at her with a smile in his dark emerald eyes that made her stomach flip. "This messy-looking creature can't possibly belong to you."

"She does indeed. I have been looking for her for forever. She ran off a half-hour ago. Vera, come." But the blasted creature just rolled over on her back with her paws in the air, her panting smile inviting him to scratch her belly. "And why can't she possibly belong to me?"

"I'd expect an incomparable such as Lady Kat to own the best-groomed canine in town." He smiled down at the dog. "Not a hopelessly mangy whelp like this fellow."

"Now you've gone and insulted a lady."

He looked up quickly. "I meant no insult to you."

"Not me," she said, amusement in her voice. "That messy

*fellow* is female."

He grinned at her and light came into his eyes. For a moment they fell back six years—to when they had talked easily and enjoyed each other's humor. "Ah, then I must offer my apologies." He favored Vera with a doubtful look. "Although, while she may be female, she does not appear to be a lady."

She looked at Vera, sprawled out on her back with her loose hanging tongue, her fur matted and wet. The dog looked utterly relaxed, half asleep actually, thanks no doubt to Edward's ministering hands on her belly. "I'm afraid you have caught her at her worst. She decided to take a dip in the pond."

He came to his feet, as if belatedly realizing he'd been sitting in the presence of a lady. "That explains the malodorous scent."

He was dressed in a casual manner which still retained a certain military precision. The form-fitting nature of his clothing emphasized how lean he'd become. His chocolate jacket was slightly wrinkled from his crouched stance against the tree, and his mushroom-colored breeches bore traces of grass and twigs.

Vera remained on her back, watching Edward with one open eye, clearly hoping he'd return to the task of scratching her belly. After a moment, she appeared to give up because she rolled over onto her legs and sauntered over to press her nose against Kat's thigh.

She petted the dog's damp, furry head. "Suddenly Vera recalls that she belongs to me."

"Vera, is it? What breed is she?"

"No one really knows. We're not certain how my father's

Pomeranian came to be *enceinte* at the country estate." Her face warmed to be discussing breeding with him.

Turning his attention back to Vera, he didn't appear to notice her discomfort. "She has the look of a pointer to her. Perhaps her mother had a clandestine meeting with a neighbor's hunting dog."

"A female of easy virtue." She arched a brow after Vera, who wandered away, distracted by a fluttering butterfly. "Thereby proving your point that Vera is no lady."

He laughed out loud, a chest-deep expression of amusement this new Edward had seemed incapable of until now, and she noted his complexion had lost some of its pallor. "I'm surprised to encounter you here. Isn't Kensington Gardens a little out of the way for a shining star of the *ton*?"

She brushed a hand down her skirt, his perusal making her self-conscious of her appearance. She wore a simple old day dress, nothing like her usual modish ensembles that set young ladies of the *ton* rushing to their modistes to copy her latest look. "I like it because it is quiet here."

"I thought it paramount for all of the incomparables to appear in Hyde Park to see and be seen."

She lifted a shoulder with deliberate insouciance. "Haven't you heard? I, sir, am the *only* reigning incomparable this Season."

"And have been for many years, from what Tobias tells me." He regarded her with obvious appreciation. "I can't say I'm surprised."

Her insides warmed under his gaze. She turned to follow the dog, castigating herself for allowing this man who had deserted her to have any impact on her at all. "I mustn't let Vera escape again. We might find her assaulting another unsuspecting admirer of nature."

He followed. "Are you alone?" He looked around as they strolled, spotting her maid following at a distance. "Good lord, is that Fanny?"

"It is indeed." For some reason, it pleased her that he had remembered her maid. Fanny was part of their shared past.

"Well, I'll be." He squinted to get a better look at the dark-clad woman. "From the disagreeable expression on her face, I gather I'm still not a great favorite of hers."

"Fanny sees herself as the guardian of my reputation. And you are the only gentleman who has ever tempted her mistress to misbehave."

"Is that so?" Probing eyes fixed on her face. "Your Lord Sinclair doesn't provoke you to naughtiness?"

Her cheeks grew hot. *No. No one has ever had the power to provoke me but you.*

A shout pierced the air. "I say, you there, is that a dog? Canines are not allowed in Kensington Gardens."

She looked back to where three gentlemen of middle age pointed in their direction. "Oh no."

"Is that so?" He followed her gaze. "Are dogs not allowed here?"

She averted her eyes. "It might be so."

His brows rose. "Are you breaking the rules?"

"It's a silly rule and I just wanted some privacy and quiet for my walk."

"I'll take that as a yes."

She looked back at the approaching men. "Perhaps if we ignore them—"

The man was gesturing wildly now toward his servants.

"You, go get the constable." Pointing to another servant, he yelled, "You, capture that canine."

Turning to face them, Edward squared his shoulders, his face hardening. "Don't worry. I won't let them take your animal."

A shiver of consciousness swept through her. On the battlefield, commanding an army, he must have appeared much as he did now: the lean lines of his body tense with anticipation, his emerald eyes dark and stormy, the hollows in his cheeks made more pronounced by his braced jaw and the fierce set of his features.

She put a staying hand on his forearm, surprised by the hard turn of warm muscle apparent beneath his jacket. "Let us away from here." She tugged at his jacket. "I cannot be caught here with you *and* Vera. The gossips would have a field day."

An arrogant rise of his brow. "Are you suggesting that we run rather than face them?"

She nodded with vigor, still pulling at him. "That is exactly what I am suggesting. The rags love to write about me. And you are a new earl, a war hero. If we are discovered, it will be in all of the papers. Mama will have an apoplectic fit."

He appeared reluctant at first, his planted feet not budging. "Please, Edward," she pleaded, yanking on his sleeve more vigorously.

His stern expression shifted, as though he'd reached a decision. "Vera, come!" Grabbing Kat's hand, encasing it in his large, firm grasp, they made a run for it.

The dog yapped, cavorting alongside, clearly enjoying the game. Kat raced with Edward as they ducked into the wood line, her heart pounding and her blood soaring in a way that made her feel like a carefree girl again. When her hat snagged on a branch and swept it off her head, tousling her hair, she wanted to laugh. She had no idea how long they ran, but finally, out of breath, they spun around the trunk of a large tree in the wooded area.

Peering in the direction they'd just come from, Edward ran a hand over his close-cropped hair. "I think we've lost them."

Kat bent over, panting, trying to ease a cramp in her side. "Oh my, I can't remember the last time I've run like that."

"Are you well?" Concerned tinged his question.

She dropped to the ground, still trying to catch her breath. "I'm wonderful," she said between laughing gasps. "That was marvelous! We showed them, didn't we?"

He eased down next to her. "We certainly did. Although I doubt they'd drag us down to Old Bailey for bringing a canine to Kensington Gardens."

"Certainly not an earl," she said between heaving breaths.

His lips curled into an ironic smile. "Finally, a useful privilege to go along with this infernal title."

She looked at him and they shared the smile, the impartial coldness in his deep green eyes replaced with a penetrating spark of cognizance. A fine sheen coated his face and neck from their exertions and the tang of perspiration mingled with the bergamot scent of his shaving soap. Having been starved for him for far too long, she breathed him in, relishing the sensation of his masculine warmth in such close proximity.

He reached out and touched a loosened golden strand

at her shoulder, fingering it as though it were something precious. "Like sunshine, just as I remember."

Her heart slammed. "I must look a mess."

"You are beautiful as always." He slid both hands up behind her head, caressing her for a moment before drawing his fingers outward through the strands of her hair, shaking it loose of its pins so that it streamed down her shoulders. "I have always loved your hair. When it is loose and flowing like this, you look like a goddess."

He cupped her face with his large hands and she brought her own hands up to rest over his, relishing their rough softness. Her heart sped up when he lowered his head toward her. His lips met hers with a tender touch, taking soft nips, as though his body was reacquainting itself with hers again. Her body recognized him at once. She felt edgy and wet all over, and a restless energy throbbed between her thighs.

She kissed him back, reveling in the softness of his lips. Nothing and no one else existed. The kiss deepened, becoming hot and full of hunger, nothing like the sweet considerate kisses Laurie gave her. Edward's tongue drove hers lips apart and he lapped inside like a starving man. He plundered deeper, demanding more, his kiss raw and hungry, lacking any restraint or finesse.

He tasted like tobacco and something much darker and sweeter. Her greedy tongue tangled with his, taking as much as she gave. She'd waited six interminable years for this, for him. Damn him.

Then he was shifting her onto the soft ground. He came down over her, and the scent of grass and wet leaves and tree bark engulfed them. His lips left hers, trailing down her neck, then back up to suckle the tender lobe of her ear. She moaned at the exquisite sensations, writhing against his hard body as it pressed down on hers, loving the feel of his unrelenting lean form against her woman's softness.

"You are exquisite," he murmured as his hands ran down the sides of her body, his thumbs brushing provocatively over the sides of the sensitive flesh of her breasts. When they reached her hips, he grasped them and pulled her against him. She gasped at the titillating sensation of his aroused flesh grinding against the throbbing wetness between her thighs.

A band of tension tightened inside of her. Then his lips were back on hers, his tongue tasting and stroking. His hand moved to her breast, cupping and then tweaking at the tip through the thin fabric of her dress until she thought she would scream from the intense sensation. It felt as though the sun's hottest rays radiated from that place between her legs outward through her entire body—every part of her was alive and pulsating.

Somewhere out there, Vera's bark penetrated her consciousness, followed by the crunching of leaves and approaching footsteps. "My lady!" Fanny's sharp tone shattered the spell, dragging Kat unwillingly back to the reality of a world where she and Edward no longer belonged to one another.

He jerked away and rose to his feet in one swift motion. Sitting up, still dazed, she took the hand he offered to pull her to her feet. The maid stood just a short distance away, arms crossed over her chest, shocked disapproval stamped on her face. She glared at Edward before running her disappointed gaze over Kat's flushed and disheveled state.

"We must return, my lady," she said tightly. "Lord Sinclair will be waiting for you."

Edward gently disengaged Kat's hand from his. She hadn't realized she'd been grasping onto him so tightly. "It is good to see you again, Fanny."

"I wish I could say the same, my lord." She said the honorific in the same tone one would say an epithet.

"Fanny!" Kat said, shocked by her maid's insolence.

"Come along, Lady Kat." She jerked her chin in Edward's direction. "This one here is nothing but trouble to you." Edward's face remained expressionless, his skin stretched taut over sharp cheekbones.

"Hush, Fanny. You don't know what you are talking about."

She bustled over and took a firm hold of Kat's arm. "Yes, I do, my lady. Now come along. You don't want Lord Sinclair to come upon you looking as you do now. There'd be no explaining it away."

She glanced back at Edward, who'd remained frozen where he stood, his eyes an inscrutable opaque. He gave a brisk nod. "The redoubtable Fanny is correct. It is best that you go with her."

"Will you call on me?" she called over her shoulder.

Watching her go, he did not answer.

Once they'd walked far enough to lose sight of him, Kat tugged away from Fanny's grip. "You may return my arm to me now."

Letting go, the maid made a tsking sound with her mouth. "I would have thought you would know better than to involve yourself with the likes of him again."

"We are not involved. It was just a moment that took us

both off guard."

Fanny halted and fixed a hard look on her. "After that man left you that last time, I thought you would never recover. It took months before you began to act alive again, but in truth you were never the same."

She opened her mouth to dispute Fanny, but then shut it again. She thought she'd hidden her despair so well, but no one understood her better than Fanny, who had known her since girlhood. And her maid had seen through her performance. Kat hadn't been the same after Edward's desertion. And she would not survive another of his rejections.

"Oh, Fanny." Her lungs ached. "You have the right of it, of course. What do I know of this new Edward?"

"Nothing, my lady. And men return from war much changed."

Edward had certainly changed. Who was he now? Was he the distant stranger who rarely gave her a second glance? Or the laughing, tender lover who'd just kissed her in the woods? More confused than ever, she followed Fanny out of the park and on toward home to receive her betrothed.

...

"Bloody hell." Rand cursed, loud and foul. Six years—*six years*—had done nothing to temper his attraction to her. If anything, absence had solidified the pull between them. Kissing her soft willing lips had stirred something in him that he thought had died at Talavera. With Elena, the sex was always good, but it hadn't gone beyond kinship and physical pleasure. Merely being in Kitty's presence managed to twist something deep inside him. That she still had that kind of power over him shocked and disconcerted him.

In her plain dress, with her hair almost carelessly tucked under an unadorned straw bonnet, she couldn't have looked more different than the glamorous peacock who'd commanded Sinclair's drawing room. And she'd elected to take a solitary walk in the relative seclusion of Kensington Gardens, rather than reign over admiring crowds in Hyde Park during the fashionable hour. Strange behavior for a toast of the town. The lack of artifice did not detract from her appeal; in fact, she'd never looked lovelier. God help him. He was far from cured of Kitty Granville

Even worse, he'd kissed her after suffering another episode. As though losing himself in her eager warmth would somehow obscure the harrowing truth of the madness that haunted him. He shouldn't have touched her, especially when he had nothing to offer her, except the very real possibility of a lifetime tied to a bedlamite.

Something wet slobbered against his hand, interrupting his internal rant. He looked down to find Vera practically smiling up at him, her water-sopped tail swishing back and forth. Kat had forgotten her animal.

"Come on then, you mangy whelp," he said, not without affection as the dog frolicked alongside him. "I can't very well leave you here."

Picking up a stick, he threw it into the distance and watched Vera lope after it with a good-natured bark. He should be annoyed to find himself stuck with Kitty's animal. Instead, he was happy for the company on the walk home.

As he and Vera neared Grosvenor Square, they encountered Toby Hobart, wearing the brightest blue tailcoat Rand had even seen, with an orange striped waistcoat beneath.

"How fortuitous," Toby said, the sun glinting off his upswept coppery hair. "I was just coming from your mausoleum."

"Hobart. To what do I owe your colorful presence?"

"I came to deliver an invitation to a country house party my mother is planning in a fortnight. She's keen to have the most talked-about peer in attendance." Vera's restless whine drew his attention. "Is that Kat's hound?"

"As it happens, yes."

"What are you doing with her?"

"Lady Katherine and I met by chance in Kensington Gardens. She recalled a forgotten engagement and rushed away." He was careful to keep his tone bland. "It was only after she'd gone that I realized she'd left the creature behind."

"No doubt it is the garden party Nugent is throwing today that disconcerted her. If I don't exert myself, I, too, will be late to the affair."

"Don't let me keep you. We wouldn't want to leave Sinclair and his betrothed to their own devices for too long."

Toby chuckled as he took his leave. "I daresay Sin wouldn't mind. He's absolutely besotted." As Rand continued homeward, he wondered if there was any man who wasn't under Kitty's spell.

Beside him, Vera barked and nuzzled into his hand. The sour expression on his valet's face when Vera trotted into the front hall behind Rand suggested Burgess did not share his affection for the canine. "Your solicitor awaits your pleasure in the parlor, my lord."

"Yes, we have an appointment to go over matters related to the earldom." Rand wasn't sure which room in this mausoleum was the parlor. Had it been up to him, he'd have contented himself with a much more modest home in town, but a man did not decline a gift from his sovereign. "Send him to the study, will you, Burgess?" He trotted up the stairs and into his bed chamber with both Burgess and Vera following. "And see that our little friend here is bathed."

Burgess made a moue of distaste as he regarded the canine, and Rand could have sworn the animal's eyes narrowed in response. "Surely, you don't mean to keep it."

Pulling off his cravat and shirt, Rand rinsed his face and neck. "Indeed I do. See to her bath, if you please."

Burgess placed a towel in the hand Rand held out. "If you had a butler, he could arrange the matter. An earl's household should maintain a butler."

"Why do I need a butler when I already have you?" He dried his face and neck with vigorous strokes. "A shirt, if you please."

Burgess already had a shirt at the ready and handed it to him. "Your staff is inadequate to your station."

"I should think a butler would challenge your role in this household."

"Not at all. As valet, I'm quite safe from challenge." He eyed Vera as she made herself at home, curling up into a ball on the carpet at the foot of the bed. "That creature has a most unpleasant odor."

"Which is why she needs a bath."

"I shall have a footman attend to her," Burgess said with an exaggerated sigh. "I suppose you'd like me to confer with Cook about the evening meal?"

Rand pulled the door open and stepped through it. "I don't see who else is going to do it. Unless you've gone and hired a housekeeper while I was out."

"What you need, my lord, is a countess to oversee your household."

An image of Kitty flashed in his mind. He shoved it away. She had no place in this bedlamite world of his. No. Everything was as it should be. Kitty would marry Sinclair, a man who was clearly devoted to her and could offer her a husband of sound mind.

"Just see about the dog, will you?" he said brusquely before slamming the door behind him.

# Chapter Five

Kat remained distracted throughout the luncheon, replaying the taste and feel of Edward's kisses over and over again. The intimacy in the park proved he wasn't indifferent to her after all. Far from it.

Frustrated, she shook her head against the emotions swirling through her. The man had devastated her with his abandonment, yet she'd allowed him to kiss her, to touch her. Even worse, everything about this new Edward entranced her—perhaps even more so than the soft, sensitive boy who had left her. The sharp angles and long lines of his body, the almost harsh turn of his nose, all contrived to give him a dangerous edge that enthralled her.

The guests' laughter brought her back to the reality of her parents' intimate garden party. The small, amiable group included Bea, Toby, and their mother. And Laurie, of course. These days, he always seemed to be underfoot.

Guilt stabbed her at the uncharitable thought. As her

betrothed, Laurie should be attentive. While he treated her with the highest regard and gentle kindness, she'd betrayed him by allowing Edward liberties Laurie would never think to attempt.

"Are you well?" Laurie's solicitous voice broke into her thoughts.

"Of course," she answered, while her conscience continued to berate her. "Why do you ask?"

"You seem out of sorts."

She bristled inwardly, but answered with calm civility. "I am a little. I've misplaced Vera."

That caught Toby's attention. "Not to worry, Kat. I just saw that mutt of yours with Rand."

Kat's cheeks warmed. Cutting a guilty glance toward her parents, she found them engrossed in conversation with her aunt. "Oh well, thank goodness for that," she replied in an easy tone. "I should go and retrieve her this afternoon."

"Why would the earl be in possession of your animal?" Laurie asked, taking a sip of his wine.

"Fanny and I came across him in Kensington Gardens." She favored her betrothed with an engaging smile — one that usually distracted him sufficiently enough to head off any uncomfortable exchanges. "Then I remembered you were due to arrive shortly, so I rushed back to prepare myself to receive you."

It had the desired effect. The heat of interest sparked in Laurie's admiring eyes as they ran over her. "You *are* in excellent looks today." He reached for a hand and placed a kiss at her fingertips. "I'm a most fortunate man."

"And don't you forget it," Kat replied in the playful saucy manner she knew he loved.

Laurie's heated gaze held hers until Bea's words drew their attention. "I am surprised Vera let you leave her behind."

Laurie leaned back in his chair and crossed his arms. "It is peculiar. Usually the animal is stuck at your side."

Kat frowned. They were right. She'd been so wrapped up in her encounter with Edward that she hadn't given Vera's strange behavior much thought. A most loyal creature, the dog rarely left her side. And yet the animal had instantly fallen under Edward's spell. Apparently the man had the same effect on all females. It was strange, though, how staunchly Vera had stayed by Edward's side—almost as if she were guarding him.

The gentlemen rose and followed Kat's father to the library for drinks and cheroots. Kat's mother and Aunt Winifred rose and headed to the parlor, leaving Kat and Bea alone in the garden.

Bea moved closer, taking the seat next to Kat with a conspiratorial expression on her face. "I saw the Amazon today."

Bile rose in Kat at the thought of the woman who could very well be Edward's mistress. "Where?"

"She was at Madame de Lancy's." The Amazon patronized the same fashionable modiste that Kat herself frequented? "You should have seen her in the dressing area, walking around without a care for modesty. She even took off her chemise when Madame's girls took her measurements."

Kat was truly shocked. "No!"

"Yes." With a vigorous nod, Bea gestured to her own décolletage. "And they are enormous."

Kat regarded her own modest attributes in that area.

Had Edward compared her breasts unfavorably to the Amazon when he'd touched her intimately in the gardens? Chagrin arrowed through her at the thought.

"She ordered all sorts of things, even intimate things," Bea was saying. "And you'll never guess who she said the bill should be sent to."

"Who?" Kat asked with a sinking feeling.

"The Earl of Randolph."

Her stomach felt queasy. "So not only is she his mistress, but she doesn't even attempt to hide the fact."

"She didn't announce it loudly or anything, but I was behind the curtain changing and I overheard her."

Unable to contemplate hearing any more, Kat rose in a strident motion. "Let's find Laurie and Toby and insist that they amuse us."

Bea stood and linked her arm with Kat's as they walked through the French doors that led into the empty dining room. "She was most kind."

"Who?"

"The Maid of Malagon, of course."

"You conversed with her?"

"Oh yes. Elena said we must go riding in Hyde Park."

"Elena?" Kat's eyebrow rose. "You are on familiar terms?"

Bea nodded. "I quite like her. She is most amusing. Fighting off an entire regiment of French soldiers. Whoever heard of a female receiving a commendation for war-time bravery? She is quite the heroine."

• • •

The Maid of Malagon was also the topic of conversation between Laurie and Toby in the library. They stood off in the corner while the Earl of Nugent sat at his desk, conferring with his man of business about some newly-arisen emergency at his country estate.

Laurie eyed the amber liquid in his glass. "I gather she is Randolph's mistress," he said, not bothering to disguise his distaste.

"Most assuredly," Toby answered.

Laurie thought of the proud, unapologetic way the Spanish woman carried herself. "Has he set her up in an exclusive arrangement?"

Toby laughed. "Not likely. No man will ever own Elena, not even for a contracted period of time."

Somehow that did not surprise Laurie. Elena Márquez-Navarro did not seem particularly conquerable. He had to admit though—however inappropriate her public and private conduct—the Maid of Malagon was a handsome woman. Her appeal was nothing like the exquisite delicate beauty his betrothed possessed, of course, but she was an appealing specimen nonetheless. And the body on her. Only a molly would fail to take notice of her bountiful curves. "She's a lightskirt then."

"I wouldn't say that. She is a woman not bound by any sort of convention. Elena does what she wants, when she wants."

They were interrupted by Kat and Bea, who took them off for a game of whist. Later, when the time came to depart, Laurie lingered after the others had gone. Casting an indulgent look in his direction, Kat's parents tactfully withdrew to allow them to say their good-byes in private.

Taking advantage of the opportunity, Laurie pulled Kat into the cloak room beneath the stairs.

"What are you doing?" she hissed, darting a look at the servant stationed in the front hall. "What will the footman think?"

Pulling her into his arms, he inhaled the subtle scent of violets. "He'll think I want to steal a kiss from my betrothed." He nuzzled her neck. "And he'd be quite correct in his assumption."

A delicate blush bloomed on her cheeks. "You are incorrigible." Despite her stern tone, she relented a bit in his arms.

Laurie had been unaccountably randy all afternoon so he took advantage of her softening. Bringing his lips down to taste hers, he nipped at her lower lip before allowing his tongue to invade her mouth with slightly less restraint than he usually showed in her presence. She stiffened for a moment and then seemed to decide to allow him the liberty.

He pulled her body up against his so that they were touching from hip to breast, her soft chest pressing against his while his tongue stroked hers. What would it feel like to have Elena Márquez-Navarro's ample bosom crushed against him? The unbidden image caused the temperature of his blood to soar. He broke the kiss on a muttered oath, mortified to have insulted his betrothed by thinking of the Spanish jade during such an intimate moment.

"What is it?" Kat whispered, her cheeks flushed.

He inhaled. "You are just so lovely that if I don't restrain myself now, I fear I won't be able to stop."

Doubt flashed in her eyes, making him hate himself. "Are you angry with me?"

"Not at all." He pressed a gentle kiss on her lips before guiding her out of their hiding place. "I just can't wait to make you my wife so I can have you all to myself."

Taking his leave, he bounded down the front outside stairs with his blood still running hot. For the first time in his memory, he was relieved to be out of his betrothed's company. What was wrong with him? To think of the Spanish jade while kissing his future wife was the height of disrespect. He'd been faithful to Kat since before their betrothal, which could explain his body's current state of agitation. And since the Maid of Malagon made no secret of being free with her favors, perhaps it was natural for a man to think of her in a carnal way.

His thoughts turned to Gentleman Jackson's. Throwing a few punches would be just the thing to settle his body. Dismissing any further thought of Randolph's mistress, he quickened his step in the direction of the boxing saloon.

# Chapter Six

Rand directed his mount off Queen's Road and through the high gates leading to the King Street Pensioners' Hospital, a home for elderly and injured soldiers. Some of his men lived here now and he was of a mind to check in on them.

Riding up to the faded brick building, he alighted and handed the reins to a groom before striding toward the entrance and into the generous vestibule. Walking across clean-swept marble floors, he made his way to the library where his men could often be found. He scanned the space where older residents, veterans of the war in the colonies, and younger soldiers from the Peninsular Wars, sat talking, smoking, playing cards, or reading. Some were missing limbs or bore other signs of debilitating permanent injuries.

Unable to spot his men, he was directed out to the courtyard where he found more than a dozen pensioners, old and young alike, gathered in a circle. Even from a distance, instead of the usual murmur of masculine voices, he heard a familiar lilting feminine laugh rise from the center of the group.

His pulse quickened. "What the devil is Kat doing here?" he said aloud to no one in particular.

"I told her not to come, but she insisted."

He spun around to find Toby, wearing a relatively muted burgundy tailcoat over a green-and-white striped waistcoat, leaning against a tall marble column. "You brought Lady Katherine here? What were you thinking?"

Toby shrugged. "Once Kat sets her mind to something, she is difficult to deter."

"This is no place for a gentlewoman." He looked back at the circle of pensioners. "How does she even know of this place?"

"The ladies were making donation baskets for the pensioners and when she learned I planned to deliver them in person, she insisted upon coming along."

"For what purpose?" This bleak environment, filled with graphic visual reminders of the vagaries of war, was no place for a maiden.

"To do what the *ton*'s incomparable excels at—to regale them with her wit, charm, and beauty, to flirt and entertain." Toby pushed off the column and came to stand next to Rand. "To take their minds off their troubles for a little while. At the moment, she is reading to them."

He shook his head in disbelief. "I trust you will not be so foolish as to bring her here again."

"I doubt I could stop my cousin. This is her sixth or seventh visit. I accompany her to ensure she comes to no harm."

Muttering a few foul words, Rand edged closer to the

group, which afforded him a view of the lady in question. Kitty sat on a stool wearing a soft blue day dress that brought out the deep sapphire color of her eyes. She read in an animated voice punctured by the occasional laughing smile. The pensioners surrounding her listened with rapt attention, obviously as spellbound by her undeniable aura as the high-born denizens of the *ton*. Kitty had surprised him again. Instead of accepting one of the numerous invitations she must surely receive, the reigning toast chose to pass the afternoon in decidedly unglamorous environs visiting wounded soldiers.

Something akin to pain shifted in his chest. He hadn't laid eyes on Kitty since their chance meeting in the park three days ago. He still had her canine—the animal had resisted his footman's attempt to return her—but once he reunited Vera with her mistress, he intended to cease all further contact with Kitty. The undeniable pull between them was too potent and too dangerous to her future for him to risk doing otherwise. Their encounter in Kensington Park demonstrated he remained as susceptible to her charms as he'd ever been. Neither time nor distance had altered the attraction. She was his sun, and when he was in her sphere, he could not resist her life-sustaining vitality.

When the story came to an end, she closed the book with a decisive snap and—appearing in no great hurry to escape the dreary surroundings—continued chatting with the soldiers, demonstrating her mastery of light flirtation.

"May I impose upon you," Toby said to Rand "to stay with her for a few minutes while I dash up to the ward and look in on an old friend?"

Devil take it. "Be quick about it. I have a pressing

engagement and must depart soon." A lie, but one that would mercifully curtail his time in Kitty's presence. Soon after Toby's defection, the pensioners were called in for tea, leaving Rand with no choice but to spend a few minutes with her until her cousin's return.

"I didn't anticipate seeing you here," she said coolly as he approached her. "You've been decidedly absent of late."

"Your cousin has gone up to visit a friend. He asked me to look after you until his return."

"Shall we walk then?" Not waiting for an answer, she turned and strolled in the direction of the gardens.

He followed. "It isn't wise, you know, for a young, gently-bred lady to visit a pensioners' home."

"I should think you of all people would deem it proper to thank these men for their service."

"Yes, well, you should be shielded from unpleasantness."

"There is much unpleasantness from which I have not been shielded," she said. "This is a trifle in comparison."

A less than subtle reference to his abandonment of her. The bitter irony of his life was that going to war to win her had created the very reason they must now remain apart. They moved beyond a hedgerow, well into the gardens. Once they were out of the sight of others, she came to an abrupt stop.

"Are we ever going to discuss it?" She crossed her arms under her bosom, the soft flesh he'd caressed not so long ago. "Or is it your custom to paw a lady and then go about your business?"

He stiffened. "Is it an apology you desire? I offer it most profoundly then."

Her blue eyes sparked. "I don't want an apology and

you know it. You return after many years, proceed to take liberties I have allowed no other man, and now you intend to proceed as though nothing occurred between us?"

Liberties she'd allowed no other man? Satisfaction swelled in him even though it shouldn't have. "You are betrothed to another man." He forced the words out through paralyzed lungs. "By all accounts, Sinclair is decent and can be expected to treat you well. Honor dictates that I withdraw, despite my appalling lapse in Kensington."

She looked stricken. "Laurie is a good man, the best in fact. But I would do him a grave disservice by marrying him when my heart doesn't belong to him."

Breath whooshed out of him. She didn't love Sinclair? "You are speaking without a care for your future. I am not the same man who left you."

She stepped closer, showering him with the scent of violets, and her voice trembled with uncertainty. "I should hate you. I think a part of me does, but it is of no use." Her eyes filled. "How can I wed Laurie when he is not the man I love?"

He couldn't bear being this close and not touching her. He turned to go. "We should return."

She gripped his arm. "Why do you keep leaving me?" She slid her hand down his arm to interlock her pale, tapered fingers with his. "Am I nothing to you?"

Heat rushed through him at the feel of her soft, delicate hand in his clumsy large one. His meager defenses crumbled. What a poor soldier he was in the battle to save Kitty's future. "You are everything."

He pulled her tight into his embrace and buried his face in the fragile turn of her pale neck, soaking up her scent. She sighed, melting into him when his lips sought hers, finding them soft and willing. He kissed her deeply, plunging his tongue into the wet cavern of her mouth with the full force of his passion for her. He explored the satiny softness of her cheek, the sweet womanly taste of her tongue, and immersed himself in the heaven of her feminine essence. Her breasts flattened against his chest, her hips pushing up into him. His arousal swelled hard and heavy against her.

"Forgive me," he said softly, trailing kisses down her neck, suddenly desperate for her to accept his apology. He could not offer her a lifetime, but she did deserve this much. "I was wrong to leave and never send word. You are the last person in Christendom that I would willingly hurt."

"I'll cry off," she said, breathless. "And then we can be together."

The words snapped him back to the reality of their situation and his insides went cold. He could never marry her. He couldn't bear it if she were to witness one of his episodes. She'd likely regard him with a combination of pity, fear, and disgust. It was better that she despise him. He released her and pulled back in one abrupt motion. "You misunderstand."

"But you just apologized—" Her pink cheeks were luminous against her porcelain complexion, the vivid shade of her eyes glittered in the afternoon sun.

"I do regret my treatment of you," he said stiffly. "However, I don't intend to marry anyone. Ever."

Kitty's delicate brows drew together. "What is wrong with you? Why do you insist on denying what is between us?"

*To save you from me.* He turned to go, walking out of

the garden — and away from her — at a fast clip. "Toby will be looking for us. It is for the best to leave things as they are."

She hastened beside him, keeping up with his strident pace despite her petite stature and much shorter legs. "In the same way leaving me to go fight your war was for the best? I suppose you believe abandoning your music is also for the best."

"Things in the past cannot be changed." He stared straight ahead, not daring to look at her. "It is best we move on."

"Best for whom, I wonder."

Emerging from the gardens, it relieved him to see Toby crossing the lawn, heading in their direction. "Ah, here's Toby now."

"Coward," she muttered under her breath.

"Did you enjoy your walk in the gardens?" Toby asked upon reaching them.

"Yes, we had the most delightful time," Kitty said brightly. "I should like to repeat the experience soon."

Rand firmed his jaw. "Now that your cousin is returned, I shall take my leave."

"But there is something of critical importance that we must discuss," she called after him.

His heart stopped and he turned back to see her amused expression. "I can't think of what that might be."

"There is the matter of Vera, of course."

His pulse returned to almost normal. "Your canine."

"Yes. Do you mean to keep her?"

"My footman attempted to return her, but it seems she's grown accustomed to sleeping next to my bed. I trip over her every time I rise at night."

She tilted her head in contemplation. "Do you awaken often in the night hours?"

Damnation. "Not often," he lied. "I'll have the animal brought to you."

"Perhaps the parting will go easier on Vera if you deliver her yourself," she said with false innocence. "Mother and I receive on Wednesday afternoons. Will you come and bring her then?"

"You might as well acquiesce," Toby said. "Kat is decidedly hard-headed when it comes to getting what she desires."

He forced a response through his tight jaw. "Of course."

"Brilliant." She flashed a radiant smile that he felt down to his toes. "I shall look forward it."

Striding away, he scrubbed both hands down his face. The meaning of that smile was not lost on him. Kitty had just thrown down the gauntlet. She intended to fight for what she wanted and, Lord help them both, she still wanted him.

...

"This is madness." Fanny shook her head with exasperation as she finished dressing Kat's hair, readying her to receive callers for their Wednesday at-home. "How can you even contemplate any sort of courtship with the earl after what he's done to you?"

Kat met her maid's gaze in the mirror's reflection. "It's never really been finished between us. I have to see where this road takes me. If I don't, I fear I will always regret it."

Fanny scoffed. "It'll take you to misery and ruin, mark my words."

"I don't believe Edward would hurt me on purpose. He was always a good man." She'd given the matter a great deal of thought since their encounter at the veterans' home. "He left because he wanted to make something of himself before we married. He was too honorable to run away to Gretna Green, even though I begged him to." She ignored Fanny's shocked inhale. "I don't know why he didn't come back for me after the war. There is something he isn't telling me."

"Maybe he has good reason for keeping his business to himself." Fanny tugged a loose tendril into place.

"Ouch!" She rose to keep her hair out of Fanny's grasp and turned to face her. "You of all people should understand why I must see this through. This time, if it doesn't work, I shall know it wasn't meant to be."

They were interrupted by a knock on the door and a summons from her mother because their first callers had arrived. Kat stifled pangs of guilt when she saw the ever-attentive Laurie was among the first arrivals. Dear, sweet Laurie. Crying off would hurt him deeply, but she truly believed he wouldn't want to wed her once he discovered her heart didn't fully belong to him. He deserved a wife who would put his happiness above all others.

The at-home came to an end without Edward making an appearance. Climbing the stairs to her bed chamber, she wasn't entirely surprised. He'd made it quite clear that he wished to avoid her, although their recent embraces proved he wasn't unmoved by her. Voices sounded down below in the foyer followed by Vera's joyful bark. She turned on the stairs and looked down to where Edward stood with a frolicking Vera on a leash. He looked up at her, those dark eyes taking her in.

"Lord Randolph, this is a surprise." Her mother's tone was polite, but wary. As an earl, Edward was now deserving of the respect her parents had denied him all those years ago. He bowed low, showing her deference as Kat's mother. "My lady."

"Will you join us for refreshment?" Lady Nugent politely suggested, the hesitation in her tone easing. Their at-home having concluded, it would be rude for the earl to accept her invitation, and so he did not.

"No, thank you. I don't wish to discommode you. I only stopped by to return Lady Katherine's animal to her."

Kat had to restrain herself from running down the stairs to keep him from leaving, but she managed to proceed at a discreet pace. "Thank you."

Vera bounded over to her, wagging her tail in lavish, wide swishes. Kat laughed and bent to welcome the dog, allowing her to lick her chin.

"Really, Katherine," her mother admonished, her distaste clear on her face. "You mustn't let her do that."

Kat gave Vera's ears a vigorous massage before standing upright and flashing Edward an amused expression. "There's no harm in it. She's showing me her affection."

Edward replaced his hat atop his head. "Now that you two are successfully reunited, I shall take my leave."

She didn't want him to go. "Are you certain you won't stay for refreshment?"

His answer was interrupted by Vera's whine as she scratched at the front door.

"John," her mother called to the footman standing sentry in the foyer—all of the footmen were called John no matter their true Christian name—"do take that creature out before she marks up the door."

"I'll do it." Kat seized the opportunity to be alone with Edward. "I'll walk the earl out. I could use the fresh air."

Her mother flashed a troubled look between the two of them. And for a moment Kat worried she would forbid it. But then she said, "Very well. Do take Fanny with you."

"This is folly," Fanny hissed after they donned their pelisses and hurried down to join Edward.

"I would have a care if I were you," Kat retorted, unwilling to be deterred. "You might not approve, but bear in mind that Lord Randolph could one day be your new master and the true folly would be for you to cross him."

Fanny answered with a humph, and all three set out with Vera in tow, Fanny trailing behind. Edward held Vera's leash in one hand and offered Kat his opposite arm, which she took, happy to have at least this limited physical contact between them.

"You must put any idea of an arrangement between us out of your mind," he said in quiet tones. "It is for the best."

"I have decided to tell Laurie I am crying off at the Hobart's house party in a sennight." She knew Edward had been invited to the house party Toby and Bea's mother planned to hold at their country estate. "Will I see you there?"

His arm stiffened under her hand. "No, you most certainly will not. I beg you to reconsider this nonsense."

She continued as if he hadn't spoken. Her course was set now. She would see it through. "After I cry off, Laurie can retire to his country estate instead of returning to Town to face the scandal. By the time the Season begins in earnest and he returns to take up his seat in the lords, the uproar will have abated."

He halted, his face set in hard lines. "We enjoyed a childhood infatuation and nothing more. I will never court you. We will never marry."

"You are not unmoved by me. I felt it when you kissed me."

"Physical desire is not love."

"I will also stay in the country," she continued as if he hadn't spoken. "And once my parents become accustomed to my new situation, I hope you will come and visit."

"I most certainly will not."

"We shall see." She took the dog's leash from him. "We should go. Come, Vera."

The animal bounded over, nosing up against her thigh. Kat turned to leave, but felt a sudden tug on the leash after she'd gone just a few steps. She turned to find Vera planted by Edward's side.

"Well, how do you like that?" he said with clear amusement.

"One would think you were her master." The irritation roiling in her chest at Vera's blatant defection immediately gave way to a realization. "Perhaps the animal already knows what fate has in store."

"I don't take your meaning."

"Vera seems to understand that you are soon to be her new master."

His face darkened. "You don't stop."

"Exactly right." She handed Vera's leash to him. "You would do well to give up the fight."

• • •

The unbearable stench invaded his nostrils, the smell of blood and rotting flesh turning his stomach. Rand stumbled away and struggled not to spill its meager contents when he caught sight of the flies buzzing around the pile of severed limbs. All the while, the soldier's singing played over and over in his mind:

*I thought I heard the Colonel crying*
*March brave boys there's no denying*

Then the other sound joined in, the unrelenting back-and-forth rhythm of sawing. The soldier's voice grew shriller, yet he continued on.

*Cannons roaring—drums abeating*
*March brave boys there's no retreating*
*Love farewell*

He went toward the sound. Something dropped with a heavy thud at his feet. Another severed arm. His shoulder hurt like the devil. He rubbed it, but found an empty sleeve where his arm used to be.

Rand shot up to a sitting position in the dark, sweating and disconcerted, his breathing fast and shallow. The stale smell of cheroot smoke thickened the air, replacing the awful stench of rotting flesh and bone. It took a moment for him to comprehend he was in his bed in the mausoleum on Grosvenor Square and not at a wartime field hospital.

His sudden movement alerted Vera, who'd been asleep beside the bed. She pushed up on all four legs and faced him, her tail held up high and still, as if she were standing sentry. Lightheaded and dazed, he tried to remember why the animal was in his bed chamber.

Agonizing pain clenched his chest and the uncontrollable shaking began. Cursing, he lay back down, curling into a fetal position. There was nothing to be done for it. He'd experienced enough of these episodes to know there was no preventing them. A curtain of terror bled over him, his vision dimmed. He couldn't breathe.

And then everything went black.

# Chapter Seven

"Get down from there! Shoo before I feed you to the horses!"

His valet's irritated voice pierced the blackness. Something both rough and delicate lapped at Rand's face. The unmistakable scent of dog's breath closed in on him.

"Down, you mangy creature. Get away." Burgess' voice moved closer. Rand dragged his heavy eyelids open to find Vera's snout at very close range. Standing over him on the bed, she paid his valet no mind and concentrated on licking his face repeatedly.

Perspiring and shaky, his heart slamming against his chest wall, Rand placed his hand on the animal's head to push her away in a gentle manner. She allowed it, jumping off with a bark and coming to an alert sitting position on the floor by the bed. Her tail swept back and forth in slow, wide wags, and she regarded him with an expectant expression.

Then it occurred to him what had happened. "Bloody

hell. I had another episode."

"Indeed," Burgess said in his crisp fashion. His clothing, slightly askew as though he'd dressed in a hurry, was the lone sign anything out of the ordinary had occurred. "Brandy or a smoke?"

"Both." He pushed to a sitting position, wincing at the throbbing pain in his shoulder. Rubbing the tender spot, he trailed his hand down his arm to reassure himself the limb remained intact. "How long this time?"

Burgess handed him a brandy and cheroot, pausing to light it for him. "Considerably more abbreviated than the last time." He paused, contemplating the question. "A few minutes at most."

"Son of a bitch." Rand threw the brandy down his throat all at once.

Burgess reached for the decanter again. "More?" Still disconcerted, Rand nodded. "Speaking of bitches, that one there" —Burgess tilted his head in Vera's direction— "refused to be dissuaded from lapping at your face as though it were a sweetmeat."

He emptied the glass again and handed it back to the butler. Coughing, he swiped his mouth with the back of his hand. "No more brandy." He dangled his hand off the side of the bed and Vera came right to it. Standing on her hind paws, she balanced her front legs against the bed frame and nudged her furry head up under his hand. "Good girl."

The animal wiggled her body with happy enthusiasm. He petted her more vigorously, in the playful way he now knew she preferred. "Did I put the fear in you, girl?"

Burgess moved about the chamber, straightening the clothes Rand had draped across a chair when he'd undressed before bed. Even though the valet had comfortable quarters commiserate with his status as the household's highest placed servant, he still slept in the simple valet room just off the master's chamber. Rand suspected it was so he could be close at hand during these moments of crisis.

"Did I say anything this time?"

"Nothing particularly distinguishable." Burgess threw a few logs on the flagging fire in the hearth. Picking up a poker, he coaxed the flames into a burst of renewed energy.

"You're lowering yourself to tend the fire rather than leaving it to an underling." Rand spoke in a wry tone. "My episode must have been very bad indeed."

"Not to worry." He propped the poker carefully back into its stand. "There are plenty of other tasks I can assign on the morrow to remind the lower servants of their place. There's no sense in waking the entire household."

Other than Elena, only Burgess knew of these blasted episodes. He'd been on hand since the first one, not long after Talavera. Although the occurrence of the bouts had dwindled in the two years since Rand had given up his commission, they still struck occasionally with no forewarning.

He massaged behind Vera's ears. The animal practically sighed with pleasure as she rested her chin on the edge of the mattress. Rand's heartbeat slowly restored itself to a more normal rhythm. "I suppose I needed this particular episode to slam some sense into my addled mind."

"Beg pardon?"

He took a deep drag on his cheroot. "I was beginning to contemplate giving you the mistress of the house you've been haranguing me about."

Burgess turned to give him his full attention. "Indeed?"

"This episode reaffirms that it would be folly to take a bride." Pressure bore down on Rand's chest at the thought of what he must do. "I can't in good conscience subject a wife to this madness."

The valet tilted his head. "Who was the fortunate lady, may I ask?"

"You may not. Suffice to say, I must put an end to her fanciful notions of marriage."

"I imagine any lady who would release you so easily isn't worthy of your affections."

"I fear you might be correct." He exhaled, blowing smoke high into the air, remembering Kitty's kind tolerance of the pensioners. "If I explained this madness to the lady, she's liable to stay out of guilt or misplaced duty."

"Or an abundance of affection."

"What sort of drivel is that?" he said more sharply than he intended. "Don't tell me there's a romantic soul hidden under all that starch."

"Perhaps you should relay the truth and allow the lady to make the choice."

"No." He spoke in hard tones. "I will never allow that. She deserves better." The irony of it tasted bitter on his tongue. He'd left her all those years ago because he hadn't the consequence to take her to wife. Now, despite being in possession of both a title and a tidy fortune, he was even less worthy of her.

"Drivel indeed," Burgess said in a low tone, more to himself than to Rand.

"What was that?" Rand demanded, even though he'd heard perfectly.

"Nothing at all. Do you want me to put that creature

out?" Burgess approached Vera with obvious distaste. "It's liable to keep you awake." Vera's body vibrated with a low growl when the valet got too close.

"She seems to have taken an immediate dislike to you."

Burgess sniffed. "The feeling is mutual."

Rand patted the bed and Vera hopped onto the mattress, settling down beside him. "Leave her with me." He ran a hand down the length of the animal's body. Stroking her soft coat settled him somehow. "I could use the company. I doubt there'll be any more sleep for me this evening. Why don't you return to your bed?"

"As you wish, my lord."

Rand scowled. "Perhaps Vera could be persuaded to bite you in the arse every time you call me by that blasted title."

"Perhaps," said Burgess disappearing into his valet chamber, "my lord."

Rand settled back against the pillows, running one hand over Vera's prone form while contemplating the distasteful task that lay ahead. Leaving Kitty to join the war had been agony enough, even when he'd had every intention of returning to reclaim her. This time, he meant to end their association for good. He must find a way to persuade her to abandon her notions of a romantic reunion between them. In short, he needed to do something unforgivable.

Taking a long, slow draw on the cheroot, a plan of how to put Kitty off him forever formed in his mind. Now he just had to find the courage to follow through with it.

• • •

"Look at Laurie. He has the most well-formed body of any

man I've ever seen," Lexie said with an audible sigh of envy. The tangle inside Kat's stomach tightened into a hard knot. The three women had set up near the lake to watercolor for the afternoon. She looked into the distance, across the lake, where the men were fishing. Laurie stood at the edge with a pole in hand, his strong legs braced apart, his blond hair catching the sun. Soon she must tell him the truth. Normally, she'd do anything to avoid hurting Laurie. Except give up Edward.

"And have you seen many men's bodies, Lexie?" Bea asked in a teasing manner.

Keeping her gaze on the men, Lexie twirled her sable brush into a fine point. "Since Laurie is taken, I've set my sights on Lord Randolph. He's a little bit on the thin side, but still cuts a fine form."

Pushing her brush around aimlessly on the cold-pressed paper, Kat pretended to concentrate on her watercolor. What was Edward doing here? He stood by the bank, not far from Laurie, with Vera at his feet, conversing with Toby and some other gentlemen guests.

The last time they'd spoken alone, in the park, he'd planned to decline the invitation to the Hobart's house party. She smiled to herself. Perhaps he'd missed her.

Lexie's gaze remained on Edward. "He isn't the handsomest of men, but his title more than makes up for what he lacks in looks and charm."

"I think he is quite attractive," Bea said. "In a hard sort of way."

Lexie winked. "That mistress of his seems to have no problem handling him."

Bea gasped. "Lexie!"

Lexie waved her off. "What? Everyone knows the Amazon is the earl's ladybird."

Kat swallowed away the instant jealousy that gripped her throat. She'd forgotten about the Spanish strumpet. Surely, Edward would give up his mistress once they married. He had to.

Any hopes Kat harbored of putting the Maid of Malagon out of her mind were firmly dashed a few hours later when the Amazon made an unexpected appearance as the guests gathered before dinner. Resplendent in a royal blue gown that showcased her bountiful breasts, she appeared on the threshold of the salon with her jet-black hair styled high atop her head, making her appear even taller.

The air whooshed out of Kat's chest. "What is she doing here?" she whispered to Bea.

"Isn't she divine?" Bea watched Elena with a frankly admiring expression on her face. "I convinced Mother to invite her."

"And she agreed?" Kat said incredulously. "Surely she is not considered respectable?"

"She has the prince regent's admiration on account of her wartime valor, so she is now invited everywhere."

Well. That hardly seemed fair. The woman flouted convention at every turn and was still accepted everywhere, while all other females had to follow society's rigid strictures or risk being cast out permanently. Kat couldn't even walk alone in the park without courting ruin, yet the Amazon could go to war and have carnal knowledge of men and *still* be widely admired?

"Are you well, Kat?" Lexie asked. "You seem a little flushed."

Kat flashed Lexie an angry glare before remembering to mask her true feelings. "It is a little warm in here," she said in a bored tone.

"Hmmm," Lexie said. "I thought perhaps your thoughts were on the Maid of Malagon." Kat's heart froze. Had she been so obvious? She was usually a master at masking genuine emotions; even Laurie rarely had an inkling of her true thoughts. "After all," Lexie continued, "when she is about, you no longer command the entire room as you are so used to doing."

"Oh, do be quiet," Bea said. "Kat has already landed the Season's most eligible bachelor. What does she care for the attentions of other gentlemen?"

A hush fell over the room, drawing their attention back in the direction of the Spanish woman. Kat forgot how to breathe when Edward stepped in beside Elena wearing unrelieved black formal wear with a royal blue cravat, which exactly matched the shade of Elena's silk gown.

"Well, perhaps not the most eligible bachelor." Lexie stared at the couple. "After all, an earl is higher than a viscount."

Kat struggled to maintain a neutral expression despite the awful thought forming in her mind. She'd thought Edward had come for her, his future wife, but what if he'd been unable to stay away from his mistress? The color of his cravat could not be a coincidence. It was as if he'd purposely dressed to complement the gown worn by his mistress and wanted everyone to know it.

She watched Elena smile at Edward with a confidence that suggested she knew she belonged at his side. Edward's stern expression relaxed as he bowed over his mistress' hand, touching his lips to the gloved surface.

"She's a bold piece, that one. Not that I care," Lexie said with a mischievous smile. "I do not require fidelity in marriage, so long as it comes with a title."

A heavy ache throbbed in Kat's chest. Obviously, Edward not only intended to keep his mistress, he planned to flaunt her openly at society affairs.

After supper, the men rejoined the ladies not long after being left to their port. Laurie and many of the other men went off to play cards. When Edward slipped out of the room, Kat seized her chance to have it out with him. He moved ahead of her at a leisurely pace, which made following him remarkably easy. He wound his way down the corridor and around a corner until he came to the solarium and slipped inside. Kat melted back into the shadows when she heard the sound of approaching footsteps. Servants it seemed. After they'd passed her, she emerged from her hiding place and followed Edward into the solarium.

The room was dark and steeped with the tang of citrus fruits. A long row of windows faced out onto the manor grounds. A deep-throated, feminine chuckle reached Kat, and she had no doubt who it belonged to. She maneuvered around the lemon plants until she caught sight of them.

"Are you sure this is a good idea?" the woman asked Edward in that throaty voice of hers.

"Definitely." He pulled Elena's body up against his and kissed her with almost violent passion. The Spanish woman did not seem to mind. From what Kat could tell, she participated fully in the embrace.

The Amazon sighed when he kissed a trail down her neck. "Do you like that, my love?"

Throwing back her head, Elena drew Edward's head against her. "*Sí mi amor. Si.*"

"You are so lovely," he murmured against the woman's throat. "So lovely."

Kat stood frozen in place, unable to fully believe the wretched scene playing out before her: Edward's lips on that woman's skin, the terms of endearment, his breath heavy with arousal.

Elena's fingers went to the placket of Edward's pants. "Come, *mi amor*. I want you now."

The full horror of witnessing Edward in the act of copulating with another woman slammed into Kat. Before she could stop it, an indecipherable utterance of shock and dismay escaped her lips, reverberating through the air like a clanging bell. Clapping her hand over her mouth, she watched Edward pull away from the Amazon to look in her direction.

"Kat?" Comprehension moved slowly across his face when he recognized her. "You shouldn't be here."

What had she expected? Remorse? Chagrin at being caught in a blatant act of betrayal? Some expression of guilt? Instead, his face wore a polite expression, his voice almost nonchalant, as though he hadn't been pawing his mistress right before her eyes. She saw his hand move to his placket to assure himself that his privates were not exposed. Thank goodness they were not. "I beg your pardon for disturbing you," she said, her tone edged with irony, hating how shaky her voice sounded.

"No harm done," he said in a mild tone.

*No harm done?* She began to tremble with a combination of distress and fury. "No harm done?"

"Eduardo." The Spanish woman spoke his name in a warning tone. "*Basta*."

His courteous gaze remained on Kat. "Although I must apologize you were subjected to this unseemly display."

"You're sorry that I saw you?" Not sorry that he had done it. He only regretted that she had witnessed his betrayal.

"Of course, you are a maiden with tender sensibilities."

She found it hard to comprehend what she was hearing. None of it made sense. Darting a glance at the Amazon, she said, "May I speak with Edward alone?"

"There is nothing we have to say that Elena cannot hear." He gave the woman a fond look. "She is very dear to me."

Kat couldn't believe her ears. She began to shake. "You want your mistress to remain for our private discourse?"

Compassion flitted across the Amazon's face. "I shall leave you," she said in an almost gentle tone. Elena walked out of the room, leaving them alone.

"How could you do it?"

An expression of courteous inquiry came over his face. "Do what?"

"You know what I'm talking about." Her voice shook. "Don't insult me by pretending you don't."

"Oh, you mean Elena. Isn't it obvious? I enjoy her charms. Very much so."

"How can you love me and do…that…with her?"

He smiled in the indulgent manner of a father explaining a simple concept to a naïve child. "The intimacies you and I have shared are also very pleasant. Men are simple creatures. Most willing women will drive us mad with lust."

She sucked in a breath. "How dare you compare me…

what we share...to the unspeakable things you engage in with that strumpet."

"Come now, it is really not so different. I am drawn to Elena, as I am to you, and would be to any beautiful woman, especially ones with whom I can slake my desires."

His words slammed into her like a runaway carriage. His kisses, his touches, weren't anything special. He felt the same physical need and excitement with all women. "Even if we marry, you will still pursue other females?"

He shrugged. "It is the nature of men. We are a rather base lot."

"I don't believe you. You're lying," she said heatedly. "The Edward I know would never behave as you have."

His expression hardened, the skin stretching tight over his high cheekbones. "You are quite correct. I am not the same man. Your Edward died a thousand deaths on battlefields across the Continent."

Her eyes filled. "So what is left of him?"

"Nothing."

The impact of his words hit her like a blow to the stomach and she winced at the pain. "This cannot be happening."

"Shall I escort you back?" he asked in a solicitous tone. "I do hope we shall always be friends."

Friends. As if she and Edward could ever be friends. "Have you no feeling?" she whispered.

"No." Darkness clouded his face. "I've none."

Unable to bear the sight of him for another moment, she spun away and stumbled out of the room with sorrow throbbing in her chest. She bolted down the corridor and tried desperately to recall the route back to her bedchamber. She couldn't possibly face the other guests.

"There you are, darling. I wondered where you'd got to." The familiar warm voice cut through the fog of despair and misery.

The sight of Laurie standing at the end of the corridor prompted relief to flood her body. "I'm here." She went to him and took his arm, grateful for the solid strength he offered. "Oh Laurie, I'm so fortunate to have you."

His eyes widened slightly, perhaps because he sensed her remark was genuine rather than motivated by the flirtatious banter she usually employed with him. "I hope you shall always be so pleased to see me." The palpable affection in his voice soothed her jumbled nerves. "Even after I've lost my hair and my teeth."

She squeezed his arm under her hand. Dear Laurie. Honest and loyal. So good when she was so faithless. "Especially when you are old and toothless," she said fervently. "I swear it."

# Chapter Seven

Edward stood motionless in the darkness of the solarium long after Kat left him, replaying her stricken expression over and over again in his mind.

"Your plan, it appears to have worked, *querido*."

"Astoundingly well." He blinked in the direction of the familiar voice. Elena stood in the doorway. "Although that's hardly surprising. Strategy is supposed to be my strong suit." It had, after all, won him an earldom.

"She was most distressed." Elena moved closer, her eyes fixed on him. "It is as you wished, no?"

"Absolutely." He swallowed against the ache in his lungs. Erasing any lingering doubts Kitty had about wedding the viscount was his final gift to her. Sinclair would give her what she deserved: a devoted, honorable husband who wasn't mad.

"And how about you, my friend?" she asked gently. "Are you all right?"

"Of course." He gave a harsh laugh. "Despite outward appearances, I'm quite dead inside. Surely, you of all people know that."

Her expression softened. "I know nothing of the sort, *mi corazon*."

• • •

"Excellent round." Laurie bowed to Peter Fawson after a turn of fencing. "Will you have another go?"

"Not I." Fawson headed for the door. "Breakfast is calling my name. I'm hoping to catch the Spanish strumpet there."

Laurie frowned. "Rand's gel?"

"The very same. She's one hot senorita. Have you seen the dairy on her?"

"They're hard to miss."

"I'd like to squeeze my Thomas between those diddeys and grind her good and hard." Fawson chuckled. "Think she's one to take it into her mouth?"

"I'm sure I cannot say." Laurie had no fondness for Rand's mistress, yet Fawson referred to her as one would a common whore and the crude references didn't sit well with him. "She seems devoted to Randolph."

Fawson shrugged. "Word is she does as she pleases. I'd like to think she'd be pleased to entertain all sorts of possibilities with me," he said with a wink before walking out the door.

Glad to see the back of Fawson—whose company he generally enjoyed—Laurie experienced a sense of restlessness. He continued to practice his moves, thrusting and parrying with an imaginary opponent. Kat had been in a strange mood last night, clinging to him as if he were some sort of lifeline. He often felt humored and appeased by her, but last evening he'd felt needed, indispensable even.

A Spanish-accented lilt cut into his thoughts. "Do you desire a partner?"

Turning to face the Maid of Malagon, Laurie gaped momentarily before catching himself. Randolph's mistress wore tight-fitting breeches that hugged her lanky curves in all sorts of indecent ways. The gentleman's apparel lingered over her hips, caressing firm, lithe thighs before the calfskin fabric disappeared into gleaming black boots at her knees.

She gave one of those smoky laughs of hers, which made his body tense in response. "I have shocked you again."

How had this jade ever come to be accepted in polite company? She certainly defied all rules of decorum. "Most English ladies do not wear gentleman's breeches."

Those dark lush eyes sparkled with obvious amusement. "Nor do Spanish ladies with breeding. We are not so different from you English."

*She* was certainly unlike any other female of his acquaintance. Elena moved with a confident gait and bent over to pick up the foil Fawson had left on the ground. The movement strained the breeches over her bottom, giving him an astoundingly sensual view of her nicely rounded backside.

He averted his eyes. "And yet you wear breeches?"

She straightened to her full height. "It is rather difficult to man a cannon in a skirt." She whipped the foil around as though testing its weight. "Will you have a go with me?"

To his dismay, his prick swelled in reaction to her

invitation, even though she surely wasn't offering to shuck those breeches and give him a go at her. "You not only man a cannon, but you fence as well? I suppose I should not be surprised."

She lifted her chin. "Perhaps you are afraid to take on a woman."

He sighed at her obvious attempt to goad him. "Very well." Laurie saluted her with his foil and bowed.

"The *vizconde* is always so polite."

"I do try."

They began to thrust and parry, light movements to warm up. He changed his rhythm to throw her off, but she caught on and followed seamlessly. He clearly had strength and height as an advantage, but the Maid proved to be quick on her feet. "You fence well."

"For a woman you mean, *vizconde*?"

"I will not dissemble with you, ma'am." He executed an advance lunge, but she was ready for him and danced out of danger. "I do believe ladies have no business on the battlefield...or in the fencing arena."

She thrust, her large breasts quivering under the billowing white folds of her shirt. "And why is that, *patron*?"

He easily warded off her attack. "Because of their inherent physical weakness. The Lord, in his wisdom, made females the weaker sex."

Her foil passed around the tip of his. "You have discounted our strengths."

"Women undoubtedly have their own strengths, primarily related to intellect. However, I don't see their use on the field of battle."

"Oh!" She lost her footing and stumbled, handily proving

his point that women had no business fencing. Throwing down his foil, he leaped to catch her before she fell.

She felt surprisingly soft and supple as he held her tight against him, momentarily distracted by the feel of her fleshy orbs against his chest. She blinked up at him with luminous, almost innocent eyes before a look of triumph gleamed in them and he felt the blunt tip of her covered foil under his chin.

She grinned, slow and feline, prompting the temperature of his blood to soar. "Now do you see, *vizconde*," she asked, pressing the tip of her blade a little harder into his vulnerable skin, "how our female strengths assist us in our battles?"

With an inward curse, he eyed his foil, which he'd tossed away in an effort to save her. "Not all your opponents will be gentlemen who leap to save you from danger," he said with grudging admiration.

She laughed, the throaty sound reverberating all the way down to his vitals. "But they are still men, *patron*, and can be trusted to react to certain womanly charms."

With his arm still tight around her waist, he became aware of the sensual feel of her lushness pressed against him. The scent of exertion mingled with notes of cinnamon and jasmine filled his nostrils. What a cunning, lusty piece of baggage. He envied the earl his place in this woman's bed. Then he thought of Kat and shame flushed through him. He released Elena more abruptly than he intended.

She didn't appear to notice. "Friends?" she asked, drawing the tip of her foil away from his chin.

"Of course."

She replaced her foil, seeming unaffected by what had just passed between them. But when she turned around, he glimpsed — through that white shirt of hers — that the tips of her bountiful breasts had hardened.

Following his gaze, she looked down and then shrugged. "I am still a woman after all, and you are a most attractive gentleman."

Laurie inhaled sharply and his prick roared to attention. But she just smiled and sauntered out of the room with those hips swinging, once again treating him to a spectacular view of her backside.

This time, he did not avert his eyes.

• • •

"God in heaven, Kat." Toby stared at her. "Where is your hair?"

Kat fingered the short golden curls framing her face, feeling lighter than she had in years now that Fanny had chopped off the thick mane the others girls in her set had long envied. Which Edward had so admired. Only she thought of him as Rand now. Edward, *her Edward*, was dead.

"I needed a fresh start," she said, determined to put Rand out of her mind. "What do you think?"

Toby's forehead shifted upward. "Has Sin seen it yet?"

"Seen what?" Laurie asked coming around the corner, his eyes widening when he caught sight of Kat. "Oh my."

For the first time, she experienced second thoughts about her impulsive decision to chop off her hair. "Do you like it?"

"Of course I do." Laurie wiped away his expression of surprise. "It's enchanting."

Relief flowed through her. "I'm relieved you approve."

"I like everything about you, you know that," he said.

Bea, Lexie, and Peter Fawson, who'd walked up behind Laurie, came to an abrupt halt.

Bea's eyes went round. "Your hair!"

"I think it is divine." Laurie brought Kat's hand to his lips. Warmth filled her at his gallant defense of her.

Lexie gave her an assessing look. "Only Kat would be so daring to stay in the first stare of fashion."

"Wait until your mother sees it," Bea said.

Kat tightened her hold on Laurie's hand. "As long as Lord Sinclair is pleased, that is all that matters."

Toby rolled his eyes. "The two of you are aware that love in marriage is just not done."

Laurie placed Kat's hand on his arm, keeping his own hand over it. "Then I suppose Kat and I will have to resign ourselves to being unfashionable. Shall we?" They made their way into the parlor for the afternoon tea and games arranged by Aunt Winifred. A cool relentless rain would keep them from outdoor pursuits.

"Steel yourself, darling," Laurie said as a footman drew open the door for them to enter. She did, but against Rand, not against reactions to her new hairstyle. She hadn't seen him since the debacle in the solarium two nights ago.

Not that she'd hidden from him. It was Rand who had not appeared at all yesterday. Despite the misery wracking her body and the heavy headache throbbing at her temples, she was determined to continue with the normal activities. She refused to give Rand the satisfaction of knowing how much damage he'd done. He'd almost destroyed her once, but never again. This time, she wouldn't allow despair to consume her. Edward and the dream of him were long dead.

What she'd witnessed in the solarium proved that beyond any doubt.

She'd wasted far too much time pining over Edward Stanhope. Now, she meant to move forward with her life, giving Laurie the full attention he deserved. Few men were as decent as her betrothed. Breaking with him would have been the biggest mistake of her life. Thank goodness she'd learned the truth about Rand before it was too late.

Exclamations of surprise met their appearance in the parlor. With her shoulders back and chin up, Kat played her incomparable role to the hilt, easily accepting compliments about her hair, laughing and smiling, flirting and tossing about witticisms with her set.

All the while, she pretended not to feel the wrenching ache of loss deep in her belly, or to notice the dark eyes following her. Rand had finally reappeared, standing in a corner against the wall with Elena and Peter Fawson. Peter seemed intent on charming the Spanish woman, who gave the appearance of being amused by his efforts. Nursing a drink, Rand appeared to pay little attention to either of them.

Thunder clapped outside, drawing gasps from those closest to the windows. People took turns at the pianoforte, some partnering together, while others in the chamber gathered around to join the singing.

Another thunderclap boomed, so loud it seemed to shake the room. Some of the guests murmured a little nervously. Then Kat noticed Toby, standing by the window, looking even whiter than usual. Something about his posture, his complete stillness, alarmed her.

She approached him and laid a hand on his arm. "Toby?"

He ignored her, standing frozen in place, his eyes unseeing. "Toby?"

"I'll see to him." Rand's voice was curt. She looked up into his face, but his gaze remained intent on Toby. "Hobart, it's Rand." He placed an arm around Toby and guided him away from the window.

She followed. "What is wrong with him?"

"For God's sake," Rand hissed as they made for the door. "Don't make a scene."

Kat broke from them and went to the center of the room. Diverting an audience was something she did quite well. "Who's for charades?" she called gaily to others in the room. "Laurie, dear, won't you come and partner with me?"

After a lively game that lasted well over an hour, Kat slipped away and headed for her guest chamber. As Bea and Toby's cousin, she'd been assigned a bed in the family corridor, which was in a separate wing from the other guests. Approaching her chamber, sounds of distress emanated from farther down the hall.

"Don't touch them," Toby cried in an agonized voice. "Leave them alone, you vultures!"

Her heart accelerating, she hurried toward the sound, intent on offering her help. The door to Toby's chamber stood slightly ajar. When she looked inside, she saw Rand kneeling beside Toby, who sat with his hands over his ears, rocking back and forth in a rhythmic motion.

"Hobart, it's Rand. Look at me."

Toby shook his head, rocking faster. "Tell them to get away. Get away!"

"I will, Tobias. Rest assured. I will make them go away." Rand spoke in a gentle tone tinged with weariness, deep grooves lined his forehead.

Another man she didn't recognize stepped forward. "Here it is, my lord."

Rand took a cup from the man. "Thank you, Burgess." From the look of his attire, the man was a valet.

Rand offered the glass up to Toby's lips. "You must drink this now, Hobart. It will allow you to rest."

Toby stopped rocking in an abrupt motion. "Is that an order, sir?"

"That is a command, soldier," Rand said in an uncompromising voice she supposed he used with his troops. Toby allowed Rand to bring the cup to his lips and he drank fully. Rand helped him to his feet and assisted him to his bed. "There now, you rest. You'll be right as rain in the morning." Rand pulled the counterpane over Toby, who seemed to be falling asleep.

Feeling as though she'd intruded on something intimate, Kat backed away from the open door, just as Rand stepped out into the corridor.

He came to an abrupt halt, and his stern expression hardened when he saw her. "What are you doing here?"

Kat's cheeks heated. "I heard my cousin call out. Is he all right?"

Rand's uncompromising dark eyes bored into her. "He will be fine as long as you forget what you saw here."

Nodding, she hurried back to her chamber with a tight throat. Once inside, she fell back against the closed door and exhaled. Tears welled in her eyes. Bea had never been specific about how the war had ruined Toby. She swiped a tear from her cheek. After what she'd witnessed today, she now had a pretty good idea.

• • •

Passing the open library door, Laurie heard a throaty laugh he would recognize anywhere.

"What do you say?" a man's voice said in an inviting tone. Peter Fawson. "You won't be sorry." He knew he should keep on walking and leave them to their business, but he halted at the door and peered in.

Elena stood by the book stacks with an open volume in her hand. Peter stood next to her, with one hand propped up against the bookshelf over her shoulder. "I am not interested in boys," she said in a tone that seemed equal parts boredom and amusement.

Peter edged closer to her. "I'm all man, I assure you."

Elena appeared nonplussed. "Thank you, but no."

He placed a hand on Elena's bosom and she closed the book in her hands with a snap. "If you know what is good for you, *senor*, you will remove your hand now."

Instead he placed the other hand on her bosom as well. "I want to see how your gorgeous dugs bounce when you ride me."

Clenching his teeth, Laurie pushed the door open. "Am I interrupting?"

Peter, the lout, didn't bother to turn around or to remove his hands. "This is a private matter, Sin."

"I think not, Fawson." Something heated in Laurie's gut. "The lady is unwilling. Remove your hands from her person or I will remove them for you."

Peter turned to face him with an incredulous expression. "You would fight me over this strumpet?"

"Insult her again and I will call you out."

Elena's brow shot up in amusement. "He's a boy." She waved a dismissive hand in the air. "He should be sent to bed without supper, not called out on a field of honor."

Laurie's hard stare didn't waver from the other man. "Apologize, Fawson, and then make your farewell."

Fawson flushed. "Very well. My most profound apologies, ma'am."

"Now leave," Laurie said.

Fawson flashed him a disbelieving look that slowly twisted into comprehension. "I see how it is. You want her for yourself."

"Don't be absurd."

Peter sauntered to the door and paused. "I wonder what Lady Kat would have to say about that, Sin."

Once Peter was gone, Elena asked, "Is that true?"

"Is what true?"

"That you want me for yourself."

Laurie cheek's burned. "Pay him no mind. He is a rude lout with no manners."

"At least he is not afraid to go after what he wants."

Laurie's chest heated. "The man mauled you. Are you suggesting that you wanted it?"

Her eyes glittered in a way that made his temperature soar. "No, I don't want that boy."

"What do you want?" he asked sharply.

"I suspect the same as you, *vizconde*." Her somnolent gaze held his. "Only I am not afraid to admit it."

He walked over to her in quick strides. "What is it that you think I want?"

"They call you Laurie," she said in that husky voice of

hers. "That is a woman's name, no?"

He shocked himself by shoving her up against the book stack with his body, pressing himself against her. The woman made him crazy. He desired her. He wanted to do unspeakable things with her. To her. Acts he would never even contemplate with Kat. "They also call me Sin."

She chuckled low and throaty, and shocked him by wedging her hand between their bodies, brushing cunning fingers against his sex. His prick leaped at her touch, hard and full, throbbing with need. She cupped him fully, her ebony eyes intent on his. "Tell me, *vizconde*, what do you know of sin?"

"You really are a shameless hussy." He breathed hard, fighting the urge to touch her while praying her fingers would not stop their brazen exploration.

She stroked the length of him. "Perhaps you should teach me a lesson, no?"

He finally forced himself to grab hold of her hand to halt her indecent exploration. "Stop," he ground out, his breath coming in short, hard spurts, his body raging with lust.

Her dark eyes taunted him. "Tell me, *vizconde*, will you punish me for my bad behavior?"

Raw lust, hot and uncontrolled, swamped him. He grabbed her hands in one of his and forced them above her head. Fire sparked in her gaze so he jerked her hands higher. She closed her eyes and licked her lips, a shudder going through her. He lost any last bits of gentlemanly restraint. "Perhaps I know just what you want, madam."

He grabbed her around the waist with his free hand, abruptly turning her toward the shelves, her hands still hiked above her head. He gyrated into her, shocked at how good her softness felt against him. Dropping her hands, he lifted her skirts in a frenzy, baring a smooth caramel bottom. All he could think of now was being inside of her. Still clutching her bottom to his hips he pulled her back away from the book stack to bend her over. She went willingly, planting her hands against the shelves for leverage.

"*Sí vizconde, sí,*" she cried softly.

He couldn't see or hear anything beyond the pounding in his ears and groin. He unfastened his breeches and freed himself, driving into her from behind with a single strong stroke. She was wet and moaned her pleasure when he entered her. He pounded into her as hard as he could. She felt damned good, slick and tight, her femininity caressing him as he shoved himself in and out of her, banging her like she was the lowest of whores.

"Is this how you want it?" he gasped, stroking into her with an urgency he had never known before. His hands clutched her bare, rounded bottom, a smooth bronze that rocked as he drove into her. The sight of it drove him even madder.

He slid his fingers around to touch her where she was hot and wet. Beneath him, he heard her crying with pleasure. She shuddered and convulsed, her peak coming hard and fast. He quickened his pace, exploding into her with a release that left him shaken and spent. His body curved over hers while he caught his breath and regained his senses, their labored breathing the only sound in the room. The warmth of her body and her spicy woman's scent, intermixed with the earthy smell of recent coupling, engulfed him.

Good lord! What had just happened? He forced himself to withdraw from her, and something akin to regret sluiced through him at the loss of her womanly softness and heat.

"*Dios mio*," she whispered, standing up to lean against the bookshelves as though she had no strength left.

"I apologize." He stepped away from her, fastening his breeches. Remorse, shame, and guilt slammed into him all at once. "That should not have happened."

Her dark eyes fixed on him. "You do not owe me an apology, *vizconde*. We didn't do anything I didn't desire."

"It won't happen again."

"That is a pity." She shook out her skirts. "We could enjoy each other a great deal, I think."

He had to get away from her and this abomination he had just allowed to happen. He was betrothed to Kat and had just betrayed her in the worst possible way. But as he hurried down the corridor it wasn't Kat he thought of. But rather of Elena's soft, warm bottom moving back against him, of her ready response and slick heat. He'd never experienced anything like it—the passion, the desperation, the unparalleled physical pleasure.

God help him, but he already wanted more.

# Chapter Eight

The following morning when Rand went to check on Toby, he found him with his mother and a gentleman of middle years with untamed salt-and-pepper side whiskers, who Mrs. Hobart introduced as Doctor Drummond. Rand didn't recognize the doctor, yet the name struck him as familiar.

He turned to Toby, who sat on the edge of his bed, still in the rumpled clothing he'd worn to sleep last evening. "How do you fare this morning?"

"Rand." Toby regarded him with bleary eyes. "Come to join the cavalry?"

"Beg pardon?"

"The doctor here wants to dissect my brain in hopes of locating the faulty valve."

"Nonsense. Doctor Drummond is my cousin." Mrs. Hobart's mouth firmed. "He is showing familial concern for Tobias."

"And I assure you, I only dissect the dead," Drummond

said with some humor.

Drummond. The reason the name sounded familiar clicked. "You're Will's Doctor Drummond. He attends your dissections to gain a better understanding of the human form."

The doctor blinked at him. "You are acquainted with the artist?"

"Very much so. He is my brother."

Drummond regarded him with some confusion. "Yet you are not the Marquess of Camryn."

"No, the marquess is my elder brother."

"He is the Earl of Randolph," Mrs. Hobart interjected, "and was recently awarded a peerage on account of his brilliant service in the war."

"Indeed, we have all heard of Randolph, the great war hero." Drummond's eyes were watchful. "You served with Tobias?"

"He was my commanding officer," Toby said. "Have a care, Rand, the sawbones will want to start dissecting your brain as well as mine."

"Tobias!" his mother exclaimed. "You forget your manners. Doctor Drummond is family and can be relied upon to be discreet about your…discomfort."

Hobart lifted an amused brow in Rand's direction. "My discomfort."

"Nostalgia is a common reaction to the traumas of war," Drummond said. "The purpose of my research is to determine why that is."

Toby pushed up from the bed. "Well, go experiment on someone else. I need to see to my toilet."

Satisfied that Toby seemed sufficiently recovered from

last evening's incident, Rand followed Mrs. Hobart and the doctor out of the chamber. Toby's mother excused herself and Rand accompanied the doctor to the dining room for breakfast.

"Did you see many instances of nostalgia, my lord?" Drummond inquired.

"I've seen my men in various degrees of upset." The muscles across the back of Rand's shoulders clenched. "I cannot say whether it qualifies as nostalgia."

"The condition seems to affect some more than others. I'm interested to know why that is."

Rand stiffened. "If you are suggesting Hobart is a coward, you could not be more wrong. He served with all distinction in the battle arena."

Drummond put his hand to his chest. "You misunderstand me, my lord. I do not believe lack of courage is the cause of nostalgia."

His interest piqued. "Then to what do you attribute it?"

"It is entirely possible battlefield trauma causes lasting changes to the brain."

"If that is so," he said, keeping his tone purposely neutral, "is this change to the brain irreversible?"

"Ah, that is the big question, is it not? Whether these men are permanently marked or whether their affliction can be reversed over time."

"How would one reverse it, do you suppose?"

"By social healing. Exercise helps manage some symptoms. As does keeping oneself occupied." He regarded Rand with a thoughtful air. "You seem most interested in the affliction, my lord."

"Some of my men were so affected." He forced an

easy tone despite the tightness in his chest. "Naturally I am interested in seeing to their welfare."

The doctor paused and Rand could see his mind working. "If you should ever have need of my services, you have only to ask."

"For my men?"

"For your men, of course," Drummond said. "Men who are so afflicted often find sharing their difficulties with a medical expert can provide some relief."

They reached the breakfast room, where several guests were already seated. "I shall take that under advisement."

Drummond followed Rand in and they headed to the sideboard where breakfast was laid out. "Perhaps you might care to call upon me when you return to Town to further discuss the matter."

"We shall see." Rand's cravat felt tight around his neck, impeding his flow of breath. "Eggs, doctor?"

• • •

"I think we should move up the wedding," Laurie said between bites of kidney pie.

Kat nibbled on her toast and pretended not to notice when Rand seated himself at the long breakfast table, choosing an available chair across the table as far away as possible from her. His mistress hadn't appeared. She was no doubt sleeping late after a long night.

"Kat?"

She swung her attention to Laurie. "Hmmm?"

"What do you think about us marrying earlier than we planned?"

"I think it is an excellent idea." The sooner they married, the further behind she could put the catastrophe she'd almost made of her life. She slid another glance at Rand, who appeared to be concentrating on his breakfast. Yet his plate remained full. "I can't wait to be your wife."

"Excellent. I'll speak with your father as soon as we return to Town."

Cradling her chin in her hand, she gave Laurie her full attention. He seemed on edge. His handsome face was drawn and deep lines creased the areas around his eyes and mouth. "Did you not sleep well?"

He darted a look at her. "Why do you ask?"

"You seem out of sorts."

He exhaled. "I'm anxious to marry you so we can put all of this behind us."

She held her breath. Did Laurie suspect something was amiss? "All of what?"

He stilled. "The anticipation, of course. This endless waiting can drive the sanest man to bedlam."

"Is that all?" She smiled with relief. "What shall we do today?"

"The rain has let up," Laurie said, recovering some of his usual easy manner. "Perhaps we can arrange an excursion into the village. Mrs. Hobart mentioned it is market day."

After breakfast, a small group—including Lexie, Bea, and Peter Fawson—went along with them to the village. They started out together checking out the wares, and Kat couldn't help noting a subtle tension between the two men. Eventually, she and Laurie drifted away from the others. "What is going on between you and Peter?"

Laurie paid for two sweetmeats and handed her one.

"What do you mean?"

She took his arm as they resumed walking amid the stalls and vendors who'd laid their wares out on blankets on the ground. "You've been very short with him today. I thought the two of you were friends."

"It's nothing."

"It must be something," she insisted. "I've never known the two of you to be at odds."

He finished chewing his sweetmeat before answering. "I discovered him insulting a lady."

"Peter? Truly? Perhaps you were mistaken. He has always been a perfect gentleman."

"It was no mistake."

"Who did he insult?"

"It doesn't matter." He pulled her behind the church, where they were out of sight, and pushed her up against the wall.

"What are you doing?" she asked, knowing perfectly well he intended to steal a kiss.

His eyes blazed as he looked into her face. "I have a fierce hunger for you, Kat." His lips pressed against hers in a demanding kiss.

She opened to him and kissed him back, fully participating with concentrated eagerness, desperate to experience the same urgent need with Laurie that she had with Rand. Once Laurie bedded her, she'd forget all about Rand. She just knew it. "Why don't we anticipate our wedding night?" she murmured against his lips.

He pulled back, his shock apparent. "You can't mean that."

She planted another kiss on his lips. "I do mean it. We

both want to and we are going to marry anyway. Where's the harm in it?"

Warring emotions flashed in his face. He kissed her again, pulling her body tight against his. "Are you certain, Kat? Once we do it, there will be no turning back."

"I don't want to turn back. I want to belong to you fully. You are the most decent person I know, Laurie. So good and honorable."

He paled. "I want to do right by you, Kat." He pulled back from her and released a shuddering breath. "It would be wrong to anticipate our wedding night. But I will speak to your father about moving the wedding up the moment we return to Town. I want this done as much as you do."

Walking back among the vendors on Laurie's arm, a lingering uneasiness followed her. Laurie had always been anxious to marry her, yet something had changed. Not only did he seem distracted and on edge, but there'd been a note of grim desperation in the way he'd kissed her. She shoved the concerns out of her mind. Marriage would cure whatever was wrong with Laurie. As it would for her. It had to.

・・・

"Come on, girl, we'll slip out the library doors." Vera jumped a happy circle around Rand as they made their way through the darkness, moving quietly so as not to wake the sleeping guests. He walked along the corridor to the library with Vera following. Pushing the door open, he saw the fire still blazed, and its flickering light cast dim dancing shadows about the room. It was most unusual for a fire to be burning in the middle of the night.

He made for the doors that led to the gardens, but the dog veered away from him toward the hearth. "Come, Vera. Let's go for a walk."

The animal yelped a short, happy bark, nuzzling into a high leather chair that faced the fireplace. He gave a low whistle to call the dog back to him.

Wagging her tail vigorously, Vera gave the chair her full attention. Frowning, Rand stepped toward the dog. Someone must have left food on the chair. As he neared, he caught sight of delicate pale feet first, folded under feminine legs and dangling a bit off the chair. The scent of violets reached him next, leaving little doubt as to who occupied the chair. His heart pounded.

"I see I haven't completely won Vera over from her mistress," he said, forcing an even tone.

She leaned forward in the chair to look around it and back at him, color high on her cheeks, the firelight dancing in her short curls, making them glisten like specks of gold around the glittering sapphire of her eyes. "*Now* she comes to me," she said in a wry voice, her eyes following him as he stepped in front of the hearth. "When I would prefer to stay concealed."

His chest contracted at the thought of Kat hiding from him. Regret slammed into him anew for having hurt her, even though he had done it to ensure her future happiness. "She is a stubborn-minded female. I've learned Vera does as she pleases."

She ran her hands over the dog's head and wiggling body, allowing Vera to lick her chin with great enthusiasm. "Hello girl. I've missed you, yes I have."

He wondered why she'd cut her hair. He'd loved those

long silken tresses. Even now, he could almost smell the delicate floral scent her bathing soap left in the gleaming mass of strands, which he'd buried his face in not so long ago. "Why did you cut your hair?"

She paused for a moment, her eyes fixed on the motions of her hands moving up and down the dog's soft fur. "I needed a change."

Surprisingly, he found he did not regret the loss of her hair. Even though he'd always thought the gleaming strands contributed to her considerable beauty. Now Rand saw they'd actually distracted from her delicate allure. These short curls framed her face in a way that showcased her fine-drawn features, highlighting enormous blue eyes in a fragile, heart-shaped face; the adorable upturned point of her slender nose, and the slight upper lip resting atop a lush lower one. "It suits you."

This time she did look at him, her eyes rounding and flickering with obvious surprise. He realized then that she'd done it because of him, as if chopping off her hair would shed their shared past, cutting him out of her life or her heart. If only it could be that easily accomplished.

He suppressed the wild urge to tell her she was even more beautiful to him now, a mix of sensual earth goddess and ethereal nymph. For him to have believed, even for a moment, that this radiant creature could ever be his, was laughable. "I'm sorry to have disturbed you. We were just going for a walk."

Holding Vera's jowls gently in her slim, tapered fingers, Kat regarded the animal with mock reproach. "Have you awakened the earl in the middle of the night to tend to your needs?"

That she referred to him as *the earl* was not lost on Rand. No longer was he her Edward. The reference to his title emphasized the new chasm between them. He pushed away the crushing regret, reminding himself that he had intended for things to fall this way. His planning here, as on the battlefield, had been to perfection.

He did not correct Kat's mistaken assumption that Vera's needs had pulled him out of bed to wander in the night shadows. No need for her to know this sleeplessness occurred often, or how glad he was to have the animal's companionship when it did. "Has sleep eluded you as well?"

Sitting back in the chair, she looked into the fire, the flames flickering in the vibrant shade of her eyes. "So it would seem."

"Would you care to walk with me?" The invitation breached the uneasy lull between them before he'd even realized his mind had formed it.

She blinked away from the fire to look up at him, inquiry evident in her gaze.

"I comprehend I've proven something of a disappointment to you," he said in gentle answer to her unspoken question. "I understand if you wish to decline."

She pushed up from the chair. "There is no harm in taking Vera for a walk."

A spurt of gladness flowered in him at the thought of spending a little more time with her, even though the thinking part of him knew it to be a grave mistake. But he pushed it out of his head. Soon she would be Sinclair's and quite safe from him. He tamped down the howling protest deep in him at the thought of another man taking possession of her. Stepping aside, he allowed her to pass by him toward the library doors.

She wore a dressing gown over her night rail, the white of which peeked out at her smooth throat. Walking behind her, he noted how the belted dressing gown emphasized her tiny waist and the soft curve of her hips in a way that her formal gowns—which fell loose over her midriff—did not.

She stopped in front of the doors to allow him to pull them open, which he did, coming close enough to catch the beguiling whiff of violets again. The night air rushed in to greet them, doing little to cool the heat gathering under his skin.

Vera slipped past them both, bounding out onto the terrace and out of view as Rand stepped out after Kat, closing the door behind them with a soft click. They stepped down off the terrace in silence and set to walking at a pace slightly faster than a mere stroll, the full moon providing the only light over the Hobart's rolling, well-kept lawns.

Even though he did not look at her, his body felt her presence beside him keenly. His senses were alert to her every movement, to each soft inhale and exhale. He closed his eyes and swallowed, determined to drive the intense awareness between them away. "I understand you and Sinclair are moving up the wedding."

"Yes. We see no reason to delay."

He fixed his gaze ahead into the darkness, watching the blurry bouncing mass he knew to be Vera. "Indeed."

"What was wrong with Toby?"

He stiffened. "What do you mean?"

Impatience edged her response. "I'm not a complete fool. His sister, Bea, says the war has…affected him."

"He'll be fine. I imagine it will take time."

"He seemed to be seeing things, as though he was dreaming yet he wasn't sleeping."

"It is like a waking nightmare that keeps reoccurring," he said.

She stilled, her eyes on him. "And yet it does not happen to everyone. Like you, for instance, you don't suffer so, do you?"

He drew a sharp breath. "When one witnesses horrors most civilized beings cannot even begin to imagine, it is bound to have an impact."

"I always hated the war and everything about it. I blamed it for taking you from me. But now I know that wasn't the truth of it at all."

Actually it was the complete and total truth, but she could never know it. She must always assume him to be a philandering rakehell with no hope of reform. "Some men are not meant to be faithful," he said.

"Where is the fair Maid of Malagon this evening?"

"Sleeping in her bed, I presume. We are not in each other's pockets."

"I do expect faithfulness from Lord Sinclair, you know. He is very devoted to me."

Pain lanced his chest at the thought of her in Sinclair's bed. "The viscount's devotion to you is clear for all to see." She didn't speak, but he heard her breath hitch and feared she was near tears. "You could never be happy with me, Kitty. I wish it were otherwise, but it is not."

She stared straight ahead as they walked, refusing to look at him. "I know that now. It is well and good that I discovered it before it was too late." Her words were punctuated by a distant bark followed by a splash. She groaned. "Talavera, you bad dog."

He froze. "What did you call her?"

She walked ahead, shielding her face from his view. "We must retrieve her."

He caught her arm, feeling the soft warmth of her flesh through the thin dressing gown fabric. "You called her Talavera. Is that her full name?"

"Yes."

"Why did you name her that?"

She still looked out ahead, refusing to meet his eyes, the blue-green light of the moon slanting over her soft features. "You know why."

"Tell me."

She finally looked at him, a hard glint in her glistening eyes. "Must you complete my humiliation by forcing me to say it aloud?"

Talavera. He'd been badly injured and left on the battlefield for days while the killing raged around him. Both sides had claimed victory and the outside world saw Talavera as a great military triumph for Wellington, winning him a viscountcy and, eventually, a dukedom. As the great commander's chief strategist, the acclaim had extended to Rand. Many saw Talavera as the battle that won Rand an earldom.

For Kat to pay him tribute by naming her beloved dog after his greatest wartime achievement both stunned and humbled him. He'd had no idea she'd followed his military career. "I'm honored," he said in a soft voice. "Truly."

She snatched her arm away from him. "Don't be," she said sharply, gesturing toward the sound of Vera's yapping amidst splashing sounds. "Keep her. She's yours now."

"Don't be ridiculous, you adore Vera. As she does you."

"I don't want anything that reminds me of you." She spun around and left him, striding back toward the house, the hem of her dressing gown flapping indignantly about her ankles, making her look almost like an apparition in the blue night light. His emotions in chaos, he watched her disappear into the shadows of the house, just as she would soon vanish from his life for good.

# Chapter Nine

"It is good of you to come, my lady. Your visits seem to help tremendously." Mr. Milbank, the hospital administrator, escorted Kat to her carriage after she'd spent the afternoon visiting residents at the soldiers' home.

"It is the least I can do." She flushed with pleasure at having done something useful. The more time she spent visiting the soldiers, the more superfluous her social pursuits became. "I understood Mr. Ledworth is to leave soon."

"It is so," Mr. Milbank said as they stepped into the afternoon heat. "His episodes occur less frequently than when he first came to us."

"Episodes?" Something tickled down Kat's spine. "I have heard some soldiers are afflicted. Is it very common?"

Mr. Milbank's expression shuttered. "This is hardly appropriate conversation for a lady's ears."

She halted in front of her father's carriage. "Please be frank, sir," she said in a firm voice. "If I am to be of any assistance at all to these men, surely it is best I know something of what ails them."

Mr. Milbank swallowed hard. She knew it would be difficult for him to deny a lady's command, even though she'd cloaked it in a polite request. "You will have heard of nostalgia."

"Yes." She hadn't known what afflicted Toby had a name. "Go on."

"It is characterized by a certain moroseness, as well as a loss of strength, sleep, and appetite."

"And the waking nightmares." Like Toby experienced.

He shot her a startled look. "I'm surprised you know of such things."

She waived aside the comment. "How do you treat it?"

"We do not allow them more rest than is necessary. We attempt to keep them busy and to vary their occupations. Keeping regular hours and taking gymnastic recreation seems to help."

"I see." She nodded to the footman who rushed forward to open the carriage door and put down the step. "Thank you for your frank words, Mr. Milbank. It relieves my mind to know your good care has helped Mr. Ledworth become well enough to rejoin his family."

He flushed with pride, bidding her farewell, his discomfort with her probing questions vanishing at her flattery. She settled in the carriage where Fanny awaited her.

"Was he there?" Fanny asked.

"Was who there?"

"You know who. The Earl of Randolph."

"No, of course not." She had not seen Rand since returning from the country a fortnight ago and was glad of it. She needed time away from him to recover from it all; his lack of devotion and her chagrin that he knew about Vera's full name. Now he could easily surmise just how desperately she'd tried to follow his battle campaigns. How he must have laughed to know she'd pined for him all those years he'd been gone.

The earl hadn't made a public appearance in weeks, but Rand remained a topic of great interest in the finest circles. If anything, his absence heightened the enigmatic and eligible new peer's allure.

"He's probably holed up with his mistress." Kat grimaced at the thought. "She looks like she could keep a man busy."

"Hmmm."

Kat eyed her maid with suspicion. "What does 'hmmm' mean?"

"Not a thing." Fanny lifted a shoulder. "I am merely your servant. What do I know?"

"But you have an opinion. Come now, Fanny, out with it."

"I find the earl's recent behavior to be out of character."

"How so?"

"The earl is many things, but I never took him for a rakehell."

"I saw it with my own eyes, as you well know. I thank the Lord every day that I didn't cry off of my betrothal to Lord Sinclair. You were right about Randolph all along."

"Hmmm."

There it was again, the noncommittal noise that suggested Fanny had a definite opinion on the matter. "What is it?" Kat allowed her aggravation to show. "Surely you agree that Lord Sinclair will make a fine husband."

"Yes, he'll make you a good husband. But, mark my words, there's something strange going on with the earl."

Kat swallowed against the grief expanding in her chest. "Even if that is true, I've wasted too much time pining for Edward Stanhope. I must look forward." It was the only way she'd survive this latest heartbreak. Analyzing and examining his character and motives would only prolong her suffering.

Fanny's expression softened as if she understood. "Of course, soon you will be the Viscountess Sinclair," she said, forcing a cheerful note into her voice. "That is something to celebrate."

"Indeed," Kat said with a firm nod. Yet, in her stomach, something sank a little further.

...

"What is she doing here?" Laurie asked sharply. His heart skittered at the sight of Elena Márquez-Navarro standing on the threshold of the Campbell's parlor, looking like an Amazon queen ready to conquer all of London.

A large smile crossed Lexie's face. "I invited her," she said, leaving them to go to Elena's side.

"Whatever for?" he asked, even though Lexie was too far away to hear.

"Both Lexie and Bea admire her greatly," Kat answered somewhat sourly. "I know Bea thinks the Maid of Malagon is a paragon of progressive womanhood."

Laurie's face warmed. "The woman defies all convention."

"Exactly, that's what Bea seems to like most about her."

"I don't see Randolph with her." Beside him, Kat seemed to stiffen. Laurie's heartbeat stuttered. Surely she didn't suspect his indiscretion with Elena? Casting a quick glance at her, he noted his betrothed appeared pale and on edge. "Are you unwell?"

She blinked up at him and her mask fell into place, just before she hit him with the brilliant smile that always used to distract him. Yet, for some reason, it no longer carried the same potency. Instead, the slow, sensually-confident smile of the Maid of Malagon came to his mind, warming his body. He shoved it away, angry at himself for playing Kat false.

What was the matter with him? He'd landed London's reigning beauty, the incomparable who'd ruled the *ton* for five Seasons. Her father had even consented to move the wedding up several months, from just after Easter to late September. They would wed during the little Season, rather than waiting for the spring, doing away with the grand spectacle they'd originally planned for at the height of the Season.

Every eligible man with a title had pursued Kat and most still expressed considerable interest in her charms. Only Randolph showed no overt interest in her, perhaps because he had Elena in his bed. Laurie escorted Kat into dinner and focused his full attention on her, determined to put the aberration of his attraction to Elena out of his mind.

When the ladies withdrew after the meal, leaving the gentlemen to their port and cigars, Laurie grabbed the chance to escape unnoticed. Stepping out onto the terrace, he hurried down the stairs into the small, darkened garden, anxious to avoid anyone who might come out for air.

The smell of cheroot smoke alerted him that he had

failed in his quest to be alone. He wondered why the fellow had come outside to smoke his cheroot instead of remaining in the dining room partaking with the other gentlemen. His eyes sharpening in the dark, he watched the glowing tip of the cheroot move toward a full, curved mouth that could belong to no man. "Good Lord! You smoke cheroots, too?"

Elena chuckled on her exhale, the throaty sound firing off all of his nerve endings. "It is why I am hiding in the garden, *vizconde*, I do not want to shock my hostess."

"Is there anything you don't do like a man?"

Dark eyes rested on him as she tilted her chin up to take another pull on the cheroot. "I don't make love like a man, although I do take my pleasure when I desire it. I suppose that is as a man, *vizconde*."

Or a whore. Those were the women who took carnal pleasure as they wanted, not well-born ladies. Yet he no longer thought of her as a strumpet, but rather as someone who did things on her own terms and relished doing so. Like how she savored that cheroot. The same way she'd enjoyed fencing. And making love.

She paused for a leisurely exhale of curling smoke which enveloped her in a gray-tinted haze. "I certainly don't have the body of a man."

"Where is Rand?" he asked sharply, trying to eradicate the image of her smooth bottom moving against his groin from his mind.

"Rand has decided to become a recluse, I think. I have not seen him in several days."

"He does not require you to stay by his side?"

She smiled at that. "It might interest you to know the earl and I are no longer lovers."

His body reacted to her unexpected announcement with distressing alacrity. Blood raced through his veins in an apparent rush to fill his groin. "Why do you think that would interest me?" he said curtly, barely able to get the words out above the roaring in his brain.

She chuckled again. "Because I think everything about me interests you, *vizconde*. Especially the idea of making love again."

Beads of perspiration tickled his upper lip. "I beg to differ, *senorita*," he said stiffly. "What passed between us can hardly be described as making love."

He meant it as an insult to drive her away, but she gave no indication of taking offense. Instead, Elena stubbed the cheroot out against the tree in that unhurried way of hers. Moving to stand in front of him, her languid dark eyes held his captive. "Whatever you call it, *vizconde*, you would like to do it again, no?"

The scent of cinnamon and jasmine washed over him and he was drowning in her all over again. Like a magnet helpless in the face of an undeniable attraction, he stepped closer to her and dragged her into his arms, his lips slamming down on hers.

Lord, but she knew how to kiss. Her tongue teased his, boldly exploring his mouth, her teeth nipped and scraped against his lips, sending shivers of pleasure down his spine. The woman kissed as he suspected she did everything else; with a full interest and engagement he hadn't experienced in a female before.

Sounds of music and muted chatter drifted out to them. Someone had thrown open the terrace doors. He pulled away with great reluctance. The men would have joined the ladies by now. "We should return," he whispered in a pant against her neck. "It won't be long before someone notes our absence."

"Will you come to me later, *vizconde*?"

The thinking part of him screamed against it. To accept Elena's invitation would be thoroughly disreputable, not to mention unspeakably disloyal to Kat. Only a true cad would accept. And, besides, he didn't even know where she lived. But he would find out.

"Yes."

. . .

"It's not the best day for a riding party" —Lexie eyed the gray clouds— "but as I am in excellent company, the weather hardly matters."

Rand murmured some appropriately gallant response to the chit's tiresome flirtations. Miss Campbell was clearly out to land herself an earl. She might be a suitable marital candidate if he didn't find her incessant chattering so damn irritating. After all, he wasn't looking for love and had no interest in courting any woman except the one he could not have.

Glancing up ahead to where Hobart rode, he noted Toby's pallor and subdued countenance, yet detected no trace of the madness that had gripped him in the country a fortnight ago. They'd left the city to spend the day in Richmond, where they could enjoy wider expanses of space in which to ride. Keeping an eye on Hobart was the sole reason he'd consented to join this tiresome all-day riding excursion. The last thing he desired was to spend the day in close company with any group that included Kitty and Sinclair.

She hadn't spared him a glance beyond the polite greetings they'd exchanged this morning. The betrothed couple rode up ahead, Kat talking animatedly with Sinclair, who for once did not have that usual love-struck expression on his face, although Rand couldn't understand why.

Kitty was at her loveliest today, gleaming with radiance despite the dour weather, in a deep blue riding costume which showed her slender form to extreme advantage. The sapphire blue of her eyes glistened in the outdoor light and those cropped curls, under a jaunty feathered hat, illuminated her delicate facial features. Just looking at her made his chest ache.

More masculine parts of his body responded as well. Normally, he was a man with strong sexual appetites, which he'd routinely satisfied. Yet he hadn't had a woman since ending carnal relations with Elena. Lately his body only stirred with interest when Kat was in the vicinity, and it was almost as though being with another woman now would somehow be disloyal to her. That ridiculous notion should resolve itself once Kat became Sinclair's wife. He shoved the image of the viscount rutting over Kat out of his mind before it could fully take root and drive him into an unreasonably jealous furor.

Forcing his eyes away, he let Lexie's incessant chatter roll over him for a few more minutes before edging his mount closer to Toby's. "You are quiet today."

"You should know that I've come to a decision."

"And what is that?"

"I'm going away in a few days' time."

"Going away? To where?"

"Doctor Drummond has a clinic in the country." Toby's pale determined eyes met his. "He is an expert on matters of nostalgia and believes he can help me with my episodes."

"In what way?"

"He says there are things one can do."

Hope shafted through him. "Such as?"

"Keep busy, keep a regular schedule, and take exercise. Perhaps even music."

"Music?" Something shifted deep in his chest. "How can that be of any help?"

"Drummond believes the appropriate music can soothe the mind."

Their conversation was interrupted by Fawson, who made some laughing noises about a racing bet to Toby, and before long the two of them galloped off, racing across the wide open space. Rand noticed Miss Campbell heading in his direction and, eager to shed himself of her cloying presence, he gave his mount his head. Content to ride by himself, he cantered across the open field away from the riding party.

He indulged himself by racing across open spaces on his own, slowing when he moved through trees, taking the occasional jump that caught his fancy. After a particularly daunting jump, Rand slid off his mount to give the animal a break. With the horse sampling some nearby grass, he rested on the trunk of a felled tree. His damn shoulder throbbed and he gave it a vigorous rub to help lessen the pain.

The sounds of galloping hooves cut into his peace, growing louder as the animal neared. Someone else had apparently veered off from the crowd since it sounded like a lone rider approached. Instead of slowing, the pounding hooves picked up speed as they neared.

The rider must be heading for the jump he'd just cleared. Pushing to his feet, Rand moved into the clearing to watch, hoping the swell was a seasoned rider because the jump was a treacherous one. His eyes sharpened on the approaching chestnut mare and the feminine, blue-clad figure upon it.

His heart froze. *Kitty*. Heading straight for calamity. The jump would be risky for anyone riding astride, but she rode sidesaddle, encumbered by the fabric of her riding habit. She whizzed past, heading straight for the jump, not seeming to notice him standing in the trees.

She might well break her neck. The image of Kitty's broken body lying on the ground gouged his insides. "Kitty, no!" he yelled urgently, just as she sailed upward. Time seemed to slow; it felt like forever before her mare touched down on the other side with Kitty still safely in the saddle. He released a breath of extreme relief, trying to calm the chaotic pounding of his heart.

She turned her mare around in a smooth motion, steering the animal in Rand's direction. Now that she'd skirted danger, he couldn't help but admire her excellent form in the saddle. "Are you mad?" she yelled at him when she approached. "I could have been thrown!"

"Exactly." Fury filled his chest, replacing his sense of relief. "You almost got yourself killed."

Her blue eyes blazed with anger. "Thanks to you. Bellowing at me like that, startling both me and my animal."

"What were you thinking to take that jump?"

She slipped off her mare and marched up to him. "What I do, and when I do it, and how I do it"—she poked his chest with her finger to emphasize her point—"is none of your concern."

He couldn't believe she was jabbing him in the chest. "Have you taken complete leave of your senses?" He grabbed her hand to stay her annoying assault. "You almost broke your neck."

"My neck is none of your business any longer." She tried to snatch her gloved hand away, but he tightened his grip, holding her in place. "Nor should you be concerned about any other part of my person."

"If you think I am going to sit by and watch you kill yourself, you are sadly mistaken," he said furiously.

"Why you—" She growled with frustration as she struggled to loosen his grip on her. "Unhand me, you lout."

"Not until you calm down." She met his gaze, her eyes glowing with angry defiance. The agitation lit up her face, making her even lovelier. For a moment, neither of them spoke while anger arced through the air. Red bathed her cheeks and her breathing became more apparent beneath the fine pelisse cloth which hid her flesh from him.

The passion of his fury transformed into something else, fueling a furious arousal. He pulled her into his arms and kissed her hard, forcing open her lips to taste her. She kissed him back with just as much aggression and he could sense the co-mingling of anger and desire each time her tongue stroked his. He widen his lips over hers, devouring her mouth as his blood surged through his veins.

He ached to touch his lips to her neck, but her blasted cravat impeded him. He broke the kiss, his hands going to loosen the neck cloth. Her hands fumbled into his and for a crushing moment, he thought she intended to deny him. But then her eyes caught and held his, the blue in them catching the light, and she loosened the perfect bow of the soft muslin fabric.

His pulse roared in his ears as she pulled the cravat free, baring a sliver of pale flesh. He pressed his lips against the tender spot. "Your neck is definitely my concern," he growled, before nipping the spot with his teeth. She moaned and pushed into him and he soothed the spot with his tongue.

He returned to press his lips against hers, to taste her again, as if he could never get enough. He embraced her, running his hands down her back and over the rounded flesh of her bottom. "Every part of your person is most definitely my concern," he said against her lips, giving the womanly flesh in his hands a firm squeeze.

"Stop talking," she said in a breathless voice, drawing him back into a hungry kiss, mating with his tongue, their lips and teeth teasing, tasting, and clashing with each other.

He brought his fingers up to her riding jacket and began to unfasten the frogs that held it closed. She helped him, pulling off her jacket while he pushed it down her arms, throwing it to the ground. His seeking hands roamed over the cambric fabric of her habit shirt, with its high collar trimmed with lace.

"Just tear it," she said between urgent kisses.

He cupped her breasts, giving them a light squeeze while teasing the hardened tips with his thumbs. "You have no idea how much I would like to. But you can't possibly return with a torn shirt without being irrevocably ruined."

She tugged at the shirt collar, seeming intent on tearing it herself. "The cravat and jacket will hide any damage to the shirt."

"Then I am happy to oblige." He tore the collar of her

shirt open to bare the smooth cream of her décolletage and the upper swells of her sweet breasts.

His arousal swelled to the point of pain. He'd never thirsted for a woman as much as he wanted her at this moment. He pressed hungry kisses down the smooth warmth of her neck and across her chest. He tongued the mounds that were still mostly covered by her corset.

She grumbled in frustration. "I've always hated corsets."

He smiled against her breasts. "It would take more than a bit of fabric to deter me."

She caught her breath when he eased one breast out of the confines of her corset. He stopped and looked for a moment at the exquisite mound with its eager pink tip. "If I live one hundred years, I don't believe I shall ever see anything so fine."

He lowered his head to her breast, pressing worshipful kisses along the tender flesh, flicking teasing licks at its point. He lost himself in the taste of her womanly flesh, her breathy cries of arousal, and the heady scent of lavender.

A sudden awareness hit him. He stilled and straightened, the hairs on the back of his neck tingled. "Someone's coming."

Leaning against his strength, she listened for it too; the sounds of an approaching riding party, theirs in all likelihood. "We're sheltered by the trees," she whispered. "Perhaps they'll ride by us."

"No," he said briskly, stooping to grab her discarded jacket. "They'll see the horses. They probably already have and that's what brought them here."

"Laurie." Panic crossed her flushed face. "He can't see me like this."

He stifled the urge to curse at the mention of her betrothed's name. Instead, he helped her don the fitted jacket.

"Damnation," she cried in frustration struggling with the jacket. "Why are these things so tight?"

He managed to get it on her. As she struggled to fasten it, he looked for the cravat. Spotting it nearby, he picked it up, shaking out the grass and leaves.

Feminine laughter trickled through the trees, followed by Miss Campbell's voice. "Perhaps they're hiding from us." She came into view, but did not see them at first because she was looking behind her, calling back to whoever accompanied her. Then her foot stumbled over uneven ground, causing her to face forward to regain her step. She almost bumped into Rand before catching sight of him.

"Oh, there you are Lord Randolph," she said with a beguiling smile.

Kitty must have moved because Miss Campbell looked in her direction. "Hello Kat," she said breezily. But then she froze, the color bleeding out of her face, her eyes riveted on Kitty's torn neckline. "What happened to you?" she whispered.

Clutching her torn blouse closed at her neck, Kitty stared back at Lexie, speechless, her lips apart. Pink stained her cheeks, her breathing coming hard.

Miss Campbell's gaze darted between them, narrowing in on the mangled cravat lying useless in Rand's hand. "You beast." Horror washed across her features. "You attacked her."

It took him a moment to process her words, to understand that she accused him of the most dishonorable offense possible. He saw immediately that Miss Campbell had also handed him a way to save Kitty from complete ruin, and so he seized it. "Yes. I have no excuse for my behavior."

Miss Campbell's eyes widened in shocked disbelief. "You cad," she hissed at him. "Laurie will call you out." She turned to call out to her companions.

Kitty came to life, leaping toward Miss Campbell and grabbing her arm to keep her from alerting the others. "No, Lexie, hush!"

"Everything will be well, dear." She patted Kitty's arm. "I'm going to summon Laurie."

"No," Kitty gasped, her eyes wild with panic. "You mustn't."

"No one will blame you, Kat. Least of all Laurie. Surely you know that." She spoke in a soothing tone which boosted Rand's estimation of the lady. Then her tone hardened. "But Lord Randolph is no gentleman. Laurie must be allowed to deal with him accordingly."

Kitty's fingers whitened as they clawed Miss Campbell's arm. "No, Lexie. You don't understand—"

"On the contrary, she understands all too well," Rand broke in, desperate to keep her from saying anything that would further damage her reputation. "I am completely at fault."

"You, sir, are no gentleman." Miss Campbell shot him a poisonous look. "Laurie will see to it that you are never accepted in polite company after this."

"Lexie, listen to me." Kitty's urgent grip tightened on Miss Campbell's arm.

"Kat—" Rand said in warning tones.

She ignored him. "Rand didn't do anything that I didn't

want." She gave Miss Campbell a direct, determined look. "Do you understand what I am telling you?"

For a moment Miss Campbell stood there staring. "No, it cannot be," she finally said.

"I welcomed Lord Randolph's attentions," Kitty said in a firm voice. "You cannot sully his name over this."

She shook her head in patent disbelief. "But you are betrothed to Laurie."

Kitty held her gaze. "I would not lie about something such as this."

The confused look on Miss Campbell's face twisted into overt disgust. "Why would you do it?" She shrugged Kitty's hand off her arm in a violent motion. "Was one man not enough for the Great Incomparable? Must you have all of the Season's most eligible bachelors paying you court?"

Kitty paled, swallowing hard. "I have no excuse."

Fire blazed in Miss Campbell's eyes. "I'll tell everyone. You'll be ruined." She turned to go. "We'll see if Laurie still wants you after this."

Rand stepped in front of her. "Perhaps you'd like to reconsider."

"Get out of my way."

"Think, Miss Campbell," he urged. "Are you certain Sinclair will cast her aside? If he does not, where will that leave you?"

The girl's voice trembled with anger. "I will not allow the two of you to cuckold Laurie." She glared at Kitty. "Everyone knows he is marrying her for love."

Kitty appeared stricken. "Yes," she whispered. "I do believe he is."

"And you would dishonor him," she said in a scathing

tone.

Rand cleared his throat. "Miss Campbell, you mistake this situation."

She looked pointedly at the cravat in his hand. "Do I?"

"You do. It is not well-known, but Lady Katherine and I enjoyed a brief flirtation before I purchased my commission." He moved toward Kitty and casually handed her the cravat. She took it, her eyes never wavering from his face. "When I returned after years abroad, I still thought to make her my countess."

Miss Campbell stared at him. "You intend to marry Kat?"

He dipped his chin in acknowledgement. "As an earl, I will naturally require a hostess."

Miss Campbell shot a look at Kitty, who stood watching with a slightly dazed look on her face. "You are going to cry off with Laurie to marry the earl?"

Rand answered before Kitty could. "We gave in to our mutual curiosity today and immediately realized what occurred between us years ago was a youthful infatuation that is best left in the past."

"I don't take your meaning." Miss Campbell shifted an uncertain looked between the two of them. "You don't want Kat? Every gentleman is smitten with her."

Excellent. He had her wavering now. "Not I. At least not in that way." His gut churned as he forced out the lie. "We've found that our feelings for each other are no longer engaged."

Miss Campbell tilted her head in thought. "So she is not going to marry you."

"Lady Katherine and I realize the regard we share is

friendship rather than any deeper affection."

"So you don't want her," she repeated slowly, her incredulity plain.

Rand's stomach curled at the thought of giving this insipid girl false hope, but he would do anything to secure Kitty's future happiness. "Correct. I must look elsewhere for my countess."

She took the bait. If the sudden interest that flashed in her eyes was any indication. "And Kat is still going to marry Laurie."

"Most assuredly," he answered.

Rand could see Miss Campbell's mind working and realized he had underestimated her. She was no fool; the tittering miss routine was perhaps the persona she assumed because she thought it would land her a husband. Yet her hidden canniness just might end up securing her an earl. Once she thought on it, Miss Campbell would comprehend that revealing his and Kitty's indiscretion would force a marriage between them, obliterating her own chance of becoming his countess.

He offered her his arm. "Now, shall we forget this unfortunate incident and rejoin the others?"

Miss Campbell took his arm with a pleased smile. "Of course." She glanced back at Kitty. "I suppose no real harm was done."

If only that were true. As he escorted Miss Campbell into the clearing, her hand tightened on his arm, and he had the sinking feeling he'd just fallen into an iron trap of his own making.

# Chapter Ten

Fury rendered Kat speechless. Seeing Rand flirt with Lexie for the remainder of that day and then again two evenings later at Lady Clover's musicale left her so heated she was liable to self-combust at any moment.

Instead she seethed, pretending to be engrossed in the music, even though she neither saw nor heard the performance. She was too busy casting surreptitious glances at Rand and Lexie, trying to keep her internal scowl from usurping the serene mask plastered on her face.

It wasn't the most overt of flirtations, but Rand definitely made his interest clear; his hand at Lexie's elbow, the way he inclined his head toward her with sincere interest whenever she uttered a word. As though Lexie ever had anything interesting to say. Lexie preened under the earl's attentiveness in a manner that twisted Kat's innards into painful knots.

Rand clearly preferred to countenance marriage to plain

Lexie Campbell than to be forced into a scandalous match with her. Humph. So much for being the *ton*'s incomparable. It certainly didn't land her anything she desired. Especially not Rand. He could barely stand to look at her since their indiscretion at the riding party.

Then there was Laurie's puzzling behavior of late. He remained as present as always, escorting her everywhere, but his attentiveness seemed forced now, his manner more brittle beneath the genial facade. In the past, she'd longed for relief from the intensity of his unwavering regard, but now his distracted manner unnerved her. She missed the good-natured, dependable warmth she'd come to count on from him.

"Cozy little duo, wouldn't you say?" She started at Toby's voice. She'd been so lost in her own ruminations that she hadn't heard her cousin slide into Bea's empty seat next to her. "Where is Sinclair? And what happened to my sister? It appears everyone has abandoned ship."

"Shhh." Kat kept her eyes on the performance. "Laurie begged off. Bea pleaded a headache and excused herself," she murmured, trying not to move her lips.

"This performance is headache inducing," Toby whispered.

Suppressing a smile, Kat elbowed him. "People are looking at us."

"Doubtful." He pretended to give the performance his full attention. "They're far more interested in Rand and Miss Campbell. One could suspect he's courting the lady."

A sick feeling stirred in her belly. "Perhaps he is."

"She's a departure from his usual type. He's not the sort to attach to any one gel for long."

*His usual type.* So he had a usual type. While she'd pined away for him for years, he'd been racing across the Continent planning battles and littering his path with discarded lovers. Polite applause erupted around her as the music came to an end. She clapped like an automaton and rose with Toby.

"Be a dear and do escort me to the carriage." She was impatient to depart lest she witness more of Rand's fawning over Lexie. There was only so much she could take.

Toby accompanied her outside. "I understand you visited the soldiers home again. Better be careful, cousin." He handed her up into the carriage. "You wouldn't want people to suspect the *ton*'s reigning princess cares for anything other than frocks and baubles."

"Am I really so frivolous?"

"Far from it." He leaned into the carriage with a conspiratorial expression on his face. "Even as you took the *ton* by storm, you never seemed to truly enjoy your popularity. I've always seen past your facade, Kat. Although, I confess I've never understood the need for it." He stepped back and closed the door, leaving Kat alone in the dark. "Farewell. I am away for a month or so."

"What?" She leaned her head out the window as the carriage began to pull away. "Where are you going?"

"Away. But you must give me your word not to tell anyone," he called after the moving carriage. "Rand will know where I am should an emergency arise."

...

Rand forced a thin smile and asked Miss Campbell to take a turn with him. She acquiesced with a triumphant flush of color in her face. Curious eyes followed their progress as he escorted her about the room.

"I trust you are well," he said.

"Supremely well," she answered quite matter-of-factly. "It was well done of you to ask me to take a turn. Tongues will certainly wag this evening."

This new version of Miss Campbell certainly didn't dissemble. "I'm gratified if my attentions have assisted in increasing your popularity."

The corner of her mouth lifted. "The attentions of an earl will do that, even if the maiden is a chatterbox who is plain of face."

For the first time he paid attention to Miss Campbell's looks. It had been hard for him to see any woman other than Kat. It was true that she was not particularly pretty, but neither was she unattractive. Her features were pleasant enough and her complexion a creamy white. And there was life in those deceptively plain brown eyes. "Hardly that."

"Come now, my lord," she said. "I know you are putting up a pretense of a flirtation with me to save Kat's reputation."

The woman continued to surprise him. "Why play the mindless chatterbox, Miss Campbell, when you are nothing of the sort?"

"According to my mother, it is what gentlemen expect of a wife."

Her mother was an idiot. "I much prefer this version of you."

Her straightforward gaze caught his. "Enough to make me your countess?"

He suppressed the urge to laugh at her gumption, yet he admired her for it. "I fear you would be much disappointed.

I'm not the sort to give my heart to anyone."

"That suits me. I am not interested in your heart, just your title."

He smiled, surprised to find himself intrigued by the conversation. "I see."

"And if you wish to keep your Amazon that is nothing to me."

"I confess, Miss Campbell, that you have shocked me."

"I would make you a good countess," she said. "I have always enjoyed excellent health. My mother bore six children, four of them sons."

"You do seem eminently qualified for the role," he said mildly, noting the calculating gleam in her eye.

"I've been trained to run a large household, to manage servants and the accounts. I shan't let anyone cheat you."

At least the old mausoleum would never be quiet with Miss Campbell ordering servants about while playing at being his countess. Good God, was he actually considering it? "I see I have much to think on." He paused. "And if I were to decline your generous offer?"

For once she seemed at a loss for words. "I haven't decided." The expression on her face hardened. "But I am weary of Kat reigning over all of us as though she were the Queen of England."

"I took the two of you for friends."

"We both know she isn't perfect and I think maybe Laurie should know it as well, before he binds himself to an inconstant woman for life."

"You would take pleasure in hurting Kat."

"Someone needs to knock her down a peg or two. We came out during the same Season and she's ruled all of this time. It is tiresome to see how all of the gentlemen flock to her."

Miss Campbell's jealousy was certainly understandable. She was a colorless shadow next to Kitty's vital beauty. If marrying her would ensure Kat's future happiness, he would gladly do it. He and Miss Campbell might actually deserve each other. After a few more minutes, Rand escaped Miss Campbell by heading to the cards room, where he found his brothers, except for Will, assembled at a table.

"Why if it isn't the estimable Earl of Randolph," said Basil, the youngest of the five brothers. "I'm surprised you've time for a round of cards."

Rand took a seat between Cam and Sebastian. "And why is that?"

"I'd have thought you'd be far too engaged entertaining Miss Campbell," Basil said with a smirk as he dealt the cards.

Cam sipped his drink. "I confess it surprises me to see you paying court in that direction."

"It should not surprise you in the least." Rand reached for a cheroot, already beginning to regret joining the game.

Blue eyes twinkling, Basil leaned forward and lowered his voice. "You do realize that as an earl and a war hero, you could aim much higher than Miss Campbell? Hell, I'm a youngest son in possession of neither a title nor a fortune, and I could do better."

"Perhaps your real attentions are focused elsewhere." Sebastian's unwavering dark gaze accentuated his dusky good looks. "If so, you should not delay."

"*I* should not waste time?" Rand lit his cheroot and took a long inhale. "This advice from the man who left his bride untouched for the better part of seven years."

"She was a child bride and ours was an arranged match," Sebastian said.

Basil grinned. "And once she was of age she traveled across the Continent to escape you."

Sebastian played a card. "But I ultimately succeeded in tempting Bella to my bed." His probing gaze returned to Rand. "You should not waste time pursuing the woman you desire."

Basil reached for his drink. "Sebastian has the right of it. With your title, you could lure the toast of the *ton*." His expression turned contemplative. "As a matter of fact, I do seem to recall you carrying a torch for Nugent's daughter, and she is the reigning incomparable."

Rand didn't look up from his cards. "She is also very much betrothed."

"She certainly waited long enough to accept an offer," Cam said.

"It was almost as if she awaited someone's return," Sebastian murmured.

"Nonsense." Frustration roiled in his chest. "This discussion has no purpose. She is to be wed."

"But she isn't yet married." Cam spoke in serious tones. "There is nothing here that cannot be undone. As a family, we could survive the scandal it would cause."

"Wrong." Anger and frustration stirring in his belly, Rand threw down his cards and pushed to his feet. "There is much here that can never be undone. Nothing will be as it was."

He left them, striding out of the cards room and through the front hall, eager to make his escape. He almost bumped into Toby coming through the door in the opposite direction.

"Leaving so soon?" He about-faced and followed Rand down the steps. "I'd have thought the lovely Miss Campbell's company would entice you to prolong your stay." Lengthening his stride, Rand shot him a dark look. "Doesn't seem your type, that one."

They set off in the direction of Rand's townhome. "And you know my type."

"If Elena is any indication, you like them dark and buxom."

Of course, he couldn't tell Toby his tastes ran toward only one woman; a wisp of a beauty with flaxen curls framing her delicate face. "In truth, I admire Elena's character more than her form."

Toby guffawed. "That seems to be the minority opinion when it comes to men, Elena, and her…ah…more voluptuous attributes."

"Elena and I are no longer involved."

"I cannot claim to be surprised. You never do stay with any one woman for long. Did you break her heart?"

"I doubt it. I'm rather certain she's already entertaining a new admirer."

"Indeed? Who is the lucky sot?"

"I've not a clue. She's been surprisingly discreet about it."

"Elena? Discreet? Not a behavior I'd attribute to our fearless Maid of Malagon." Toby pursed his lips. "Perhaps he's married."

They rounded a corner. "Unlikely. Elena is not the sort to consort with married men."

"True. She does have standards. Just not the same ones as the rest of polite society."

They reached Rand's doorstep. The idea of entering the big, empty structure alone did not appeal. "Join me for a nightcap, Hobart?"

"No, thank you. I'll just push on." He raised his hand to hail a passing hackney. "I depart on the morrow with Drummond. We'll see what he can do for my addled mind."

Rand raised a hand in farewell to his friend before turning to ascend the stairs. The huge manse cast a hulking shadow across the square. A few doors down, one of his neighbors was entertaining. Lights blazed from every window, and the chatter of people and music filtered out onto the street.

He wondered what Kitty was doing at the moment. He'd seen her this evening, of course. How could he not? She wore a silver gown that glittered in the candlelight, her short curls adorning the delicate beauty of her features. He noted others had copied her style. There were a number of debutantes sporting short curls at this evening's musicale. Of course, none of them to the effect of Kitty. Incomparable indeed.

Entering the house, he dismissed the footman who'd waited up for him and made for his study, the clicking of his boots echoing through the silence. At least if he married Miss Campbell, the house wouldn't be so damned quiet. Although having her incessant chatter crowding his mind for the rest of his days might well drive him to bedlam.

He slowed as he neared the music room. Coming to a stop on the threshold, he exhaled and stepped into the darkness. No one lit candles or a fire in here because he never entered this chamber, yet tonight he felt the familiar old pull to lose himself in his music. He paused by the pianoforte to run his fingers over the cool keys and thought of the beauty he could coax from the instrument. Once, long ago, he'd entertained the idea of becoming a serious musician, which was pure folly for a gentleman. Now he no longer played at all, not even for himself.

Music brought back memories which were best left buried; remembrances of Kitty, who had happily sat beside him when he'd practiced for hours. He hadn't touched an instrument since the night he'd left her. Music opened something deep inside of him and laid him too bare. He would never allow himself to be that vulnerable again.

He turned and strode from the music room, trotting up the stairs to his bedchamber. The happy yelp that greeted him when he entered his chamber immediately punctured his somber mood. Vera trotted up to him, wagging her tail in ecstatic welcome. He smiled. "Hullo there, girl." He knelt to pet her in the robust way she liked and immediately felt some of the tension inside his body ease. She slipped away with a playful yelp and danced in little circles. He laughed. "It looks like you're as restless as your master. Let's go for a walk, shall we?"

...

"I am the worst kind of cad."

Laurie closed the door and fell back against it. Elena sat at her dressing table wearing nothing except the shiny mass of ebony hair cascading down to the small of her back. His hungry eyes feasted on the smooth bronze of her back, the strong, sleek arms, and the feminine indentation at her waist.

She'd been expecting him. She rose from the chair with her usual languor, allowing him a full view of her strong, streamlined form. His eyes were riveted by the movement of her abundant, perfectly-formed breasts. They overflowed in his hands, a bounty of femininity he couldn't seem to get enough of. "Every time I visit, I swear it will be the last time. But I just can't seem to stop myself."

Her deep throaty chuckle rippled through him, sizzling down to the place between his legs. She moved to the bed, and climbed on, giving him an excellent view of her firm bottom as she scooted upward to settle herself back against the pillows. "How would you like it this time, *vizconde*?"

His vitals surged. Pulling off his neck cloth, he kept his gaze on her. "Let me see you." She raised a dark brow in question. "Spread your legs. All the way."

Bending her knees, she planted her feet on the mattress and spread her legs far apart, letting him look his fill at the very center of her. Sheltered by a fluff of black curls, she was pink and glistening. "Do you want it?" she said in a voice husky with arousal.

"You know bloody well that I do," he said harshly. Blood pounded through his body, swelling in his groin. If he'd thought shagging Elena a few times would get her out of his system, he couldn't have been more wrong. He'd never known such temptation. In the past fortnight, he'd had her every way he could think of; in her bed, bent over the dresser, up against the wall, even on the servants' staircase at the opera.

None of it slackened his desire. Even now, struggling out of the rest of his clothes, all he could think of was shagging her senseless. Finally naked, he climbed onto the bed and came to a stop between her legs. He lifted them further apart, bending them back toward those luscious breasts, stretching her even more open to his appreciative gaze. Then he stooped down to lick the moist place between her thighs.

"*Sí mi amor, sí,*" she cried, urging herself up to him.

He had never wanted to pleasure a woman like this before but, with Elena, he wanted to do it all—to give her complete indescribable pleasure. He licked and sucked, tasting her musky arousal. Listening to her cries, he followed her urgings until he hit the perfect spot for her pleasure. He became relentless, demanding more with his mouth until she cried out and shuddered against his tongue.

Giving her no respite, he prowled up and shoved into her, moving with demanding strokes, setting an unforgiving rhythm for both of them. She locked her ankles behind his back and bucked against him. Her peaked breasts quivered with her movements and he fell on them like a ravenous animal, giving her his full weight, relishing the warm slide of full body, skin-on-skin contact.

Holding each overflowing orb in his hands, he rubbed his face into the plush flesh, taking in the earthy scent of her skin before latching onto a hardened tip and savoring its pert, rippling texture. He indulged himself in this way for several minutes while she moaned and quivered beneath him. Then she spun him around until he lay beneath her. Her dark eyes holding his, Elena smiled in that slow voluptuous way of hers. His heart kicked with excitement, his groin grew heavier.

She threw her head back and began to move atop him, her black hair gleaming about those smooth bronze shoulders and breasts. He watched, mesmerized by the sight of her as she rode him, her succulent mounds undulating with each movement. He'd never seen anything more beautiful. Closing his eyes, he gripped her hips and moved with her, losing himself in the feel and scent of her.

"Forgive me, my dear. I didn't realize you were entertaining."

It took a moment for Laurie to register the droll masculine voice sounding from the doorway. A dog barked. Mired in the haze of urgent lust, he barely managed to direct his attention past the sensuous goddess moving atop him. When he did, his gaze slammed into the Earl of Randolph standing rigid in the doorway with Kat's dog on a leash by his side. Laurie's blood iced. The crushing indecency of his liaison with Elena hit him anew. Remorse cleaved through him at being caught in the act of betraying his betrothed in the worst possible way.

Atop him, Elena stilled with a reluctant sigh. Rolling off she said, "Rand, *querido*, I did not know you were coming."

"Obviously."

His heart slamming, Laurie bounded off the bed in one quick motion and reached for his clothes. If he had to fight Randolph, at least he'd do so with his breeches on. Tugging them on over his bare hips, he regarded the earl with an unflinching gaze. "Do you intend to challenge me?"

To his surprise, Randolph's mouth curved in amusement, though one could never really tell with the man. He was such a cold fish. "Good lord, no. Elena is her own mistress. She belongs to no one."

Why did Randolph have Kat's animal? And what was he doing here? Hot jealousy seared his chest at the thought of Elena shagging both of them at the same time. "I was led to believe you two were no longer engaged in a liaison."

"We are not. I confess to being surprised at your lack of

discretion, Sinclair. You are betrothed after all."

A sick feeling swirled in Laurie's stomach at the truth of Randolph's words. He, who had always prided himself on his decency, proved to be nothing more than a common scoundrel. The lowest of the low. If his behavior with Elena didn't prove that, he didn't know what did.

He reached for his shirt and pulled it over his head. Grabbing his boots in one hand and the remainder of his clothes in the other, Laurie made for the door. Pausing on the threshold, he turned to face the other man. "I trust I can rely upon your discretion in this matter, Randolph. I wouldn't want Kat harmed by this."

"Of course not." The steely courtesy of the earl's tone sent a shiver through him.

He glanced over at Elena, who had put on a dressing gown and stood, arms crossed under her chest, watching his exchange with Rand. "Ma'am," he said with a stiff bow.

"You can see yourself out, *vizconde*," she said as if understanding his urgent need to be far away from her at the moment. He took her dismissal for the gift it was, striding out of the room and hurrying down the stairs. Pulling the door open, he welcomed a blast of moist heat, though nothing could warm the self-loathing icing his insides.

. . .

Once he heard the front door slam, Rand raised his brows in Elena's direction. "Are you planning to make a habit of being caught *in flagrante, querida*?"

She smiled when she realized he referred to the amorous performance they'd put on for Kitty. "No. Some things are better left in private."

"Indeed." Struggling to control his anger, he walked over to a small table that held a decanter of brandy to pour himself a drink. "What are you doing docking Sinclair of all people?"

"I desire him, of course."

"And the fact that he is betrothed means nothing to you?" He threw the brandy down his throat. "I never took you for a toffer, Elena."

"Toffer?" She frowned. "*No comprendo.*"

"A toffer is what we English call a superior whore."

"Why are you so angry, *querido*? I thought you would be pleased."

"Pleased? You thought I would take satisfaction in seeing Kat's happiness destroyed again?"

"Don't be foolish." She sat at her dressing table and picked up her brush. "The *vizconde* has come to my bed many times now."

"And you are proud of that?"

"It shows you are much mistaken about his devotion to your Kat."

"She is not my Kat," he said through clenched teeth. "Sinclair is a whole man. He can make her happy."

"It surprises me a brilliant strategist would make such a grave miscalculation." She pulled the brush through her hair in an unhurried motion. "How can she be happy with a husband who desires another? You, at least, would be faithful. And you have never truly desired any woman but her."

Her cool logic maddened him and he longed to shake some sense into her. "What if these bouts of madness are just the beginning? Have you considered that?" He fought the urge to throw something. "These episodes could worsen and grow more frequent until I am a complete bedlamite."

She continued stroking the brush through her hair in slow, rhythmic motions. "No man is without his imperfections."

"You would have me saddle her with that kind of future?"

"Most women would give anything to be cared for by a man as you care for her." She caught his gaze in the mirror. "You think to offer your lady a life free of turmoil, but it will also be absent of love."

"What balderdash." He exhaled his exasperation. "Don't tell me you're docking Sinclair as part of some misbegotten stratagem to reunite me with my true love?"

She put down the brush and turned in her chair to face him. "Now that you comprehend the *vizconde* is not the perfect match for your lady, what will you do about it?"

He narrowed his eyes as realization washed over him. "You're toying with Sinclair to prove a point."

She rose and walked over to him. "You know me better than that, *querido*. I only bed men I desire." She took his glass from him and finished the brandy in one long gulp, her throat working as she swallowed. "But, perhaps you *have* learned that he is not so much better for her than you are. You at least can offer her complete devotion. Sinclair cannot."

"Perhaps you believe you can command the viscount's total devotion," he said in a voice rich with scorn.

"I would have a better chance at it than your Kat." She dragged the back of her hand across her upper lip to wipe away any remaining traces of brandy. "She is enchanting, but she is not for him. And he is not for her. One day he will find the right woman for him, one who not only captures his heart but also satisfies his deepest manly needs."

He had to get out of here and away from this maddening woman. Whistling for Vera, who'd settled at the foot of Elena's bed, he stalked toward the door. "Devil take it. You've gone and made a mess of things."

"*Donde vas?*" she called out from behind him as he and Vera barreled down the stairs. "You haven't told me why you came to visit."

He swung around to look up at her standing on the landing. "I was going to discuss the merits of my offering for Miss Campbell."

That got her complete attention. "And now?"

He favored her with a dark look. "Obviously, in light of what I discovered this evening, that's completely out of the question."

She nodded her approval. "Perhaps now you will cease being a coward and pursue what you truly desire."

Anger ripped through his chest as he took a reflexive step up toward her. "If you were a gentleman, I would call you out for that grave insult."

"For telling the truth?" She came down the stairs to meet him, halting a step above so that they stood eye to eye. "What else would you call refusing to claim the woman you love? You act as though you died on that field in Talavera."

His stomach churned with emotion. "Shut your mouth."

"You are afraid to live." Her dark eyes burned into him. "Will you stay shut up in that old mausoleum forever because you are fearful of ever feeling anything again?"

His fury at her instantly gave way to an overwhelming

flood of grief. Suddenly, he was drowning in it. Staggering backward onto the landing, he braced a hand against the wall to steady himself. To his horror, he choked back a sob. "I cannot—"

"You can."

"You have no idea what you ask." Desperate to be away from her, he turned and staggered toward the door. He fumbled for the latch and pulled it open, darting from the house like a man deprived of oxygen.

Later, he didn't know how long he and Vera walked, striding silently through the darkened streets, his mind in turmoil, contemplating Elena's words. It was true that he was afraid of being found out, of not being the man Kitty thought she loved. He couldn't bear her disappointment. But if he refused to claim her, he'd have to stand by and watch her marry a faithless man. Conflicting thoughts continued to swim in his mind as he and Vera covered a great distance with no particular destination in mind, until he found himself at Cam's door.

"Is something amiss?" Cam trotted down the stairs at a fast clip as he belted his dressing gown, clearly surprised to see Rand twice on the same evening.

"I've interrupted you. It is late." Feeling foolish for disturbing his brother, he turned to go. "I shall call in the morning."

"Nonsense. Charlotte and I were just preparing for bed." Cam put a gentle hand on his shoulder to impede his departure. "Come to my study. You look like you could use a drink."

When the brandy was poured, they settled into two chairs before the unlit hearth. Vera sat on the floor by

Rand's feet, her ears back in an alert posture, almost as if she sensed his distress.

Cam regarded him with a serious gaze. "Do you want to tell me why you're here?"

"Bloody hell." He scrubbed a hand down his face. "I've made my mark as a leader of men, but at the moment I've no idea how to conduct my own life."

Understanding lit his face. "Is this about Lady Katherine?"

"Is it that obvious?"

"To me it is. She's always been the only person who can turn you inside out."

"I discovered Sinclair screwing another woman this evening."

"Sinclair?" Cam's dark amber brows rose. "I wouldn't have thought he had it in him."

"Exactly."

"Is the lady aware?"

"Kat? No." He drained his glass and set it on the table with a resolute clunk. "And I don't plan to enlighten her. She has been hurt enough."

"You mean to allow the woman you love to marry a faithless man?" He shook his head. "I could never have let Charlotte go."

"It's not at all the same. Being with me could ruin Kat's life."

"Do not be so certain." Cam's smile was wry. "Charlotte has certain associations that, if known publicly, could ruin me."

"Truly?" His mouth slackened. "Then why did you marry her?"

"She was worth the risk." He smiled at the memory. "She put up a formidable fight to protect me, but I wouldn't have it. I seduced her."

"You seduced Charlotte?" he asked, incredulous.

"In a manner of speaking," Cam said in a mild tone. "Does Lady Katherine care for you as you care for her?"

"She does." Restless, Rand pushed out of the chair and paced away. Vera stood, her ears and tail alert. "She intended to cry off from Sinclair so we could wed."

"What happened?"

"I led her to believe I would be a faithless husband."

"I won't even ask how you managed to convince her of that." Cam rose to refill their drinks. "Why do you think you are unworthy of Lady Katherine? As Basil said, you are an earl and a war hero."

He paused. "The war left more of a mark on me than the scar on my shoulder."

Cam stilled. "Meaning?"

His heart accelerated as he forced out the words. "I experience…bouts."

Concern lit Cam's green eyes. "What sort of bouts?"

"Episodes that can best be described as waking nightmares. Sudden movements, sounds, smells, anything can trigger it. I panic, sometimes I blank out and can't remember what occurred."

"I see." The words were gentle. "Can anything be done to ease your distress?"

"There is an expert, Doctor Drummond, who believes so."

"Doctor Drummond? The fellow Will mentioned during our walk in Kensington Gardens?"

"The very one."

"Have you consulted with him?"

"No, a...friend of mine is doing so now." He exhaled. "I'm at a loss as to what is best for Kat now. Is she better off with a scoundrel for a husband or a probable bedlamite? Both are pathetic options for the toast of the *ton*."

"You are not a bedlamite and I will not have you speak as if you are, or ever could be." He walked over to Rand and handed him his refilled glass. "Perhaps you should see this Doctor Drummond to determine whether he can help ease your distress. If this is the reason you are condemning yourself to a life without the lady you love, it's pure folly."

"I couldn't stand her pity if she were to see me in that state."

"It is inevitable that our wives will at some point see us at our worst. It is part of marriage," Cam said. "If the love is strong enough, it can be overcome. In the case of you and Lady Kat, I do not believe your issues are insurmountable."

"You think I should pursue her, despite everything?"

"You are the great strategist, so why don't you strategize? Fight for the lady with the same fierce determination you battled the Corsican. See this Doctor Drummond about your episodes and go and claim your lady."

"*My* lady? That is a bit premature."

"Not at all. If anything you are late. She's always been yours. You've just taken overlong to claim her."

Rand returned home after taking his leave of Cam to spend a long, restless night. He could not see a life with Kitty as he was now, but he also could not envision one without her. By early morning, he'd reached a decision. He rose from his bed and searched for the calling card he'd received weeks ago at the Hobart's house party. Both relief and trepidation filled him when he found it. Flipping it over, he saw that Doctor Drummond had scribbled his direction on the back. He dressed with haste, before he could change his mind, and set out for Drummond's home, hoping to reach the doctor before he left town today with Toby...and before Rand's own resolution faltered.

...

"My lady, you cannot visit a bachelor residence."

Fanny's words barely registered with Kat, who fingered her short curls as she peered through the carriage window at the imposing Palladian-style structure with pilasters running from the ground to the roof. So this was where Rand lived.

He was the last person she wanted to seek out, but she could think of nowhere else to turn. Toby had vanished two days prior without a trace. Aunt Winnie and Bea were beside themselves. She remembered Toby telling her he was going away and that Rand would know how to reach him.

"We must." She tapped on the roof and the footman appeared immediately to open the door and pull down the step.

"My lady, this won't do at all," Fanny said.

Ignoring her, Kat stepped down. "You may wait for me here if you prefer." To the coachman, she said. "Drive around the block please."

"I most certainly will not." Fanny scrambled down after her, clearly agitated. "I know what the two of you get up to when you are alone."

Kat quickened her stride. "Not any longer." A fresh

wave of hurt and anger washed over her. "He can't stay far enough away from me." When Fanny made a derisive sound, she added, "It's true. He's courting Miss Campbell now."

"Hmph."

She hated it when Fanny did that. Making her opinion clear when she hadn't actually said anything. "What does that mean?"

"That man only has eyes for you. Any fool can see it."

"You are not present at the gatherings where he constantly attends her." It was enough to turn her stomach, and it often did. Her stride faltered and she considered turning back, but then Aunt Winnie's aggrieved face came to her mind along with Bea's pale, quiet worry. She straightened her spine and marched up the stairs to sound the knocker before she could lose her courage.

No noise came from inside. A servant should have opened the door immediately. She frowned at Fanny. "Obviously his staff is not very well trained."

She pounded the knocker again, and this time sound of a barking dog followed. Her heart gladdened. She could recognize Vera's bark anywhere. But where was the blasted butler? She could hardly make a discreet visit to a bachelor establishment if Rand's staff kept her waiting on the front doorstep all afternoon. Impatient, she sounded the knocker again, this time hitting it louder.

The door swung open as she did so and she almost fell into the tall man standing in the doorway. "What is that infernal knocking?" Rand barked before his probing emerald gaze focused on her. "Kitty? What are you doing here?"

Her cheeks grew hot. "Do you mean to keep me on your

doorstep all afternoon?"

He glanced up and down the street before pulling her inside. "Have you taken complete leave of your senses," he hissed, "to call on a bachelor residence?"

"Precisely what I asked her," Fanny said, following her mistress inside.

Vera yelped, looping excited circles around Kat. Distracted for a moment by her happiness at seeing the dog, she knelt down to give her old friend a proper greeting. "Hello, you fickle girl," she said with a smile, running both hands over the animal's soft fur. "I've missed you."

Rand slammed the door shut and turned to face Kat with his hands on his hips. "Are you determined to ruin yourself yet again?"

She shot to her feet. "Yet again? You are the one who nearly ruined me in Richmond." She ignored Fanny's exclamation of surprise. "You're a fine one to talk."

"And I've spent the time since trying to salvage your reputation," he said furiously.

"You have?" She crossed her arms over her chest. "I should like to know how."

All expression smoothed from his face. "That is of no matter. I trust your wedding planning is coming along well?"

For the first time, she realized he was not dressed to receive company. He wore no cravat or jacket, only a linen white shirt which laid bare the pronounced cords of his neck and throat. His fawn-colored riding pants skimmed over strong, lean thighs before disappearing into well-worn brown boots. Her skin warmed. "I assure you this is the last place I would willingly come."

"And yet, here you are."

"I need your help."

His expression tensed. "Is it something to do with Sinclair?"

"Laurie? No, of course not." She hugged herself against the chill of the house, unexpected on a late summer evening, and wondered why an earl would answer his own door.

He noticed her discomfort. "Forgive me, let us go to the study." He motioned for her to precede him down the hall. "I have a fire built up there."

Stepping ahead of him, with Vera trotting by her side and Fanny following, she snuck furtive looks around as she walked. Despite an absence of decent lighting, she could see the servants weren't keeping the place up very well. The house's bones were undoubtedly grand, but thin layers of dust coated almost every surface, tickling her nose.

They stepped into a large warm chamber which smelled of old leather, brandy, and tobacco. Smoke whirled upward from a still-lit cheroot on the large rosewood desk.

"I beg your pardon." He stepped past her in a quick motion to snuff it out. "I was not expecting guests."

She inhaled, sneaking a look around while he put things to rights on his desk. Shelves full of leather-bound books almost reached the ceiling. A huge limestone hearth dominated the opposite wall, its crackling flames imbuing the space with cozy comfort. She could feel Rand's presence in this chamber; it even carried his scent.

Fanny remained just outside the open door, keeping a watchful eye on events inside the chamber. Vera sauntered over to a large stuffed leather chair near the fire, settling down on the floor beside it as though she belonged there. "She's certainly made herself at home."

Rand glanced at the animal. "You can have her back at any time. She still belongs to you."

Vera practically smiled at her before propping her chin on her front paws and regarding Kat with a watchful gaze. "No," she said, feeling the weight of her loss. "She is well and truly yours now."

"Perhaps I should ring for tea, to help warm you."

She forced her eyes away from Vera. "No thank you, the fire is taking care of that. This is not a social call."

A man stepped around Fanny to enter the chamber. "My lord, may I be of service?" Kat recognized him as the man who'd been with Rand while Toby had his episode. The valet, she presumed. But if that were the case, why was he attending to matters a butler should see to?

"Ah, yes, Burgess." Rand cleared his throat. "If you could be so kind as to see to Lady Katherine's lady's maid."

"Of course." The man looked at Fanny, gesturing for her to follow him. "Perhaps Cook has some tea in the kitchen."

Fanny shot her a look and, for a moment, Kat thought her maid would refuse to leave her with Rand. But then Fanny turned to follow Burgess, taking care to leave the door wide open.

A smile cracked Rand's still face. "Still protecting your virtue, I see."

"She won't have to for much longer. The wedding is in four weeks."

He let her words hang in the air while he examined her face. "Does he make you happy, Kitty?"

His soft, almost caressing tone caught her off balance. "It is a brilliant match."

"Indeed." His keen gaze met hers. "Are you happy?"

Suddenly she felt angry. After casting her aside more times than she cared to count, he dared to toy with her yet again, making her think he cared. "You overstep, sir. I am not here to discuss my private affairs."

"Pray tell, what are we here to discuss?"

"Toby. He's gone missing. Aunt Winnie and Bea are most distressed."

He frowned. "Surely he left a note."

"A very brief missive that only said he was going away and that they should not worry about him."

"Which naturally caused them to worry."

"Precisely and you're the only person who can set their minds at ease."

His forehead lifted. "And why do you presume that to be the case?"

"Toby told me he was going away and that you would know where to find him."

"Then you know no harm has come to him. Surely you can relay that to your aunt to ease her mind."

"That's just it," she said. "I cannot. Toby swore me to not tell anyone he was going away. I can't betray his confidence in any way. That's why you must go to his mother straight away."

"Very well. I shall pay a call on Mrs. Hobart later today. I cannot betray Tobias' confidence, but I will assure her that he is well. Will that suffice?" He took a breath. "Now I wish to discuss another matter."

She tensed at the grave intent in his eyes. "And what is that?"

He cleared his throat. "I think we should marry."

# Chapter Eleven

Incredulity filled Kat's rounded eyes. "What?"

"I realize this is unexpected. However, I have given the matter much thought." He stood in a rigid posture with his hands clasped behind his back, his heart pounding. "Marriage is the best course for us."

Bright spots of red colored each cheek. "You cannot be serious."

He cursed himself inwardly. This ham-fisted conversation was not how he'd meant to offer for her. His initial meeting with Drummond had gone moderately well, enhancing his hope that he might one day be able to bring his episodes under some semblance of control. But he'd only just concluded they should marry and she'd thrown him off balance by unexpectedly appearing on his doorstep, prompting him to blurt out his intentions in the most oafish way possible. "I assure you that I am."

"You want us to marry," she repeated the words, as

though certain she'd missed something critical.

"Yes."

She licked her lips. "Why?"

He followed the trail of her little pink tongue as it washed moisture onto her abundant lower lip. "Although I am an imperfect man," he continued in an even tone, "marriage to me will carry certain advantages for you."

She regarded him with a suspicious stare. "Such as?"

"For one, you would be a countess, which is considerably higher than a viscountess."

The cloud in her brain seemed to clear, to be quickly replaced by furious indignation. "Let me see if I take your meaning," she said in an icy tone. "You expect me to jilt Laurie, a kind and devoted man, in favor of you, an inconstant, cold philanderer who has made it quite clear he will lie with any woman who takes his fancy."

He stiffened. Sinclair was hardly devoted, but he'd vowed never to tell her of the man's repeated indiscretions. "The one other thing I can offer you is my complete devotion."

She tilted her head and narrowed one eye. "Meaning?"

"From this day forward, I shall forgo…carnal relations… with all women except you." His heart beat a little faster at the thought of Kitty in his bed, of her sweet pale breasts and their pink tips, her milky white thighs parting to welcome him. He swallowed hard. "When you are my wife, of course."

"Naturally." Crossing her arms, she wandered closer to the fire before turning back to look at him. "Not so long ago you were rapturous in the arms of your Amazon and you made it abundantly clear that I alone would bore you."

Shifting his weight onto the opposite foot, he resisted the urge to rub his aching shoulder. "I've reconsidered."

One of those delicate brows lifted. "Have you told your mistress that?"

"Elena and I are no longer involved. We are friends. No more."

"Will you continue to see her?"

"As a friend only. On that you have my word."

"Because your word can be depended upon."

"I have never broken my word to you."

"No. Only my heart." Her sapphire eyes flashed. "Pulverizing and stomping on it wasn't enough for you. Now you expect me to marry you."

"I realize we haven't had much of a courtship."

She snorted. "This has been a courtship? I'm intrigued by how your mind works. Do tell, what exactly will you expect of me as your countess?"

He frowned. "I don't follow."

"Is this to be a marriage of convenience?"

"Most assuredly not." His body quickened at the thought of taking her to bed. "We will engage in sexual congress. I trust you are not adverse to that."

Something hot flashed in her eyes. "I don't understand you at all."

"I will devote myself to your happiness. You will have the running of this house to do as you see fit. I will be generous with my purse."

A mixture of emotions crossed her face: frustration, anger and, he might well be imagining it, but perhaps even a bit of elation. "For many years, I've dreamt of this moment. I've longed to be your wife. But something is terribly off here." Her gaze sharpened on his face. "What sort of game are you playing at?"

"It is no game."

"Really?" Her words dripped with scorn. "First, you leave me and go to war. Then you travel on to India, obviously in no rush to return. And when you do come back, you ignore me, and then you practically ravish me. Repeatedly. In the meantime, you either flaunt your mistress or dance attendance on Lexie Campbell."

"I have behaved regrettably in some instances. However, I am quite clear on the path going forward. We should marry."

"Stay away from me. I'm marrying Laurie in one month and no one and nothing will stop me." She crossed over into the hall, toward the front door, calling Fanny's name, with Rand following at a distance.

Her maid rushed forward with Burgess close behind. "My lady?"

"We are leaving." Kat planted herself before the front door to allow Burgess to open it for her. "Thank you," she said to the valet, before shooting a disdainful glare at Rand. "I wouldn't marry you if you were the last person in England, you arrogant, insufferable man."

She flounced out the door without another glance at him, her maid scurrying after her. Closing the door behind them with a gentle click, Burgess turned to face Rand.

"I think she's the perfect woman for you," he said.

• • •

Fanny held up a gown in each hand. "The white or the pink?"

"You choose." Kat stood at the window with her arms crossed, looking down at the gardeners trimming the hedgerows beneath her window.

"The white then." Fanny laid it carefully on the bed before disappearing into the dressing room to put the other away.

"Can you believe the temerity of that man?" Kat said when Fanny reappeared and began smoothing out the white gown. "*He has reconsidered.* As though I am going to jump at the chance to jilt Laurie to marry him."

"Perhaps you should think on it."

"What?" She spun around to face her maid. "How can you say such a thing? All of these years, you couldn't keep me far enough away from Rand. Now you think I should *marry* him?"

Fanny eased Kat's robe off. "It is clear you two cannot stay away from each other."

"That doesn't mean he is good for me," she snapped. "If I were an opium eater, would you encourage me to take up residence in an opium den?"

"Your addiction is an earl." Fanny helped her into the gown and fastened it. "You must marry someone. And you have always loved him."

She plopped into the chair at her dressing table to allow Fanny to put the finishing touches on her hair. "Rand has toyed with me ever since he returned. Raising my hopes and then dashing them. Even if I could be so cruel to Laurie, I would likely be miserable with Rand and his army of females."

"The earl did tell you he would be faithful." Fanny adjusted one last pin. "Do you not take him at his word?"

She stood, steeling herself to go down and greet the guests. "He is the most exasperating person. I no longer know what to credit, but that man has toyed with me for the last time."

She made her way down the stairs. Her parents had arranged an informal affair with twenty guests or so. Her usual group of friends would be attending, including Laurie. She looked forward to his warm, calming presence after the tumultuous day she'd had.

Her mother met her at the bottom of the stairs. "You look beautiful as always, my dear."

"Thank you, Mama," she said, kissing her cheek.

Her mother moved an approving glance over her. "Lord Sinclair is certain to take notice. Oh, I did tell you I invited the earl, did I not?"

She shot her mother a sharp look. "The earl? Which earl?"

"The Earl of Randolph, of course."

"Edward?" Disbelief knocked the breath out of her. "Why would you invite him here? You and father hate him."

Her mother fussed with Kat's bodice. "Nonsense. Why would you say that?"

"Why would I say that?" The insides of her hands began to itch. "You couldn't throw him out of here fast enough when he asked to marry me."

"That was an age ago, dear." Her mother adjusted Kat's sleeves. "He is an earl and a war hero now. Everyone accepts him, even the regent himself."

"I see." She brushed her mother's hands away. For once, she didn't care how she looked. "Now he's not beneath our notice, so you deign to invite him here."

Surprise filled her mother's face. "Your father and I are not like that. I presumed including the earl would please you."

"Why ever would that please me?"

"To show that we harbor no ill feelings against him, of course. What is all this about, Katherine? I thought he was your friend." Her mother gave her a curious look. "You seemed more than happy to walk with Lord Randolph and Vera a few weeks ago."

The heat of irritation bled across her chest. "And what of Laurie?"

"What about Lord Sinclair? This has nothing to do with your betrothed. Your father and I are pleased that all is well and truly settled."

"Not exactly," said her father, coming from the direction of his study, dressed in his formal clothes. "I don't trust Randolph around Kat, I never have."

At least her father remained consistent. "Then why is he coming?" she asked.

"Your mother was determined to invite him."

"All that silliness is in the past, Albert." She took her husband's arm. "Even Laurie seems to have taken a liking to the earl."

He brushed a kiss on his wife's cheek. "And I still say you shouldn't have invited that Spanish woman either. She's barely respectable."

Kat resisted the urge to throw up her hands. "The Spanish woman?" she echoed in disbelief.

"Don't be silly, Albert," her mother chided. "The Maid of Malagon is accepted in the highest circles. Why, they say she's been to Carlton House more than once."

"On account of Prinny being a horse's ass," her father mumbled under his breath.

"Albert!" Warning filled her mother's voice. "Someone might hear you." Noise sounded at the front door, distracting her mother, who rushed off to greet the guests.

"They might agree with me, too," her father mumbled, following after his wife.

Scratching the insides of her hands through her white kid leather gloves, Kat trailed her parents. She just had to endure this one last evening with Rand. Tomorrow they would leave for her father's country estate to celebrate the bringing in of the harvest. They'd return to Town a week before the wedding. After tonight, she could easily avoid Rand until the nuptials.

The parlor began to fill and Kat assumed her cheerful public demeanor, chatting with both her friends and those of her parents, wondering where Laurie was. He usually arrived first at these gatherings, often to steal a private kiss before the crowds descended. She suppressed a groan when Rand appeared before her betrothed.

"Where is Laurie, Kat?"

She turned toward Lexie's voice, forcing her most pleasant smile. "I'm certain he is on his way."

"Are you?"

She and Lexie had not spoken since the incident with Rand in Richmond. In fact, Lexie was so busy being courted by Rand she'd barely seemed to notice Kat. Little did Lexie know her fickle beau had already moved on. She breathed a sigh of relief when Laurie entered the parlor and came toward them.

"Are you well?" she asked eyeing his flushed face.

"Yes, supremely," he answered in a clipped, somewhat harried manner, quite at odds with his usual easygoing warmth.

"I was beginning to worry. You are never late."

Looking chagrined, he brought her hand to his lips. "I am sorry, Kat, truly."

The seriousness of his tone took her aback. "It is of no matter. You are here now." Taking his arm, she smiled in a manner that usually brought an admiring—and vaguely lustful—look into Laurie's eyes. Only this time, he didn't even appear to notice. Instead, his attention fixed on the arrival of a new guest. She followed his gaze to see the Maid of Malagon standing on the threshold. "Don't be angry," she said. "My mother insisted on inviting her."

"What?"

She lowered her voice so no one could overhear. "Elena. Mother says she is respectable because the regent invites her to Carlton House."

He seemed to snap out of his strange daze. "No matter," he said crisply. "She has nothing whatever to do with us."

"I wonder why she is so late. She came in just after you."

The butler announced the meal, bringing their conversation about Elena to an end. Supper was an informal affair, with small tables set up for people to sit at. Laurie went to fill a plate for Kat while she took a seat at one of the round tables.

"Surely your viscount hasn't deserted you already."

She stiffened at the sound of Rand's voice. "My betrothed has gone to fill a plate for me."

"How obliging of him."

"Yes, isn't it?" She watched with rising alarm as he took a seat next to her. "You don't mean to sit here?"

"I don't?"

She turned her gaze back to where Laurie stood filling a plate for her. "Oh, do go away and stop pestering me."

"I'm surprised you would treat a guest so rudely." He settled his plate before him. "And here I thought you were beginning to look more favorably upon my offer."

"I'm sure I have no idea why you would think that," she said coldly, still refusing to meet his gaze.

"You did invite me this evening."

Her gaze snapped back to him. "I had nothing to do with that. My mother seems to think we are friends."

"Does she? How interesting. Although we both know we are far more than that."

"No, we most certainly are not any more than that," she retorted. "We are barely even friends."

"Soon to be husband and wife."

"Is there something wrong with your ears?" she hissed, looking around to make sure no one had heard him. "I will not marry you."

"And lovers." He continued as though she had not spoken. His voice turned low, intimate. "I've waited a very long time to hold you in my arms as my wife."

"Yes," she said tartly, trying to ignore the tingle fluttering down her spine. "I am sure you thought of me every time you visited your mistresses."

"I have no mistress," he answered with a slow upward curve of his mouth. "I've decided to save myself for my wife."

Her cheeks flamed. "How fortunate for her."

"Absolutely. On our wedding night, all of that pent-up energy will be completely at your disposal."

Her wayward heart almost somersaulted out of her chest at the image of the two of them together in that way.

"Hush, you are disgusting. I will never marry you."

He picked up his wine glass and brought it to his lips. "We shall see."

"I warn you, you are wasting your time. I never will."

"Never will what?" Bea asked, taking a seat at the table. "I hope I am not interrupting."

Kat exhaled, happy to turn her focus away from Rand's intense gaze. "Not at all." She patted the seat next to her. "Come and sit."

Laurie appeared and set Kat's plate in front of her, his wary gaze sliding to the earl. "Randolph."

"Sinclair." Rand returned a measuring gaze.

"Elena!" Bea gestured to the Amazon, who stood by the buffet table with a full plate, looking for a seat. "Come and join us."

Rand's mistress smiled, but her face dimmed as she surveyed the people at the table. "Perhaps I'll sit over with Miss Campbell."

"Do join us." Rand sent a languid look in Laurie's direction. "The more the merrier, wouldn't you say, Sinclair?"

A muscle danced in Laurie's left cheek. "By all means."

Kat wondered at the guarded look Elena shot between the two men before relenting and joining their table. They were all quiet as they began to eat. A perplexing tension wrapped itself around their table. Having lost her appetite, Kat pushed her food around on her plate.

Rand noticed. "You haven't eaten your quail. As I recall, it is one of your favorites."

Laurie glared at Rand. "How would you know what Lady Katherine's favorites are?"

Kat resisted the urge to fling the quail carcass at Rand

for the inappropriate intimacy. "Our families were neighbors in Town before my come-out," she said as coolly as she could manage. "We had occasion to meet."

"Did you not know the earl and Lady Katherine are friends?" Elena asked him.

"I may have heard some such thing." Laurie dissembled in a most casual tone, yet his fingers were white against the glass he gripped. "It's not the sort of matter I would remember."

Bea turned to Rand. "They say you are a brilliant strategist, my lord. Do regale us with some of your greatest victories."

"Yes, do tell, Randolph," Laurie said stiffly. "Do you learn the enemy's every move in order to best counter his attack?"

"To the contrary, a sound strategist twists the battle to his own advantage." Rand took a leisurely sip of his wine. "He does not allow his opponent to set the rules of the challenge."

Laurie set his fork down in a deliberate motion. "How exactly does he manage that?"

"He ensures his opponent is drawn into playing his game. According to his rules."

Laurie placed his hands palm down on the table on either side of his plate. "And tell us, is this strategy always successful?"

Rand's smile held no warmth. "I suspect the Corsican would say so." The competitive tension arcing between the two men befuddled Kat. When had these two become outright adversaries?

Bea cut into the silent standoff. "I would imagine after

the frogs, my lord, you can take on just about anyone."

Rand maintained eye contact with Laurie. "I do always play to win."

"It's just as well that there is nothing here to be won," Kat said pointedly.

"Not for me at least." Laurie took her hand and pressed a gallant kiss upon it. "I have already won the moon."

"Some would say the moon is unattainable," Rand said.

"Tell us about your country," Bea said quickly to Elena, in an obvious attempt to divert the conversation. "Is Spain as beautiful as I have heard?"

"Oh yes. I think you would find my home very inviting," Elena said. "Perhaps you will come and visit me there."

"What about you, Sinclair?" Rand said in an easy tone. "How do you find Spain?"

"I'm afraid I have never had the pleasure of visiting Miss Márquez-Navarro's home," Laurie said stiffly.

"Do tell." One of Rand's brows lifted. "I was given to understand you are enamored of all things Spanish."

Elena stood abruptly. "I think I shall get more food."

Rand rose. "Allow me to fetch it for you."

"No. Thank you, my lord." Her dark eyes snapped at him. "You have done quite enough."

To Kat's relief, the remainder of the supper conversation turned to more neutral subjects, and when her mother signaled for the ladies to leave the men to their after-dinner port, she breathed a sigh of thanks. However, the reprieve was short-lived because the men joined them soon thereafter.

Laurie spied her and started in her direction, but paused for a moment to exchange a few words with the Amazon, who stood alone by the window. Elena's brows rose at something

Laurie said. When she responded, the lines of Laurie's body went very still. He spun away from her, making a direct line for Kat, his expression tense.

She smiled in welcome, but his countenance only tightened. "What is Randolph to you?"

Her heart dropped into her stomach with a heavy thump. "Whatever do you mean?"

"First the bit about the quail and now Elena informs me the two of you once harbored a deep affection for one another."

*Elena?* "You call her by her Christian name? How could you discuss my personal business with…with a woman of questionable reputation?"

His gaze drilled into her. "Randolph is personal business to you?"

"It's not what you think." No, it was far worse than he could imagine, but as her betrothed, he deserved the truth. At least as much as she could bear to share with him. "When we were very young, before my come-out, we had an infatuation. That is all."

He paled. "What happened? Why didn't he ask for you?"

"He…did," she stammered. "My father refused because he felt Edward didn't have any prospects. He was a second son with no fortune."

"Edward." His tone flattened. "You use his Christian name."

"It means nothing." Guilt pecked away at her as she took in his rigid demeanor.

"He wants you back," he said curtly. "That show at supper was all about letting me know it."

"It doesn't matter." She placed a hand on his arm, noting

the hard tension in it. "I don't want him. I'll be *your* wife in a few weeks."

Laurie's attention locked in on Rand standing across the room chatting with Kat's mother, who appeared unexpectedly flushed and delighted. As if he sensed hostile eyes upon him, Rand turned in their direction. He met Laurie's gaze and raised his glass in silent salute.

Clenching his jaw, Laurie inclined his head as though silently accepting Rand's unspoken challenge. "He'll try to separate us. He's made his intentions quite clear."

"There is nothing he can say or do to come between us," she said in a firm voice.

Laurie exhaled, looking visibly shaken. "Would that were true."

"In all likelihood we won't see him again before we are wed." Kat desperately hoped that was true. "We leave for the Harvest Home on the morrow. After that, the Earl of Randolph will be out of our lives forever."

# Chapter Twelve

Kat spurred her horse through the fields where her father's tenants—men and women—used scythes to cut the last of the corn. Many paused to call out a greeting of welcome before resuming their task. The day was fair and it appeared they'd finish their work before rain set in and threatened to mold the crop.

She searched for her father, whose custom it was to take to the fields with his tenants on the final days of the harvest. She loved this part of the season. Soon the workers would fill the wagon with one last load of corn and crown it with flowers. They would parade it through the village before bearing the laden cart to the barn.

She inhaled, taking in the earthy smells of sunshine and fertile fields. Watching her father work the land with his people reminded her of the centuries of tradition and heritage behind each harvest. This was home, a place of peace and comfort for her. Her throat ached at the realization this would be her last harvest at Nugent Manor. Next year, she would preside over harvest festivities at Laurie's Wiltshire estate. Her stomach cramped as reality hit her anew.

*Laurie's viscountess.*

Fighting back tears, she bit her lip, resisting the impulse to weep at the mammoth sense of loss that assailed her. It was not only the finality of leaving home that made her emotional; her marriage would also forever shut the door on Rand.

She forced her thoughts back to tomorrow's Harvest Home. The celebration meal would be an inclusive event, with the master breaking bread with his tenants this one meal of the year. And then the singing and dancing would begin—again with the master and servants enjoying the festivities together. She would dance with Laurie, of course, who was due to arrive today, and quite possibly with some of the people from the village she'd known since childhood.

She spied her father among the workers. His perspiration-laden white linen shirt clung to his back. He'd retained his fit looks as he'd aged; she could detect just a bit of extra flesh gathering around his middle. He laughed as he and a worker lifted the load and carried it toward the wagon. The movement drew Kat's eye to her father's companion and she lost her breath.

*Rand.* How could he be here? He'd shed his shirt in the heat, baring an impossibly lean form with no evidence of extra flesh; there scarcely seemed to be sufficient skin to cover all of the taut muscle stretched over bone. There was an angry-looking, mottled scar where his shoulder met the lean sinews of his arm. Her gaze traveled over the smattering of dark amber curls on his chest, toward the thin line of hair that trailed down his stomach, disappearing into the mysterious fold of his breeches.

Together with her father, he heaved the load of corn onto the wagon. The lean cords of muscle in his arms and back slid beneath sweat-glistened skin, which had taken on some of the sun's golden color. He must have been at this for hours. Rand paused for a word with a small group of workers by the wagon. He seemed to move easily among the people of her childhood.

Perspiration trickled between her breasts and her skin felt unbearably hot. She thought she'd successfully removed herself from temptation, yet here it was in the form of laughing emerald eyes, strong shoulders, and miles of bronzed, bare male skin. Her father caught sight of her and hailed her over. She forced her mare forward despite an overwhelming instinct to turn and flee.

"Kat," her father said in cheery greeting as he helped her from her horse. "Come to see us take in the final load?"

She nodded, murmuring something in response that she hoped sounded distinguishable. Rand turned away and reached for his shirt, pulling it on as a gentleman ought to in the presence of a lady.

Once he was decent, he bowed. "Lady Kat."

"My lord." She licked her dry lips. "What a surprise to see you here."

Her father mopped his brow with the back of his hand. "It seems your mother invited Randolph just before we left town."

She schooled her features into polite impartiality. "How unexpected."

Rand smiled, and she detected the subtle amusement

beneath his courteous demeanor. "Yes, I mentioned to Lady Nugent that I have much to learn about managing an estate now that I have one of my own to oversee in Devon."

"I see."

"So when she invited me here to observe the Harvest Home, naturally I could not refuse."

"Naturally."

Her father sent a broad smile in Rand's direction. "And a fine lord of the manor he shall be. A man must be willing to get close to the land and work with his people."

Rand returned the older man's smile. "I've a great deal to learn from you, my lord."

Kat swallowed a snort of disbelief. First her mother, and now her father. Rand had succeeded in charming both her parents. It was almost as if this offensive was part of his battle plan to win her—amassing his forces like a wave gaining momentum before it finally slammed into her. Only she couldn't be overwhelmed if she refused to stay on the beach. "I will leave the two of you to it."

Her father regarded her with obvious surprise. "You're not staying for the crop parade through the village?"

"I think not. Mother will have need of me to help in preparing for tomorrow's mell supper."

Sadness tinged his expression. "I can't recall the last time you missed the bearing of the cart. You've always loved it so. And this shall be your last at Nugent Manor."

Something akin to regret crossed Rand's face. "Please don't go on my account."

She fixed him with a haughty look. "It is time I put girlish whims into the past. Next year I shall preside over the harvest at Sinclair Hall."

Her father beamed. "Indeed you shall." He moved to help her into the saddle. "My Kat, mistress of the manor."

But Rand stepped forward with a polite "Allow me." Wrapping large, long-fingered hands around her waist, Rand lifted her easily onto the mount. His man's scent, intermixed with the earthy smell of exertion, filled her nose. "I shall look forward to seeing you at supper, my lady."

Heady with his scent and the raw power of his proximity, she mumbled something in response before blindly turning her mount in the direction of home.

...

The following day at noon, the long tables that had been laid out for the mell supper were filled with tenants and their families. Kat's father stood at the head of the principal table carving the meat, in keeping with the tradition started by the first Earl of Nugent more than a century ago. After he sliced a few ceremonial pieces, footmen whisked the meat away to finish the job of trimming and serving. Likewise, Kat and her mother proceeded down the main table with beer jugs—as the first earl's countess and daughters of the house had once done—serving a few of the tenants before footmen swooped in to take over their task as well.

A boisterous, cheery energy swirled among the tables as the tenants, happy to see the year's harvest come to a successful end, indulged in beer and ale and mounds of food prepared especially for the occasion. Tables were stacked with boiled hams and roasted sirloins, plum puddings made by the Christmas recipe, and fresh plum loaves, some of which were still warm.

Laurie sat to her father's right while Rand had the spot to her father's left, having been given the other place of honor at the table. Laurie's jaw had braced when he'd arrived to find Rand in residence, but he had not remarked upon it to Kat.

"You still hold to the traditional mell supper," Rand was saying to her father.

"Yes, indeed," he answered taking a swig of his ale. "Here at Nugent Manor we keep to the old traditions. On this day, the master and tenant sit at the same table."

Rand nodded his approval. "I believe the term 'mell' is derived from the French *mesler* meaning 'to mingle together.'"

Laurie winked at Kat as she slid next to him. "I never thought to see the *ton*'s incomparable serving beer to the lower orders."

"Every daughter of the house has done so since the first earl," her father said. "Do you hold a mell supper at your estate, Sinclair?"

"Not exactly. We hold a day of food and games," he said. "But perhaps when Kat is my viscountess, she will bring a bit of Nugent tradition with her."

Laurie seemed more himself today—the old friend and companion who made her feel safe and protected. "I hate that you will have to leave us on the morrow."

He smiled with his usual easy fondness. "I must away to the Harvest Home at my estate. Next year, you shall be by my side."

"That will be most agreeable." She forced a light tone, determined to ignore the tangle twisting in her belly at the thought of how much her life would change in a few short weeks. Her attention went to the end of the table, where the Maid of Malagon sat near Mama. She forced herself not to grind her teeth at the sight of Rand's mistress, who had also been invited to witness the English harvest tradition. It seemed she'd have no escape from either of them.

After supper, the sports and games began. Some of the older people congregated under trees to sip their ale and gossip while children loped through the crowds chasing each other and stealing the rare treat of a sweetmeat passed around by footmen. A large group of men congregated around the boxing challenge, chanting and roaring their approval with each swing.

To her relief, Kat managed to avoid Rand for most of the afternoon by sticking close to Laurie. Although she couldn't help noticing that Rand mingled with the tenants as easily as he did with her father.

Late in the day, as twilight approached, she and Laurie strolled to one of the last events before the evening's music and dancing. The climbing of the pole was a favorite Harvest Home game among the tenants. One of Kat's blue satin ribbons was tied atop the tall pole.

"Lady Kat," called one of the farmers. "Will you offer a boon to the gentleman who retrieves your ribbon?"

Kat gave her best coquette's smile to the appreciative audience. "I would be pleased to, Mr. Ogilvie." At Laurie's questioning brow, she added, "If my betrothed husband concurs."

"What say you, my lord?" Ogilvie called. "A maiden's kiss for the man who conquers the pole?"

"That depends," Laurie answered in an affable tone. "Are all allowed to participate? Myself for instance."

Good natured cat-calls and whistles came from the gathered men, but Ogilvie shushed them. "By all means, my lord. As the lady's betrothed, we'll give you the first chance."

"They've rendered it as slippery as a glacier," Kat warned. "With soap and wax and who knows what else."

"I'm a competent climber." Laurie approached the pole, rubbing his hands on his flanks as if to dry them. "No harm in trying. Especially with so lovely a prize to be won."

"No harm at all," Ogilvie agreed, amidst more calls and whistles from the growing crowd of curious revelers who wandered over as word spread that the viscount intended to give the climbing pole a try.

Approaching it, Laurie embraced the pole with a strong grip, clenching his knees as he began his ascent. An agile athlete, he managed to climb a bit, before sliding back and having to regain lost ground again and again, continuing upward with a determined expression on his sweat-glistened face.

At length, he reached the first prize fastened to the pole, a sweetmeat which he retrieved and tossed to the appreciative crowd. Many lunged for it, but a young boy emerged from the crush with a triumphant grin on his young face holding up the prize.

"Well done, lad," Laurie called from his perch above them before continuing his climb. Kat laughed and clapped at Laurie's gallantry, enjoying his good-natured interactions with her father's people. Yet the act of halting to retrieve the prize impacted Laurie's momentum and, even though he repeatedly tried to regain his grip, he finally acknowledged defeat by sliding down the pole, amidst cheers and ribbing from the onlookers.

With now tousled hair, he approached Kat with a rueful grin, his blue eyes sparkling. "I guess I shall have to wait until my wedding day to gain the lady's kiss," he called out to the appreciative crowd, kissing her hand with exaggerated gallantry.

On it went, candidate after candidate taking to the field with little luck. Partway into the contest, her father beckoned Laurie away to make him known to some neighbors, but Kat stayed since she was essentially the prize for any man who managed to conquer the pole.

"Will none of you rustics take up this challenge?" Ogilvie called when they seemed to have run out of takers.

"I will." The familiar masculine voice, polished yet roughened by experience, dragged shivers down her spine. Her breath hitched when Rand emerged from the crowd like a gladiator ready to do battle. In keeping with the casual tone of the event, none of the gentlemen wore waistcoats. Rand had on buff breeches and a white linen shirt. He cast a playful pitying look around to those who had tried and failed. "Behold how the climbing of the pole is done," he said to benign jeers from the crowd.

He wrapped himself around the pole with steady hands and pulled his body upward, those long, lean lines radiating self-assuredness. Each time he hoisted his form another hard-won inch, the sleek muscles in his thighs slid under his breeches. Despite his apparent confidence, Rand had difficulty making his way up the pole. Halfway up, he seemed to falter, stopping and slipping a bit. She caught her breath and waited.

Keeping his position with one hand, he drew the other away from the pole and slipped it into the pocket of his breeches, only to withdraw it laden with sand. The crowd gave a roar of appreciation for this display of the earl's wiliness. Dipping his chin in wry acknowledgement, Rand clasped the pole with his dirtied hand, while he repeated the same action with his other one. He began to progress quickly now, thanks to the traction gained by the sand, amidst the laughing and cheering below him.

The gazers hooted when he reached the top and seized the prize, giving it a triumphant wave over his head before sliding easily down the pole. Casting a wild look about, Kat exhaled in relief to see Laurie had not yet returned. Although he would, no doubt, hear of Rand's success later. She pushed that worry from her mind when the crowd parted for him as he approached her—tall, lean, and most definitely dangerous to her peace of mind.

Coming to a halt in front of her, he bowed and offered her the ribbon. "Your prize, my lady."

"What about *your* prize, my lord?" someone called from the crowd.

"Aye," said another. "A maiden's kiss he surely deserves for prevailing where so many others have failed."

With an acknowledging smile and wave to the crowd, Rand turned a penetrating gaze onto her. "My lady."

Her heart sped up. "My lord."

He stepped close enough for her to feel his body warmth and to detect the musk of his cologne mingled with masculine exertion. Fighting the urge to flee, she remained frozen in place, even when Rand lowered his lips toward hers. Her heart pounding, she closed her eyes and felt the warmth of his breath against her cheek. Her mouth almost twitched with impatience waiting for his kiss.

Then something brushed along her forehead. His lips. She opened her eyes in astonishment in time to see Rand step away. It took her a moment to realize he'd opted to kiss her forehead instead of taking a real kiss. She didn't know whether to feel relieved or disappointed. Rand gave her one last look, a flash of amusement lighting his eyes, before he stepped away and disappeared into the applauding crowd.

At twilight, the festivities moved to the home paddock for dancing to the music of pipes and fiddles. Kat's parents danced together before each took a turn with a tenant before saying their good nights and heading back to the main house. Kat coupled with Laurie, but saved the rest of her dances for the tenants, most of them young men she'd known since childhood. Laurie danced with the local women who practically swooned at being in the arms of the handsome, affable viscount. Winded from all of the dancing, Kat sought out the refreshment table and helped herself to some ale.

"I've been awaiting my chance to dance with the fairest maiden of them all," Rand's deep voice said from behind her.

Her heart jumped, but she forced herself to turn around slowly. She'd noticed that he'd spent most of the evening a bit away from the crowd, his back up against a tree trunk. Vera, faithful as ever, stood by his side. "I have but one dance left in me and I am saving it for Laurie."

"I see." He tilted his head back as he regarded her. "Are you enjoying yourself, Kitty?"

"Very much so. But I shall enjoy myself ever so much more when I preside over the Harvest Home as mistress next year in Wiltshire."

"Or in Devon."

"Beg pardon?" She scrunched up her nose. "What's in Devon?"

"My estate. By the inlet. You will enjoy living by the water."

Her strained patience snapped. "You are the most insufferable man. I am marrying Laurie."

He cast a cursory look about. "Where is he? I don't see him by your side."

"We are not in each other's pockets." Of course, that hadn't always been the case, but this evening she hadn't seen him since their dance more than an hour ago. "Unlike you, he is decent enough to dance with the tenants."

"That is very kind of him."

"Yes, it is," she said, her tone edged with obvious irritation. "And if you will excuse me, I shall go and find him to remind him of our dance."

"Yes, by all means, do go and run him to ground." He allowed her to pass and she flounced past him in a less-than-ladylike manner. She had no idea where Laurie had got to, but she knew she wanted to get away from Rand's probing gaze. She walked away from the party past the barn, but saw no sign of Laurie.

Mr. Ogilvie spotted her and said, "If you're looking for your viscount, I believe I saw him headed in the direction of the stable not too long ago."

Thanking him, Kat headed that way, wondering what business Laurie had there. Perhaps he'd gone to check on his mount. She passed some boys shooting marbles and smiled at them. The music grew faint as she neared the barn. Peeking inside, she acknowledged a greeting from the lone groom still on duty while the others had long since joined the festivities up on the main paddock. "Good evening, Patrick, have you seen the viscount?"

"No, my lady. Just me and the horses here." Thanking him, she turned to head back toward the party, but decided to check the gardens first.

An unusual sound from the direction of the gazebo drew her attention, slowing her gait. Slapping sounds. Followed by a husky accented murmur in a voice she recognized. "Not the ground, *mi amor*, it will dirty my clothing."

Elena. A man grunted in response—a guttural thing. Kat's heart sputtered, followed by furious disbelief that she could have the misfortune to come upon Rand and his mistress for a second time. Rand, the blackguard, who claimed to be courting her, who said he no longer consorted with his mistress.

Elena moaned. "*Sí mi amor*, just like that."

Kat edged closer to the sounds coming from the arched summer house—much as people do when stopping to see a carriage accident—knowing they might witness something horrible, but drawn to it nonetheless. The man's panting intensified along with the frequency of the slapping sounds. Elena's sighs riveted Kat because they seemed borne of both pleasure and pain. The idea that she and Laurie would soon consummate their marriage in this way made her stomach contract.

She silently approached the brick and stone structure where the couple remained cloaked in shadows, moving rhythmically up against each other. The man sat on the bench and Elena's back was to Kat. Both were clothed, although Elena's skirts were lifted so she could straddle the man as she moved atop him, obscuring her lover's face. The man's hands cupped Elena's bottom and he appeared to be helping her move. Releasing one last groan, he went still, burying his face in her breasts. And then he spoke.

"Good God, Elena," he gasped. "You've bewitched me."

Kat reared back in shock. *Laurie.* A sharp pain knifed her lungs. No. *No.*

Laurie stilled. He peered around Elena into the dark, the shadowed planes of his face coming into view. "What was that?"

Elena looked over her shoulder in the same direction. "What, *vizconde*?"

He disengaged from Elena, placing her on her feet before coming to his own. He fussed with the placket of his breeches, putting himself to rights, although in the darkness Kat could not see clearly. "I thought I heard something."

Elena shook out her skirts. "I did not hear anything."

"We should return before they realize we are missing."

"Very well." Curving a hand around Laurie's head, Elena drew him down for a languorous, deep-throated kiss before murmuring, "Come to my chamber this evening. I have a special surprise for you."

Laurie focused his full attention on the Amazon with a mixture of hunger and passion, a blatant yearning that had never been there when he looked at Kat. "What exactly do you have in mind?" he asked in a velvet voice.

Unable to bear watching them a moment longer, Kat retreated as quietly as she could, heading in the opposite direction from the party with no clear destination in mind. She couldn't stand to think on what she had just witnessed. Her mind could barely comprehend the full impact of

Laurie's devastating betrayal, much less sort it out in any comprehensible way.

Blanking her mind, she walked and walked, trying not to mull over her appalling lack of judgment, or what it portended for her future. Instead she focused on the elemental things; her moving legs, the sounds of her inhales and exhales, the sensation of her heart beating in her chest. The soothing rhythm calmed her mind, lulling it with natural cadences which reminded her that, despite everything, she was still Katherine Granville. Still herself. Now she just had to find out what that meant in this new world where Laurie no longer belonged to her.

She uttered a hollow laugh into the darkness. What folly her life was. The *ton*'s incomparable, the ruling beauty. How the *ton* would laugh to discover she was nothing but a fraud with so little appeal she couldn't command the complete devotion of any man. Not Rand. Certainly not her betrothed, despite the *ton's* belief he was smitten with her. Laurie appeared to be smitten for certain, just not with her.

A fresh hurt panged in her chest as the image of him grunting against Elena replayed in her mind. And yet, it suddenly struck her that beneath the raw sorrow, she felt unexpectedly light—buoyant almost—as though a terrible weight had been lifted.

Halting in the night, she drew a deep breath and her thoughts clarified. Yes, Laurie had betrayed her in the worst possible way. But he had also freed her. The implications of her unencumbered status—and the possibilities that came with it—washed over her. She was bound to no one and, for once, there were no expectations to fill except her own.

The way forward suddenly became obvious. She smiled

to herself, a sense of purpose and determination firming inside of her. It was time to take control of her life and finish what she had started at sixteen. She would fight for what she'd always wanted and this time nothing and no one would stop her.

# Chapter Thirteen

Where the devil had Kat got off too? Rand took a last long drag on his dwindling cheroot and threw it to the ground, grinding it with his boot heel. It was difficult enough to seduce the woman when she deigned to be around him. It would be impossible if she continued to absent herself.

Exhaling, he watched the dancers from a distance. It still made him uncomfortable to be in the center of a crowd, where unexpected noises unnerved him. Instead, he stood a bit away with Vera by his side. The alert animal peered out into the dark behind Rand, almost as though she watched his back.

At first he thought Kat had found Sinclair. His gut clenched at the thought they'd gone off somewhere to anticipate the wedding night. But no, the viscount had reappeared not long ago, rejoining the festivities from the direction of the stables. Standing apart, observing the action as he was, Rand was probably the only person to note

Elena returned at about the same time, just from a different direction. So the bugger was still joining giblets with Elena every chance he got.

Beside him, Vera rose from her sitting position to all four legs, her tail perched high in the air. Turning to look behind him, he stroked her soft fur. "What is it, girl? Is someone coming?"

Kitty emerged from the darkness. With a happy yap, Vera bounded over to her. Kitty ran a distracted hand over the dog's head, yet her gaze remained fastened on Rand. He squinted into the darkness, trying to get a better look at her face. "Kitty?"

She caught his eye, flashing him a look of such raw sensual intent that it took his breath away. She turned to walk away. Naturally, he followed. "Where are we going?"

She moved ahead of him, without a backward glance, giving no indication she'd heard the query. After a moment, he parsed they were heading to the manor. They slipped in through a side door although he couldn't be sure where in the house they were. They entered a small, dark passageway—no doubt the servants' corridor—and proceeded up a staircase, emerging through a hidden door off the corridor in the guest wing. Near his chamber. She went to it, pushed the door open, and stepped inside.

He froze in the corridor, his heart racing. "What are you about?" He swallowed hard. "Why are we in my chamber?"

"I see you were given the best guest chamber." She moved further into the room, gazing around. "Better even than Laurie's."

Following her inside, he shut the door behind him and fell back against it. "Fit for an earl, I suppose."

"One too fine for the young, untitled Edward Stanhope." She dragged her fingers over the plush velvet of the ruby settee. "But not for the Earl of Randolph, the great war hero."

He watched the changing emotions flitting across her exquisite face. "Why are we in my chamber?"

She met his eyes. "Because mine is in the family wing, rather too close to my parents. And I understand it can be a noisy business."

His pulse roared in his ears. "What is going on?" he asked, struggling to hold onto reason. One of them had to keep their wits about them and it clearly wasn't going to be her.

She looked up at him with opaque eyes. "Don't you want to?"

Blood catapulted to his nether regions, making him hard. "There is nothing I want more."

"Good." She turned back to the settee. "Can we do it here?"

His good sense screamed against it. Something was terribly off, but his baser self fully intended to take what she offered. "Are you going to tell me what made you change your mind?"

"No." She walked up to him and turned, giving her his back. "Will you undo my gown or do we keep our clothes on?"

Riveted by the enticing bit of pale flesh along the exposed area of her neck, he put his lips to it. "We most certainly do not keep our clothes on," he whispered against the warm, tender flesh. A ripple went through her. Sliding his hands around to cup her breasts, he squeezed the feminine flesh in his fingers, exultant to finally have her in his arms. He inhaled her drugging scent—violets and the outdoors, tinged with her own particular feminine essence. "Are you certain, my love?"

"I've never been more certain of anything." She sighed and softened back against him, where she surely felt his prodding erection. "I begin to see this is the only true thing I've ever desired in my life."

. . .

She didn't know where the sudden boldness came from, but she had always wanted Rand and now she meant to have him. She leaned back into his lean, solid form and allowed his powerful masculine presence to engulf her. His hands left her breasts, going to the back of her gown to work the buttons. The bodice loosened and he pushed it forward, over her shoulders and down her arms.

His lips touched her neck again, dragging gently down to her shoulders. She trembled at the sensation, at the scrape of his jaw abrading the delicate skin, commanding responses from her body in the same way he must have directed men in battle. Had they gone as willingly into the unknown as she went now?

"Will you disrobe for me?" He spoke in that roughened voice which reminded her of how little she knew this new version of Edward, this stranger named Rand. "I want to see every part of you."

She slipped out the dress, which left her in her chemise and stays, and turned in his arms, sliding her hands around his neck. He lowered his face and their lips touched. Her tongue delved into his mouth, tasting cheroots and spirits and the unique contours that made him who he was. He allowed her to explore at length—the roof of his mouth, the surprisingly sensual feel of his cheek. He groaned and lifted her off her feet, pressing her body closer to his.

She wrapped her legs around his lean hips, wanting to meld herself to him. He walked forward as she slid her hands along the skin of his throat, pressing her lips against it, tasting him.

"Kitty," he growled, loosening her stays with one hand. "If you keep at that, we won't make it to the bed." He abruptly halted and changed direction.

She nipped at his neck, marveling at the tufts of dark hair peeking out from his shirt. Suddenly he was putting her down on something soft and luxurious—the velvet settee. She blinked, focusing on her surroundings. "This is not the bed."

He smiled, heat flashing in his eyes. "I've a mind to see your bare flesh against the red velvet."

She sat up, done with games and prevarications. "What part of me do you want to see first?"

His intake of breath was sharp. "Undress for me."

With any other man, granting such a request would be unthinkable but, with Rand, it seemed inevitable. She came up on her knees on the chaise and slowly pulled off her loosened stays, tossing them away. Taking a fortifying breath, she gripped the hem of her chemise and pulled it off over her head in one quick motion before this sudden uncharacteristic boldness deserted her. Her face burning, she forced herself to look at him.

He exhaled, his gaze riveted on her body. And when his

eyes curved over her sensitive breasts, it was as if he was touching her all over again. She bent over to remove her stockings.

"No, leave them. Lie back on the chaise."

She did as he asked, her body tight with sexual tension, feeling unbearably aroused even though he had yet to touch her bare skin. "Put your hands over your head."

She did as he asked and laid there, the velvet fabric caressing her sensitive flesh, tension throbbing within her, waiting for his touch.

He walked to the chaise and knelt, his eyes devouring the wanton sight of her. "I'm going to touch you." He did not wait for her permission. He feathered a finger down her shoulder and over the tender curve of her breast.

She bit her lip in sudden apprehension. "I am not so well-endowed as some."

"You are perfect." He put his lips to the taut tip, sending a rush of sensation straight down to her toes. "This is perfect." He flicked his tongue repeatedly against the pointed tip before taking it fully into his mouth and suckling her. She felt an exquisite tug deep in her belly as though the two were connected. His hand teased her other breast, thumbing the tip, caressing the curve, before traveling down the turn of her hip to the place at the juncture of her thighs. He cupped her mound, playing with the downy hair, before spreading her with his fingers and touching her moist inner flesh. "Tell me if it feels good. Take your pleasure."

It felt indescribably good. His clever fingers played her the way he used to play his violin—with flawless mastery, plucking a sensitive spot into a quivering crescendo, before running a soothing masterful finger over it. She squirmed at the huge rush coursing toward her, holding back against the mammoth wave of almost painful pleasure that seemed ready to break. "Oh, Edward!"

He intensified the movements of his fingers. "This is the best part of it, Kitty, let it come."

Her body went taut and she began to tremble. Suddenly she didn't want to hold back. A frantic pleasure exploded over her, throbbing down the insides of her legs, leaving her body warm and pulsing. Rand moved over her and kissed her gently.

"Oh," she said once she'd caught her breath. "I had no idea."

His lip curved. "I'm glad you trusted me to satisfy your needs."

"But I am not satisfied." At his frown, she said, "You are still clothed."

He gave an appreciative laugh before a serious expression came over his face. "I don't know what transpired this evening to make you come to me so unexpectedly. But you are still a maiden and it is not too late to resume the course you were on."

She sat up, indignant, noting with satisfaction the way his eyes were drawn to the movement of her bare breasts. "Are you jilting me again?"

"Far from it." He bent to kiss the tip of her breast, mouthing it in an almost worshipful way that sent tingles through her. "I want you for my countess. More now than ever."

"Then what is this about?"

He came up to meet her gaze. "I want you to make a reasoned choice. Not one you will regret in the morning."

"I've made my choice. There is no going back."

• • •

"It really would be best if you allowed me to speak to your father alone."

Kitty kept pace with him as they headed for his appointment with the Earl of Nugent. "The last time you asked my father for my hand, you vanished for six years." She shook her head in a decisive manner. "We're discussing my future, and this time I plan to secure it properly."

Minx. He resisted the urge to smile. "Will you least allow me to do the talking?"

"To a point."

"When will you inform Sinclair of the changed state of affairs?"

She shrugged. "He departed this morning to attend the Harvest Home at his estate in Wiltshire. I shall send him a letter later today."

He regarded her with some surprise. "That's a little heartless, don't you think?"

Her brows almost reached her hairline. "Have you become a sudden admirer of the viscount?"

"Far from it." They came to a stop in front of the closed study door. "Now, remember, allow me to do the talking," he said. "I have a strategy."

She all but rolled her eyes. "Of course."

He tapped, polite but firm, and entered at the earl's behest.

Nugent stood up behind his desk. "Randolph," he said before he turned a questioning look at Kitty. "Katherine?"

"Father," she said in greeting, ignoring the question in Nugent's voice.

"Thank you for agreeing to see me, sir." He kept his tone courteous, but resolute.

"What is Kat doing here?" Nugent asked.

Rand cleared his throat. "I have something of utmost importance to discuss with you."

"I can't imagine what that could be."

"As you well know, I have always held you daughter in the highest esteem."

Nugent's gaze flapped between the two of them. "She is betrothed."

"And my feelings have not changed," Rand continued as though Nugent had not spoken.

The older man's face flushed. "What are you doing? I beg you to stop and get a hold of yourself."

"I realize this is a somewhat difficult situation—"

"It's an impossible situation." Outright alarm stamped her father's face. "St. George's is already booked. The entire *ton* is coming."

"—but I have come to ask for your blessing to marry Lady Katherine."

"Well, you most certainly do not have it," Nugent said on an outraged exhale. "Sinclair is a fine fellow and it is all arranged."

He regretted distressing Nugent, but nothing would keep him from Kitty now. "I urge you to reconsider, sir, as your daughter is in agreement."

"You've turned her head again, just as you did all of those years ago. Well, I won't have it, I tell you! She is marrying Sinclair as planned."

"I won't marry Laurie," Kitty said. "I love Edward."

Nugent shot a furious gaze at his daughter before turning it back to Rand. "This is how you take your revenge on me, is it? Because I declined to accept your suit all of those years ago?"

"Not at all, my lord. I esteem your daughter. Six years ago, you were quite right to decline my suit as I had little to offer Lady Katherine. However, the situation has changed." The words were coated with steel. "I am now an earl in possession of a substantial fortune. What has not changed is the esteem in which I hold Kat. My desire to make her my wife remains as constant today as it was six years ago."

Nugent's face reddened. "Katherine is already betrothed. She has no good reason to jilt a gentleman as honorable as Sinclair."

"Laurie probably won't want me now anyway," Kitty interjected.

"And why is that?" The cords in Nugent's reddening neck worked. "Surely you are not suggesting—"

Rand suppressed a groan. Surely, she did not mean to—

"Just that the sooner we marry, the better," Kitty said.

Color infused Nugent's face. "Why you blackguard—"

Well. That had not gone as he had planned. Thanks to Kitty's loose, lying tongue. But he could hardly dispute her insinuation that she was already ruined without looking like a complete cad. "My lord, I assure you my intentions are completely honorable. I secured a special license before leaving town. We can marry immediately."

"I see. You had it all planned out." Kitty's father glared at him. "You wormed your way back into our good graces so you could cause this scandal to embarrass us all."

"No, sir," he said gently. "However, I do care deeply for Kat and, with all due respect, nothing will keep me from taking her to wife."

"You've made certain to leave me no choice in the matter." Nugent slumped back into his chair, suddenly looking all of his almost fifty years. "Get out of my sight, the both of you."

Rand bowed and turned to go. Once they stepped into the hall, Kitty said, "That didn't go too badly."

He shot her an incredulous look. "Why on earth would you insinuate that I seduced you?"

"I couldn't very well tell him the truth."

He frowned. "I shudder to ask which 'truth' you speak of."

"That I was the one who seduced you."

"No one was seduced," he said pointedly. "You comprehend perfectly that I made certain you were not ruined. To my own extreme discomfort, I might add."

"I'm not the one who insisted on waiting. I was more than happy to anticipate our wedding night."

"I told you to leave speaking with your father to me. I had a plan all worked out."

"Ah, but someone once told me a sound strategist ensures the other participants are drawn into playing her game, according to her rules."

He narrowed his eyes. "You planned what you said in there?"

"Precisely." She smiled pertly. "You aren't the only one with a strategy."

...

"Are we here?" Kat peered out the carriage window at the rough-hewn landscape as the footman pulled the door open. She shivered against the austere nature of the North Devon coast. With its unspoiled rolling valleys and greenery, it should have presented an idyllic tableau. But instead, the stalwart shrubs and wild plants punctuated the greenery in an almost defiant way, as though toughened by time and the elements, daring nature to do its worst. Lord, but this strange place seemed far from civilization. "Is this Waterford?"

"Almost." Rand, seated across from her, stepped out first before turning to help her down. The first days of her marriage had been a weary blur of continuous travel punctuated by brief stops to change the horses or to overnight at coaching inns.

She took his hand, anxious for this tiresome, never-ending journey to be over. "Then why are we stopping?" Her bones ached from the ceaseless rattle of the carriage. Her clothes were wrinkled and she needed a bath. She'd never been so exhausted.

He pointed over the valley. "That is Waterford."

Her eyes followed the direction of his hand, and Kat's disagreeable mood floated away on a whooshing breath of wonderment. They stood on high ground and beyond the valley, across a smooth expanse of meadow and parkland, nestled among hills to one side, jagged rocks to the other and a small inlet of the bluest sea she'd ever seen, an immense brick castle shimmered in the slanting afternoon sun, as though nature had contrived to showcase it for approaching visitors.

Rand gazed out over it. "This is my favorite view of Waterford," he said, the pride apparent in his voice, "and I thought to share it with you."

She exhaled. "It's a castle."

"Of course. Waterford Castle."

She ran her eyes over the turrets and battlements. "You never said it was a castle. You only referred to it as Waterford."

Vera yelped from somewhere behind her, then both Fanny and Rand's man emerged from the back coach, a look of distaste on the valet's face. Happy to be free of the confines of the coach, the animal loped out onto the sloping hill.

"Vera seems to like it," she said. "But of course the disloyal creature seems to like everything about you."

He took her hand. "Come, the carriage will have us home in a matter of minutes."

Home. Gazing at the imperious collection of stones set against the grass-covered hills across the inlet, the beauty of this unspoiled place tugged at something in her chest. "Can we not walk?" Unable to bear the thought of another moment in the carriage, she experienced a longing to immerse herself in this place.

"As you wish." Motioning for the coachman to continue on, he offered his arm and they set off. Rand gazed back over his shoulder at Fanny, who stood uncertainly by the luggage coach, still staring at Waterford. "No need for a chaperone, Fanny, she is my wife now."

"It is wrong of you to tease her," Kat said as they started down the hill toward the castle.

"I confess, even after I've taken you to wife, she still makes me feel like an errant schoolboy off to sneak a kiss."

Would he steal a kiss? Her blood slowed thick and warm

in her veins at the remembered sensation of his lips covering hers.

"Do you approve of your new home?" he asked, breaking into her thoughts.

She refocused on the elemental majesty before her, the parapets and tall stacks with crenated caps set against the unforgiving landscape. Tears pricked her eyes. "I do believe it is the most beautiful place I've ever set my eyes upon." She regretted they would not stay for long, just a fortnight for their wedding trip. "Does it have dungeons as well?"

"As it happens, yes. But they are just cellars. And the castle is not so very old. It is really a simple country house built to resemble a castle."

"Hardly simple," she murmured. "What happened to the people who lived here?"

"The Randolph title died out after just one generation. Two brothers held the title. The first earl married, but died without issue. His brother and heir never married."

"So now you revive the title."

"It was so awarded." His dark eyes settled on her. "But, by marrying, I like to think I am well on my way to breaking the solitary tradition of the Earls of Randolph. And an heir perhaps will follow before long."

Heat flushed through her at his allusion to intimacy. He hadn't touched her since the evening of the Harvest Home. They'd departed for Dorset immediately after taking their vows and Fanny had slept with her at the inns along the way. But this evening, he surely would come to her.

They stretched their legs across a wide expanse of cultivated parkland, which appeared even more so against the raw, craggy edges of the coast beyond it. They walked past the front and side retaining walls—brick walls covered in ivy—and up the stairs to the generous stretch of drive in front of the castle.

A modest staff had lined up to welcome them. "How many servants are there?" she queried in a low voice.

"Just six for now, since most of the house is closed up," he said. "And we are only here for a short while."

And then they would return to Town. "Do you think a fortnight is long enough time for the scandal to blow over?"

"Are you regretting your decision?"

"Of course not." Her wedding to Laurie was to have been in a sennight. Instead, she was here with Edward, as his countess. No, she was not sorry. For once, she'd taken what she wanted rather than done what was expected of her.

The introductions were brief. Mr. and Mrs. Cully were married. He served as both butler and caretaker of sorts while she acted as both housekeeper and cook. There were two maids of all work, a footman, and a gardener. They stepped into the gothic-styled main entrance hall where ornately carved wooden panels reached as far as her shoulder before meeting sand-colored stone, which ran two floors up to the ceiling. A central staircase at the rear broke into two flights, each with heavy fluted banisters and carved newels. The principal room to the right had ornate geometric designs in the plaster ceiling and leaf decorations in the cornice. A fire flickered in the immense marble hearth at one end of the room while a triple bay window looked out onto the bay.

"It's breathtaking," she said, going to the window to better take in the view.

"Do you like the water?" Rand asked, coming to her side.

"I've never seen anything like it." Her gaze followed seabirds making a circle formation out above the calm blue waters. "I've been to Bath of course, but it is nothing like this."

"Yes," he said. "I had the same feeling when I first laid eyes on Waterford."

"Would Countess Randolph like to freshen up before supper?" Mrs. Cully inquired.

Countess Randolph. It took Kat a moment to realize the housekeeper referred to her. She had expected to be the Viscountess Sinclair. "I should like that very much."

Rand bowed in a formal manner. "I shall see you at supper."

Her apartment, done in faded shades of blues and greens, suited her. Consisting of a sitting room, dressing room, and bedchamber, her rooms, while not extravagant, were large and comfortable. Two banks of windows were her favorite part; one overlooked the rolling park and valley beyond, while the other opened over the inlet.

When she descended for supper a short time later, Kat was surprised when Samuel the footman led her past the dining room and outside through double-terraced doors instead. They stepped out into the courtyard which was enclosed on three sides, but the open side offered a breathtaking view of the inlet and the mountains beyond it. She spotted Rand in dark formal dress, standing next to an elaborately set table for two.

"I hope you don't mind." He came toward her with a proffered glass of claret. "I took the liberty of asking Mr. Cully to serve an early supper out here so we could enjoy the view."

She smiled and took the glass. "It is perfect."

"Perhaps tomorrow you'd like to walk down to the water for a closer look."

She tried to quiet the nerves rioting in her stomach. This evening would likely be her wedding night in truth. "I would like that very much."

Samuel and Mr. Cully appeared with covered trays of food.

Rand smiled at her. "It appears dinner is served."

...

Rand wasn't sure he'd ever seen Kat look as breathtaking as she did during supper. Her short curls shimmered in the setting sun. Gleams of light also settled gently over the gentle slope of her delectable breasts, which her gown showed to extreme advantage. For a moment, he couldn't for the life of him understand why he had yet to bed his wife. Yet he did know. A coaching inn was no place for their first intimate encounter. Especially if he were to experience one of his bouts.

As serene as she appeared, once supper was over, the way Kat fisted the skirt of her gown belied her nerves. "Are you well?" he asked.

"What?" Her expression smoothed. "Yes, supremely." When she turned away to look out at the inlet, he admired the long line of her neck, left bare by her short curls and the generously-cut décolletage of her bodice.

He walked up behind her and pressed his lips to the warm, smooth spot with its delicate wisps of hair. She shivered against him. "Are you cold?" he murmured against her neck.

"No. Do you know the history of this house?"

He inhaled the delicate scent of femininity with an underlying tint of violets. "How do you mean?"

"Mrs. Cully says the last earl was in love with his brother's widow and lived here with her, never marrying, forgoing an heir."

"I had heard some such thing."

"He must have loved her very much."

"As I love you." That he had said it aloud surprised him, but he did not regret it.

She turned to face him with luminous eyes. "Truly?"

"There has never been anyone else." He took her glass from her and walked back to set both his and hers on the table. Then he came back to her and took her into his arms, touching his lips to hers. She opened her mouth and the taste of the shared claret swirled between them, their tongues rubbing against each other.

His deadened insides swirled to life, heat pouring through him. Every inch of his being swelled open to soak in the essence of this woman. His woman. To have her warm feminine curves pressed up against him, to have her fitted so snugly in his arms, felt supremely right. And he wondered that it had taken so many years for them to arrive at this place.

He broke the kiss. "Kitty," he said, his forehead up against hers. "Perhaps you should retire and prepare to receive me."

She looked up at him with rosy cheeks. "Yes." And she moved away from him, across the courtyard, disappearing inside. He walked over to the table and picked up the claret, finishing his first and then hers, but stopping there. He wanted to have his wits about him the first time he made love to Kitty.

He followed after a quarter of an hour, slipping into his chamber where Burgess awaited him. The valet helped him undress and brought out his dressing gown, before disappearing without a word. Which was quite unlike Burgess. But then, this was unlike any other night.

His nerves stretched tight inside his chest where anxiety warred with desire. He abhorred the idea of having an episode in Kitty's bed, or anywhere within her sight. Even though he'd found the strength to reveal himself to Drummond—and prayed the doctor could eventually help control his bouts with madness—he still intended to forever hide his impairment from Kitty. Drawing a deep breath, he tightened the belt of his dressing gown and stepped up to the door that adjoined to hers. Vera rose from before the fireplace and trotted over to accompany him.

"Sorry, girl," he said, "but this I do alone."

• • •

Even though she'd been anticipating the knock at the adjoining door, Kat started when it finally came. She rose to her feet from the chair she'd been sitting in, tugging at her short curls, regretting that she no longer had the long curtain of hair to shield herself.

The door opened and Rand stepped through, dressed in a burgundy dressing gown with dark paisley designs. The open neck and swirls of dark hair on his chest told her he wore no shirt. "May I join you?"

"Yes, of course," she said, relieved her voice did not betray the cacophony of nerves rioting in her belly.

He approached her, his dark eyes shining, and ran a finger along the silk of her dressing gown.

"I am sorry it is so plain. I had a special one made for my wedding night—" The words trailed off. An exquisite lace and sheer night rail had been made for her wedding night with Laurie. It remained in London.

"It is just as well," he answered in that grainy tone of his. "You won't be in it for long."

She caught her breath, the granite intent in his voice made her insides twitch. Taking her into his arms, he brought his mouth down and pressed warm, surprisingly soft lips against hers.

He pulled away and began to loosen the belt of her dressing gown. "May I?"

She froze. "Do we put out the candles?"

"Only if you insist upon it." His hands moved down to the sides of her hips. "I should like to see my wife when I make love to her."

"As you wish." She'd quickly parsed that if he could see her, she'd be able to see him. And she wanted to. Badly.

He loosened her belt and the dressing gown fell open revealing the valley between her breasts and the private place between her thighs. "Nothing underneath," he said in a cragged voice. "Brave girl."

Going to his knees, he put his lips to the smooth expanse of skin between her breasts, his large hands sliding behind to caress the curves of her bottom. His mouth trailed down over her rib cage and belly, to the vulnerable nest of tufted hair that shielded her most feminine place. When he put his lips there, Kat gasped and made some undecipherable utterance, the shock of it almost sweeping her off her feet. "Should you do that?"

Rising to his feet in a swift motion, he caught her up in his arms and carried her to the bed. "Yes, and I will do so often."

She resisted the urge to pull her loose robe shut, to cover herself. Fear sprouted at being laid bare and vulnerable to this man who had hurt her more than anyone. Refusing to yield to cowardice, her mind swerved around the poisonous thoughts and steadied itself by latching onto the one truth that had never changed for her: no matter what he had done to her, she loved Rand. She'd chosen her course and would gladly see it through.

The counterpane had been pulled back and he laid her against the cool bed linens. She still wore her robe but it was opened wide, laying her bare to him. Standing by the bed, he loosened his own dressing gown belt. He shrugged it off, baring an impossibly thin form, all rangy musculature stretched taut over bone. A puckered, angry-looking scar marred one shoulder and a series of lighter scars ran down one arm. She could make out his ribs, the muscled stomach, the line of hair that trailed down to his large jutting member.

Climbing onto the bed, he came up over her and covered her with his body. The feel of his powerful frame against hers sent an avalanche of unschooled sensation rushing at her.

Her world narrowed to his all-engulfing presence. He was like the power of the sun, and overwhelming heat and light burned into her everywhere their bare skin met. His chest rubbed against her sensitized breasts, his hard belly on hers, their hips melded and his arousal pressed against the softness of her belly. His masculine scent filled her senses until she could discern nothing beyond the press of virility engulfing her.

His kiss was hot and openmouthed, making her blood run heavy and heated through her limbs and down to the core of her. When she felt him breech her opening, it seemed natural to widen her legs in welcome.

"Can you take it?" His dark keen gaze focused on her face. "I know I should be more patient with you, but I find I cannot."

She had wanted to be with him in this way for almost as long as she could remember. "I can take it," she said breathless. "I want it all, don't be patient or too gentle with me. I've been waiting for this forever."

He pushed in slowly and profound discomfort replaced the thick desire that had weighted her body only moments before. She tensed against the painful invasion of his body into hers. Squeezing her eyes shut, she gritted her teeth against the discomfort as he pushed further in, making her insides feel like they were being torn apart. Just when she thought she could bear it no further, he stopped pushing. "Is it done?" she whispered through the pain.

His eyes sharpened on her as a tear ran down the side of her face. Something like anguished regret flashed in his expression. He kissed away the tear as though it could take away the sting. "I've hurt you."

She shook her head and pressed a determined kiss against his lips. "Just finish it, please." She wanted it over and done with, fully consummated to seal her lifelong bond with him, to make it truly irrevocable.

He caught her mouth and deepened the kiss, unexpectedly

sweeping her up into pleasure again with drugging strokes of his tongue inside her mouth. Her muscles loosened and warmth slid into her limbs. He began to move, back and forth motions that created a delicious friction, almost leaving her body before pushing in again, until he could go no further. He quickened his pace and her body began to feel the excitement again, began to close around and caress him as he slid in and out of her. Suddenly, seated deep inside her, he froze and shuddered, whooshing an exhale of great relief. Tension seemed to flow out of his body and the weight of him came down on her.

She stilled, her own body feeling strangely unsettled as she wrapped her arms around her husband, welcoming the heavy warmth of his relaxed body against hers. She pressed a kiss into his neck, inhaling his scent, a combined sense of relief and euphoria floating through her. He was finally hers. Totally and completely.

He kissed her cheek and pulled his body off of hers, swinging his long legs over the side of his bed. Rubbing his shoulder, he shifted in his sitting position so he could look at her. "Are you all right?"

"Yes, supremely." She smiled and ran a hand along the sinewy strength of his bare back, thrilled to be able to touch him so. She could never imagine growing tired of touching him.

He bent over to reach for something on the floor, making her hand lose contact with his warm skin. Pushing to his feet, she saw he had his dressing gown in his hand. He pulled it on, giving her a distant smile. "I am relieved. I feared it went hard on you."

He helped her to a sitting position and busied himself

righting her dressing gown in gentle motions that made her feel protected and cared for. Anticipation trilled through her. She wondered what they would do next.

Once he had her dressing gown belted and put to rights, he eased her back down on the bed and pulled the counterpane over her. "Sleep well, my love," he said and turned and walked through the adjoining door, closing it softly behind him.

. . .

Kat sat up and punched her pillow before flopping back against it. She had no idea of the time, but it must early morning. The gray tinge of dawn slivered through her windows, shaking off the last of the night shadows.

She shot a look at the closed door which adjoined Rand's chamber. Amazed disbelief still clung to her at the abrupt manner in which he'd left her last night. She blinked back the tears jerking behind her eyes. Perhaps she should have expected this. She knew most married people of a certain station maintained separate bedchambers.

But her father usually passed the evenings in her mother's bed. She'd found him there often enough as a child, when she'd tiptoed away from the nursery in the early morning to sneak into the comforting warmth of Mama's bed. Her father had always been there, in his nightclothes, sleepily drawing her into the bed, settling her snugly between him and Mama before falling back into a snoring slumber.

She'd expected that same sleepy warmth and closeness with her husband. She'd assumed she'd wake each morning with Edward beside her. Shivering, she lay back down and pulled the counterpane over her, seeking its warmth. The fire had died in the night, leaving only cool gray ashes and none of its vitality. Fanny would be along soon to light it.

Her thoughts wandered back to Edward. Only he was no longer Edward. She'd married Rand, an altogether different specimen than the boy who had left her. She punched her pillow again and rearranged herself on it. She couldn't shake the feeling Rand kept a large part of him—a critical part—heavily guarded and hidden away from her. Had she jilted Laurie, and risked the *ton*'s considerable displeasure, only to fall into a cold and distant marriage?

No. Time and proximity were on her side now. This time she would wait him out. And he couldn't run. Even if it took years, she'd break through the shield of distant courtesy Rand had erected between them. Now that she was finally married to Edward Stanhope, she would settle for nothing less than having all of him.

The door clicked open and Fanny slipped in, keeping her gaze averted as she went to attend the hearth. The maid worked in silence as she built the fire.

"You needn't be so quiet, I am quite awake."

Fanny turned hesitantly before running a seeking eye over her mistress' bed. "And alone?"

Kat's cheeks warmed a little under the scrutiny. "Yes," she said in answer to the unasked question. "But I am now a wife in both name and deed."

Fanny turned to poke the fire once more, commanding the flames to leap higher. "So the two of you have finally sated your hunger." She slipped out the door, returning promptly with a basin of water. "I've warm water if you'd like to…ah…cleanse yourself."

Oh. She'd forgotten there might be evidence of what happened last night. Rising, Kat examined the linens and immediately spotted the stain. Hmmm. She didn't feel any differently. One would think the loss of innocence would leave a greater mark than the small, unobtrusive streak of rust on the bed linens. "For all of the import society places on chastity, the reality of one's maidenhead isn't particularly remarkable."

Chuckling, Fanny began to strip the bed. "That's how the culls keep us faithful, I suppose. So we won't be hopping out of their bed into someone else's."

Going to the basin of water, Kat stripped off her robe. She was a little sticky between her thighs, but otherwise felt remarkably normal. She dipped a wash towel in the water and wrung it out. Holding the linens crumpled in her arms, Fanny paused to regard her with a wary watchfulness. "Did he use you roughly?"

Kat wiped the sticky brownish streaks from her thighs, glad for the warm abrading sensation against her chilled skin. "No, not particularly."

"Then what is it? Was it terrible?"

"No, not at all. It was rather wonderful being together in that way." She cupped a breast, washing it with the cloth in her other hand. "But as soon as it was over, he returned to his own chamber. It was as if he considered his duty done. I expected more…I don't know…more interest on his part."

A knock sounded at the adjoining door. Before she could answer, it pulled open and Rand appeared on the threshold. Air from the moving door breezed across her flesh. Kat froze, naked before the wash basin with the wet cloth in her hand, her skin slick with moisture.

Rand halted, his glance spiked to where she still palmed her breast as though holding it up to him in invitation. He watched for a moment before his gaze traveled down her body in a quick but thorough perusal. Sensation skated across her skin, prompting the tips of her breasts to harden. While he watched. The column of his throat moved. Chills of a different sort puckered along her body at the way he absorbed the sight of her bare flesh.

Averting his eyes, Rand focused on something on the floor beyond her feet. "I do beg your pardon." He cleared the rasp in his throat. "I thought to see if you would like to ride this morning. If it would suit, of course." He was already dressed for riding in chocolate brown riding pants, worn boots, and a white open-necked linen shirt that revealed a rugged expanse of throat.

"It would suit very well, thank you," she said, her voice polite. As though she wasn't standing naked before him, ignoring the attraction that arced between them.

His gaze returned to her naked form and lingered a bit longer than was polite. But then again, a husband had a right to look his fill. "Very well. I shall see you downstairs." Taking a step back, he pivoted, going back through the door and shutting it behind him in precise movements.

Kat exhaled, the heightened moment still fluttering under her skin like a thousand tiny butterflies. Fanny's snort broke the spell. She looked to her maid, almost surprised to still see her there. She'd been so absorbed in Rand, she'd forgotten about the maid's presence. "What?"

Fanny pushed out her lips, amusement plain as writing on her face. "I don't think you have to worry about a lack of interest on his part. Nor on yours, for that matter."

• • •

"You are in excellent looks this morning," Rand said, greeting her at the bottom of the massive staircase a short time later.

She dipped her chin. "I'm glad you approve."

The dark slash of his right brow rose at the coquettish gesture. "Surely, you anticipated that I would."

Of course, she'd known he would. Kat knew the picture she created. She'd worn the tight-fitting, soft-blue riding gown for effect. After all, if there was one thing Kat excelled at, it was appearances. The hue of her gown heightened the color of her eyes and deepened the shine in her hair. It also emphasized the modest curve of her bosom, which he seemed to appreciate even if it didn't match Elena's mountainous proportions. As the *ton*'s incomparable, she excelled at dressing for public show, like a peacock showing its colors. Today, she'd dressed for her husband. If she could win over the sharp tongues of the *ton*, surely she could manage one man.

He offered his arm and they strode out the side doors toward the stable. "Oh," she said with some disappointment. "I'd hoped we'd break our fast first, perhaps on the terrace with its spectacular views."

"There is much to see at Waterford," he said. "And I'm keen to show it to you."

Once they mounted, he led the way, winding them back up through the hills. At first he set a sedate pace, but once he seemed assured of her riding skills, they gave the horses their heads and raced across the wide expanses of the easy sloping hills.

"Here we are," he said, stopping and dismounting.

She looked across the pleasantly grassy expanse of hilltop. "Where?"

He helped her down and then turned to untie a sack tied to his mount. Taking her hand, he smiled and led the way. "You'll see."

They walked around a cliffy edge. The breeze carried the smell of the sea and then the water came into view. They'd rounded away from the house to the hills overlooking the inlet. "Oh," she breathed in awe. "The view is even more spectacular here."

"Yes, they do seem to try to outdo each other." He unfurled a blanket he'd taken from his pack and set it on the ground. They sat with the hillside behind them and the gentle drop of land all the way to the cliffs above the inlet stretching in front of them.

She blinked, breathing it all in; the view of the expansive sea stretching in front of them and brown cliffs, the scent of the sea. Her stomach grumbled, a reminder she hadn't broken her fast yet. "Dare I hope there is more than a blanket in your pack?"

"You may," he said, pulling out figs, bread, cold chicken, cheese, and ale.

"I suppose the first rule of a great commander is to always be prepared," she said with honest appreciation. They began to eat. After her first hungry bites, she slowed herself and focused on her posture, remembering to curve her profile just so, so he would see her to her best advantage.

His teeth tore meat from the chicken leg in his hand. He chewed slowly, considering her. "You know," he said as though discussing something as banal as the weather, "you don't have to seduce me."

She scratched her hand, feeling her nerves. "I'm not sure I take your meaning."

He leaned into her, his mouth near her ear. "I am already seduced."

"Is that so?"

"Yes. I don't require those frippery wiles that you used on Sinclair and all those other gallants."

"What do you require?"

"You. Just as you are. The same Kitty I left behind."

"But you are not the same man who left me."

He looked away from her, out to the sea. "That is true." She took in his profile. There was nothing refined or soft about Rand anymore. He was much like the terrain that surrounded him; all sharp jutting angles in a less-than-welcoming environment, yet indescribably, inescapably beautiful in an elemental way.

He turned his head to catch her studying him. "I realize last evening might have been less pleasurable than you'd hoped."

She stiffened. Perhaps he'd left her last evening because bedding her had not lived up to his expectations. "I'm sorry if you were disappointed."

He laughed, a sound she rarely heard from him, a deep rumble out of his chest. "I was far from disappointed."

She tipped her head, considering him. "I don't understand."

"I was so caught up in my lovely bride, I did not see to your pleasure as I should have."

She hadn't been disappointed in the lovemaking, just in

what had followed. Still, she ventured to tease him. This new Rand was so serious; he needed to laugh more. "Are you implying you can do better?"

His brows shot up in amusement. "I'm not implying it. I'm stating an indisputable fact."

She tossed her head, flirting now, an arena she was comfortable with and excelled at. "Indisputable?" She rolled the question off her tongue with obvious disdain.

"Most definitely."

"Hmmm. I suppose I shall withhold judgment until you've convinced me of that."

He had her on her back before she knew what he was about. His rock-like form hovered over her. "You require evidence, do you?"

"Of course," she said, her heartbeat moving more swiftly.

He lowered his hips against hers, so that his arousal jutted against her. "How's that for evidence?"

"It's a sturdy start."

He gave a quiet laugh. "You need more, do you?" He moved his hips against her in an insinuating manner, pressing at her mound in a way that sent shivers of pleasure careening through her. "If I am to demonstrate correctly, you must allow me complete access to your money."

She crinkled her nose. From what she understood, Edward was far wealthier than she could ever hope to be. "What money?"

His hand made its way between their melded hips to the place between her legs. He stroked a particularly sensitive spot through the fabric of her riding habit. "This is your money. Although I'd call it a treasure, myself."

"You're gammoning me." She laughed and pushed

against his chest. "That part of a woman most certainly does not have a name."

"Oh, but it does." His finger stroked more deliberately. She arched in reflex. "It has many names in fact."

"Truly?" She found it hard to concentrate on his words, given what his fingers were doing to her. "What are its other names?"

His hand was moving, finding its way under her skirt. "This is hardly a fitting conversation for a lady." His fingers skated — ever so lightly — up her leg and along the tender flesh at the top of her thighs.

She shivered in anticipation. "We're out in the open with your hand up my skirt. It's a bit late for propriety."

"True." He brought his lips down on her for an unhurried, devouring kiss. "Very well. If you insist. One's commodity."

"One's commodity?" She kissed him back, long and thorough, sliding her tongue against his, feeling the hunger grow in him. "That makes sense I suppose. In an insulting way."

"Especially for denizens of Covent Garden."

She nodded her understanding. One couldn't help but notice the weary-looking harlots who frequented the theater district, looking for their next transaction. "Tell me another."

"This" — his fingers parted her down there — "is your sweet little cunny."

"Oh." She stopped breathing. "That sounds positively wicked."

His finger found the knot where all sensation seemed centered. "One can do very wicked things with it…and to it."

Pinpricks of pleasure shot through her. "I'm sure you know them all."

"Hardly. Do you want to hear more?" When she nodded, he continued. "This"—he stroked up and down the length of it—"is your quim, your madge, your muff."

His dark, smoky voice rumbled through her. Need welled up inside her. "What do you call it?"

He undid his placket and freed himself, nudging hard and hungry against her sensitive folds. "I call it paradise," he said, pushing into her. "And you're coming with me this time."

A moan escaped her. One she could not have stopped if she tried. His finger came back to her sensitive spot, circling it, plucking gently at it. Then he took his hand away and she regretted the lost sensory pleasure. She murmured a protest.

"What a demanding wife you are." He shifted his pelvis upward, rocking against her rather than thrusting as before. "Better?"

*Infinitely.* His pubic bone connected to hers, stimulating her with each movement, ratcheting up the delicious, almost painful spikes of sensation inside of her. Catching the rhythm, she began to move with him.

"That's it." He kissed her again, his tongue pleasuring her mouth with deep-throated strokes. "Come with me, Kitty." His voice roughened. "I want to feel your hot little cunny tighten around me."

His brazen words sent trills of excitement shooting through her, heightening everything happening to her body. He rocked against her in firm, sure movements, the friction causing her insides to contract, tighter and tighter, until something inside her burst and released. She made an exclamation of surprise as warm pleasure spiraled down her legs and pulsed through her.

He pumped urgently into her and reached his own crisis soon after, shooting his seed into her throbbing womb. A shudder wracked him, and then his heavy body came down on hers. He shifted his body weight, rolling off of her and onto his back. His breathing uneven as he pulled her into his arms. "Damnation. That was good."

She luxuriated in the earthy scent of his skin, suffused with the primal tinge of lovemaking. "I can see why," she said faintly after a while.

"Why what?" he murmured, pressing a kiss into her forehead.

"Why you call it paradise." And she felt him smile against her skin.

. . .

That evening, Kat stroked a light finger over his hard member. "Does this have a name, too?"

He tightened his grip on her shoulders. She sat on her bed wearing her chemise, her legs hanging off the side. Rand stood in front of her, naked, allowing the exploration. "It has many."

"Remarkable." Her smooth pointer finger circled the head of his throbbing erection. He gritted his teeth, forcing himself to retain control. He'd been so anxious about having an episode on their wedding night that he'd performed less than admirably. He was determined for that not to reoccur this evening. "I never realized marriage would be so educational."

He watched her inquisitive finger stroke him, and all he wanted to do was suck it into his mouth. To say nothing of what he wanted to do with his rod. "You have no idea."

She smiled up at him, her pearly teeth glistening, her eyes alert with interest. "Enlighten me."

He shifted his weight. "This conversation is entirely unsuitable."

Mischief crept into her smile. "I'll tell you what." She scooted her luscious little bum back onto the bed and fell back on her elbows. The movement hiked the hem of her shift up, baring smooth delicate thighs. He pictured them clasped around his hips as he thrust into her. "You tell me what it's called and I'll let you put it in me."

His reluctance evaporated. "Arbor vitae, plug-tail, tackle." He grabbed her knees in one decisive motion, pulling her toward him so that her bottom perched on the edge of the bed. He stepped between her legs and pushed into her sweet wetness. "Wrap your legs around me."

She did and then undulated against him. She was a fast learner, this wife of his. "Tell me another word for your... tackle."

He gritted his teeth. "If you start talking dirty to me, I won't last at all."

Her eyebrows raised, as though this was a revelation. "Truly?"

"Thomas, pole, tool, lobcock." His voice strained as he stroked all the way into her, as far as he could go. "Although lobcock is not entirely accurate at this moment."

She sighed and closed her eyes, moving against him. "Why not?"

"Lobcock refers to a man's...member...in a less than... ah...rigid state."

She locked her ankles around his hips. "Then that is

definitely not the case with you. You are most stalwart."

"I intend to show you just how stalwart."

"Mmmm." She sighed with pleasure and then a wicked light gleamed in her eyes. "Your…Thomas…feels so good inside me."

His arousal soared. He leaned over to plunder her mouth with powerful strokes of his tongue. "If you persist in allowing filth to escape your lips, I shall have to teach you a lesson."

"You've given me such incentive." She gasped when he stroked even farther in her than she thought possible. "I've decided I want your…pole…inside of me as often as possible."

He groaned, and said pole grew harder, if that were possible. He should slow down, but she had him in such an agitated state that his body took over, stroking hard and heavy. He brought his hand to the place where they were joined to see to her pleasure. She moaned and squirmed and they moved together toward their crisis. Unbearable pressure built up in his stomach and chest, sensation shot down the back of his legs, and the tension broke. Waves of immense pleasure and satisfaction, sensations well beyond the carnal, saturated his senses.

He collapsed on the bed beside her, breathing hard. "I trust I have proven my point."

She stretched, creating a wanton picture with her chemise still bunched up around her middle, baring her from the waist down. "What point is that?"

"That this business of the marriage bed could be good between us. Very good, in fact."

"Oh, yes. You've proven exceedingly adept. Both this

morning and this evening. I'm very fortunate." They lay there quietly for a few minutes and she turned to snuggle against his shoulder. Her expression turned more serious as she ran a light hand over the unsightly, puckered scar there. "I hate that you were injured and suffering on a battlefield somewhere and I didn't know."

"That is all in the past." He drew her hand away and kissed it. "I am here now."

"Will you tell me about it one day?"

His chest contracted. "No. It is not something I care to remember or discuss. These are not stories of valor that will entertain the *ton*." The words were sharp. Her eyes shuttered and he saw that he had hurt her. He drew her to him, putting his arms around her. "I apologize."

"I didn't mean to anger you. I just want to know you better."

Which he could never allow. If she ever saw the full truth of who he was now, it would disgust her. The sounds of scratching at the adjoining door reached him. "That would be Vera."

She nestled into him. Her intriguing tapestry of scents—clean soap, musky skin, and the hint of lavender in her hair—curled around him. "I can't blame her for not wanting to be shut away from you," she said. "The animal is female after all. We can't seem to resist you."

*Thank heaven for that.* Rand gathered her in, all warm woman and soft curves, relishing a feeling of relaxed fulfillment. He yawned, not wanting to move, relishing this rare perfect suspended moment. Sweet exhaustion weighted his eyelids.

Vera whined behind the closed door, breaking the spell.

Rational thought speared his contentment. He forced his eyes open. He could not fall asleep here.

He must have tensed because Kitty opened her eyes. "What is it?"

He kissed her, pressing his lips against hers, before setting her away from him in a gentle motion. "I'd best see to Vera."

She caught his arm. "Don't go, surely Burgess can see to her."

"The two of them don't exactly see eye to eye."

She released him. "Then come back after you've seen to her. I'll wait for you."

He stood up by the bed and reached for his clothes, aware she tracked his movements and awaited his response. He didn't want to leave her. He longed to run his tongue along every inch of her. To take her again and again. To hear her murmurs of pleasure and sighs of satisfaction. But, as much as he desired it, he didn't dare stay the night in her bed. Not when his dreams could trigger an episode. Hiding his regret, he forced a light tone. "No, it could be a while. I wouldn't want to keep you up."

"I want to wait up for you. I don't mind."

He forced himself to walk away from her when what he wanted to do was pull her under the counterpane with him and listen to her soft breaths as she slept. "That isn't necessary," he said in a brisk tone. "I shall see you in the morning."

Without looking back, he pulled open the adjoining door and stepped through it, closing it behind him with a resolute click.

• • •

The moans woke her on the last night of their wedding trip. At first Kat thought she was dreaming, but as sleep ebbed, she realized the sounds were coming from Rand's chamber. She rose from the bed and went to the door he always made a point of closing when he left her at night.

"No!" He cried out in anguish-soaked words. "Stay away! Go away."

Alarmed, she turned the knob to enter, only to find it secured. The realization gutted her. He'd locked her out.

"Bloody hell! *Bloody hell.*" He bellowed the words through the door.

She grabbed her dressing gown and pulled it on as she rushed into the corridor toward Rand's bedchamber door. When she turned the knob, it pushed open easily. The space was dark and Rand had gone silent, but she could make out Vera standing over something on the bed. As she came closer, she realized it was Rand curled into a tight ball. The dog licked his face with strong, determined strokes. She couldn't make out Rand's expression in the dark, but he didn't appear to be reacting.

Alarmed, she reached out to touch him. "Rand?"

"It is best for you to return to your chamber, my lady."

She turned at the sound of his valet's voice, panic rising in her chest. "There is something very wrong with him."

"I will attend to his lordship, my lady." He stood just inside the door. He was haphazardly dressed, as though he'd pulled on his clothes in a rush. How had he gotten here so quickly? "You must return to your chamber."

"What is wrong with him?" The words trembled.

"It is a nightmare." He spoke in strong firm tones. "He would not want you to be here."

"Why ever not? I am his wife. If he is in distress, I should attend him."

"I assure you, he is not in any serious peril, but I cannot see to him until you leave, my lady."

She looked back to the bed, where Rand began to shake uncontrollably. Tears filled her eyes. "Please help him."

"I shall." He put a gentle hand to her elbow, even though, as a servant, he should never lay a hand on her. "Please go now."

She stumbled into the corridor, tears and panic blurring her vision, and rushed back to her room. Slamming her door, she ran to the one that separated her chamber from Rand's and put an ear to the cool wood. She could make out Burgess admonishing the dog to get off the bed, followed, after a few minutes, by murmured tones of conversation. Rand's voice. She couldn't make out the words, but the tenor of his voice was unmistakable. The calm, even tones showed no sign of his earlier distress. Relief weakened her limbs. Maybe it was just a vivid nightmare. With her back to the door, she slid to the floor and buried her face in her hands, crying tears of both relief and worry.

At breakfast the following morning, he behaved as though nothing was amiss. "I hope I didn't disturb you too terribly last evening," he said in almost casual tones as they finished their meal. "Burgess said I woke you."

"I was concerned you might be ill."

"Not at all." He drank from his coffee. "I sometimes have wretched dreams...an after effect of the war, I'm afraid. It's a nuisance, but nothing to be concerned about." He turned the conversation to other matters, mostly their impending return to Town.

He spoke of it so casually that she was left to wonder if she'd overreacted and perhaps even dreamt some of it. It was possible; she had been sound asleep when his cries woke her. But the little niggle of worry in her stomach suggested otherwise.

• • •

"Please see to it that all of the chambers are aired." Kat bustled down the stairs of Randolph House, Rand's London townhome. Only it was now hers as well, and there was much work to be done to make this dark, dusty cave into a home.

"Yes, my lady." Mrs. Deardon, the new housekeeper she'd hired two weeks ago upon their return to Town, hurried down after her.

"The spaces we use on a regular basis should be cleaned daily, the rarely-used chambers must be attended to weekly." Reaching the bottom of the stairs, Kat stopped to consider the entry hall. The surfaces now shone and the marble floor gleamed, unlike the first time she'd seen the home, when she'd come to inquire about Toby's whereabouts. The windows facing the garden had been thrown open and the curtains in the rest of the house had been pulled back to let the sunshine in.

Mrs. Deardon cleared her throat. "I will need to hire additional staff, my lady."

"Yes, of course. Please see to it." As Mrs. Deardon hurried away, Kat consulted her list of things to be done. Randolph

House had suffered greatly for the lack of a mistress, but she intended to rectify that. She stilled for a moment, soaking in the pleasure of finally being Rand's wife after all these years. He seemed to feel the same, yet he still held part of himself aloof. Although they took all of their meals together and he came to her every evening, Rand never stayed the night in her bed. Once they made love, he'd quietly rise, wish her good evening, and return to his own chamber.

Cotter, the butler they'd recently hired, interrupted her thoughts to advise Kat that the new furniture she'd ordered had just arrived. She proceeded to supervise the placement of the sofa, tables, and chairs she'd ordered for the grand salon. As the delivery men quit the room, Toby appeared on the threshold dressed in his usual finery of bright colors—a bottle green tailcoat with an orange striped waistcoat beneath.

"Commanding the troops, I see. You'd have made a fine general."

Her heart gladdened at the sight of him. "You've returned." She gave him a warm hug. "Let me look at you. I've been so worried about your well-being." Toby had always been naturally pale and slim, but he did appear to have a bit more color in his face and a few more pounds on his person.

A pale brow arched. "One wonders how you found the time to worry. I would have thought you were too busy causing the scandal of the Season."

"Oh, you refer to my marriage." Her cheeks warmed. "It was rather unexpected."

"You'll do anything to remain the center of the *ton*'s attention." He spoke in a teasing tone. "You and Rand?

Who knew?"

She looped her arm through his. "Come and have tea and I'll tell you all about it."

When they were settled in her sitting room, she told her cousin about her youthful love for Rand. She left out the part about Laurie's indiscretion with Elena.

"What a happy ending," he declared when she finished. "Except for Sinclair, of course. Although I hear he is taking full responsibility for your unexpected defection."

"He is?"

"Most assuredly. Miss Campbell went into fits of pique when she learned of your marriage. She was intent on sullying your name, but Sin wouldn't allow it. He immediately made it known he'd behaved indiscreetly and that you were quite correct to choose another suitor. Miss Campbell's mother has banished her to the country for spreading lies. The rumor is Lexie will be made to marry her father's friend, an elderly baronet who is a widower with six children." A slow, salacious smile opened up across Toby's face. "Of course, everyone is on tenterhooks dying to know what horrible indiscretion on Sin's part drove you into Rand's arms."

She exhaled. "It is good of Laurie to protect my reputation."

"You expected otherwise?"

"I hadn't thought about it. I haven't spoken to him since I sent the note informing him of my decision to cry off."

"You jilted Sin with a note?" His eyes widened. "You wicked girl. The gossips are having a field day. They say you aren't receiving callers and haven't called upon anyone since your return."

"I'm busy making the house ready to receive visitors…

while I work up my courage to face them all. Tomorrow is our first engagement. We are to dine with Rand's family at the Marquess of Camryn's home."

"I daresay you shall be more popular than ever when you do re-emerge from your dramatic self-imposed exile. Rand is clearly the victor in all of this. He not only gets the *ton*'s incomparable"—he surveyed the chamber—"but I can't help noticing that you've already brought some life to this old crypt. When Rand lived here alone, it was as dark and somber as a tomb."

Pleased that he'd noticed, she gave him a tour of the improvements. She wanted to soften the sharp edges and brighten the dark corners of Rand's life for him. She showed Toby the red-and-gold Aubusson rug in the dining room and the new leather chairs for the library. When she came to the music room, she pushed the doors open.

"You've had it painted," he said, taking in the tangerine upper walls which met crisp, white wainscoting. Large windows faced the gardens, letting light fall across the cheery space.

"Do you like it?"

"Very much." He walked to the pianoforte and pressed a key, and the crisp dulcimer tone rippled through the room. "And this has been tuned as well." He played a few more notes. "They say music can be healing."

"Does it help you, Toby?" she asked quietly.

"Ah, I forgot." He looked up from the pianoforte with a rueful smile. "You saw my rather dramatic performance the day of the lightning storm."

Her chest squeezed. "Where have you been? You were gone for a month."

"I met with Doctor Drummond. He has expertise in dealing with melancholia brought on by the battlefield." He tilted his head, a sad smile in his eyes. "But you mustn't tell anyone, my dear, lest they think I have windmills in my head."

"Melancholia? Is that what ails you? Was Doctor Drummond able to help?"

"Somewhat. Drummond believes talking about the experience helps, although I find it rather dreadful. It was horrid enough the first time, much less having to relive the nightmare over and over again." He pressed a few more keys. "I find taking regular exercise helps. Drummond says I must keep myself busy, which is an anathema for an English gentleman who is supposed to revel in his lack of enterprise."

"You look well." Tenderness for her cousin welled in her chest, and then a thought occurred to her. "You say music is healing?"

"So says Doctor Drummond."

"I do wish Rand would play." Perhaps it would help soothe the intensity of her husband's nightmares. "He's such a talented musician."

"Rand?" Toby's forehead wrinkled. "A musician?"

"Yes. He has an extraordinary gift. He used to bring tears to my eyes when he played the violin or the pianoforte."

"Are you certain we are talking about the same person? You did marry Edward Stanhope, the Earl of Randolph, did you not?"

"He hasn't played since he went to join the fight on the Continent."

"Tobias." They both turned to find Rand standing in the threshold. "I see you've returned in one piece."

The two men met in the middle of the room to shake hands. "And of relatively sound mind," Toby said lightly.

Rand's dark emerald gaze probed the other man's face. "It went well?"

"Supremely. Drummond was quite helpful, but it is only the start of our work." He smiled when Rand darted a quick look in Kat's direction. "No need for discretion. I've told your countess where I've been."

A shadow crossed Rand's face. "I see." His gaze moved to the freshly painted wall. He turned to Kat. "You've redone this room."

Hope kicked in her chest. "As you can see, I've had the pianoforte placed near the window and I even found a violin from the very same Italian craftsman who made the one you so treasured—"

His expression hardened. "I no longer play instruments of any sort. As you well know." She couldn't stand the thought of Rand never playing music again. It was so much a part of him and he used to take such pleasure in it.

"The secrets you keep inside that somber exterior," Toby said to Rand. "A life-long care for my cousin and a musical talent you keep hidden from the world."

"Some things are best left in darkness," Rand said, turning to leave the chamber. "Will you join me in my study for some claret?"

...

That evening, for the first time since their marriage, he did not go to her. He went instead to the music room. He didn't light a candle even though the chamber was cloaked in darkness. Sitting at the pianoforte, he ran a light finger across the cool tops of the ivory keys. The urge to play, to be carried away by the music, welled inside of him. The need was stronger than he could remember since he'd abandoned his music. Especially now that Drummond had advised him music could help calm his mind.

He struck a key and it answered with a gleeful chord. A shiver moved through him. His weakness for music had cost him Kitty all of those years ago. But he had her now. Dare he attempt to take back his music as well? Playing opened something deep inside of him and laid him bare. Could he allow himself to be that vulnerable again?

He hit a few notes and a joyous sensation moved through him. He put both hands to the keys and began to play an old tune he knew from memory. His fingers floated across the keys in perfect tandem, the chords striking beautiful notes that reverberated through the chamber. He closed his eyes and soaked in the feeling. An agonizing pleasure filled his chest. Emotion welled and he became lost in the music, allowing it to transport him to a place where his mind settled and jubilance filled his chest, sensations he'd thought permanently extinguished at Talavera.

It wasn't until he finished the piece that he realized he wasn't alone. He sensed her presence before he saw her. Not turning, he said, "It seems the music room will be of some use after all."

"That was even more beautiful than I remembered." She moved into his line of vision, emotion glistening in her eyes. She wore her white dressing gown which reflected the blue light of the moon. "You played with such passion."

Suddenly, he wanted—he needed—her to know

everything. "When I was wounded at Talavera, I lay injured on the battlefield in terrible pain for three days while the fighting raged around me. I could hear and see the carnage, the smell of blood and festering wounds, but I felt like the waking dead because no one paid me any mind. When the fighting stopped, people came, local villagers, and I thought help was at hand. But they had not come to rescue me. They took everything. Not only my money and my father's fob, but also the clothes off my back. I lay in the field in my smallclothes for another day." Ignoring her sharp intake of breath, he continued. "I'll never forget the stench of the dead, the overwhelming feeling of utter helplessness. Sometimes in my dreams, I am back on the battlefield again, and I try to fight back when they come to rob me and treat me as though I am dead. And sometimes now in my nightmares, the realization comes to me that I am indeed dead and the horror of it overwhelms me."

"Oh, Edward. I'm exceedingly grateful you came home." She moved between him and the keyboard, tears glistening in her eyes, and embraced him. "Thank you for telling me."

Still seated, he put his arms around her and lay his head against her chest, inhaling the warmth of her skin and her subtle feminine scent, allowing her to banish the stench of the battlefield lingering in his memory.

She pulled back and met his gaze and something clicked in her eyes. "That was no nightmare I witnessed in Devon. You experience melancholia as Toby does."

He dipped his chin and continued in a strained tone, determined to tell her the truth. "Toby's Doctor Drummond says there are some measures that can be taken to ease the severity of the fits."

She put a hand on his shoulder. "Do they trouble you often?"

"The bouts were infrequent, but seem to re-occur more now that I've returned to England." He exhaled heavily through his nostrils. "It was wrong of me not to tell you before we married that you might be tying yourself to a bedlamite."

"You are not a bedlamite." The words were fierce. "Is this why you don't stay the night in my bed?"

"Nightmares can bring on episodes." Dread weighted his chest. He hated that she would now know the worst about him. "I don't want you to see that."

"You idiot." Her eyes glittered. "That is nothing in comparison to being with you. If you had returned sightless, I would gladly be your eyes. If you had returned legless, I would carry you on my back. Nothing else matters as long as I am by your side. Nothing else even comes close."

Emotion roiled his chest. "As imperfect as I am, I am all yours."

"You are alive. You survived." She kissed the top of his head. "It is something to celebrate."

She still accepted him. He found it difficult to comprehend. He loosened her dressing gown and drew it off. "I want you now, Kitty."

"You have me."

He ran his hands under her night rail, and up the smooth satin of her legs to cup her bare bottom. "I have a fierce need for you."

She hugged him tighter. "I'm here. Take what you need."

He stood and took possession of her mouth, kissing her with deep insistent strokes of his tongue. Exhilaration shot through him. He was alive. And he was here with Kitty. He lifted her night rail and drew it off, leaving the smooth satin of her skin to glow a soft blue in the moonlight. He lifted her leg around his hip and pulled at his placket to free himself. He entered her with one strong stroke and an audible groan of resounding relief.

He worked in and out of her in forceful movements, suffusing himself in her soft wet heat. He'd survived. His strokes grew faster and more insistent. The vigor of his exertion pushed Kitty back against the pianoforte and her bottom struck the keys with each robust stroke, sending discordant notes ringing through the chamber.

His chest ached as he mouthed her neck and shoulder. Moving to her pert breasts, he flicked the eager tip with his tongue before taking the tender flesh into his mouth and sampling its soft sweetness. He sought her lips again, feeling closer to Kitty than he'd ever felt with anyone. Kitty. *His wife.* Having her in his arms, making love with her, was excruciating in its rightness.

When his crisis came, intense relief and deep emotion welled in his chest, flooding his senses. His eyes were wet. She sighed and held him, then kissed him gently on the neck and took his hand, leading him up the stairs and into her chamber. She helped him undress and settled next to him on the bed, her soft warmth soothing his mind and body. And he slept.

. . .

When Kat awoke the next morning, Rand was gone. Disappointment panged in her chest. After last night, she'd hoped to awaken with him by her side. Rising from the bed, she tried the adjoining door to his chamber and found it unlocked. At least this time he hadn't bolted her out. His chamber was empty, his bed still neatly made. Perhaps he had spent the evening in her bed after all.

She called for Fanny, who helped her dress while they discussed which gown Kat would wear to the Marquess of Camryn's dinner that evening. It would be her first meeting with Rand's family since becoming his wife. Nerves fluttering in her stomach, she settled on a pale green creation she had never worn before.

When she went down for breakfast, Cotter informed her that the earl had called for his mount and departed directly after taking his morning meal, leaving word he would return in time to escort her to Cam's soiree. She frowned. He meant to absent himself all day? She'd awakened with a sense of hopefulness after last night; not only had he played music for the first time in six years, but he'd also shared the horrors of his battlefield experiences.

Cotter, the new butler, appeared, pulling her thoughts away from her husband. "My lady, you have a caller."

"Who is it?" she asked, surprised anyone would call so early.

"Viscount Sinclair, my lady."

"Oh." Something shifted in her belly and suddenly she wished she hadn't eaten so much at breakfast. "Well, do send him in."

She swallowed and her palms began to itch when she heard his approaching footsteps, the sound of his boots tapping the marble floor as he approached.

He entered, dressed immaculately in a dark jacket and

buff breeches, and bowed with utmost formality. "Countess."

"Laurie." Her heart gladdened at the sight of him and she realized she'd missed her old friend. Rising to greet him, she offered both her hands. "It is good of you to come."

He wore a wary expression as he took her hands in his. "We are still friends then?"

"I couldn't bear it if we were not." She gestured toward a chair at the table. "Won't you sit?"

He joined her and a footman laid a place for him before withdrawing and leaving them alone. "I hardly know how to begin," he said.

"You behaved very badly." Despite her happiness at seeing him, the shock and hurt of what she'd witnessed the evening of the Harvest Home dance still stung. "It was a betrayal of the worst kind. I entrusted you with my heart."

He winced at the scorching words. "Did you? I never felt I had your heart, not really, but that is no excuse for my behavior."

Her anger lessened, for she recognized he spoke the truth. She'd never given him her heart. It had always belonged to Rand. "Did you take up with Elena because you knew all was not as it should have been between us?"

A pained expression crossed his face. "I suppose I shouldn't be surprised Randolph told you about Elena. I cannot fault him for it."

"Rand knows about you and Elena?"

"I am the lowest of cads, and I owe you the sincerest of apologies even though I know it will be of little comfort. Nothing can excuse my behavior."

"How long has Rand known?"

"Since a fortnight before the Harvest Home. I

comprehended the instant I received your note that he had informed you of my transgression."

"He didn't tell me." Why hadn't he? Especially when he had been trying to win her? It made no sense. "I wasn't aware until this moment that he knew about the two of you."

His brow wrinkled. "Then how did you come to know?"

"It is of no matter." She had no desire to add to his discomfort. "The blame is not yours alone. As you may have surmised by now, my heart was elsewhere. Given the opportunity to be faithless, I might very well have taken it."

"With Randolph?" Surprise registered on his face. "You truly care for him?"

"I do," she said with a gentle smile. "I have since I was sixteen, when my father forbade the match since his prospects were poor."

"And he has since gained an earldom." He leaned toward her, his gaze probing her face. "You are truly happy with your choice?"

"I am."

"You relieve my mind." He sat back in his chair with a heavy exhale. "I've castigated myself these many days since learning you'd married Randolph. I feared my reprehensible actions had driven you into an unhappy arrangement."

"Far from it. I am most content with my husband, and I wish the same for you someday."

"Do you think that, in time, you will find it in your heart to forgive me?"

She hesitated. "Yes, I do believe I will, with time. You are very dear to me." She put her hand over his. "Perhaps we're meant to be the closest of friends rather than husband and wife."

He turned his palm upward to take hold of her hand. "I am fond of you, Kat, but I suppose it is in the way one cares for a sister rather than a lover."

"And what of Elena?"

"I cannot say." A troubled expression lined his handsome visage. "I confess she is not the sort of woman I expected to associate with."

"Do you love her?" At his grimace of discomfort, she added. "You can speak freely...as one friend to another."

He reddened, still clearly ill at ease with the topic. "Elena insists it is primarily a...physical attraction...between us that will soon burn out. She is convinced I have yet to encounter the woman I should take to wife."

"Do you think she has the right of it?"

He sighed. "I am not sure what to think." They spoke a bit more of Elena before turning to other matters. Laurie filled his plate at the sideboard and the conversation flowed easily until he rose to take his leave. After his departure, she spent the morning and the better part of the afternoon busy with household matters. There was still much to be done.

It also took her mind off Rand's whereabouts, although worry niggled in her stomach and she couldn't help wondering where he was. As evening neared, she went upstairs to dress in her pale green gown. Fanny was putting the finishing touches on her hair when music sounded through the door leading to Rand's chamber.

Her heart shifted in her chest as the warm, bright violin notes flowed over her. She smiled at the short sharp exclamations in the music. She rose and followed the sound, the harmony calling her like a siren's song.

Rand stood at the center of his chamber, a look of

intense concentration marking the strong lines of his face, playing the violin she'd ordered for him. The glistening wooden instrument was tucked under his chin and the bow moved in sharp, precise movements. He was already dressed for dinner in his formal clothes, all black except for his snowy cravat. Before him, a small round table with two chairs had been set in a formal fashion for supper, with candles, crystal, and their finest tables settings, which she'd ordered just days ago.

Her chest aching, she closed her eyes to absorb the beauty of it all—the music, Rand, and the splendor of being with him. As long as she lived, she doubted she'd ever know a moment as perfect as this one.

"Are you going to stand there all evening with your eyes closed or do you plan to join me for supper?"

She realized the music had stopped and opened her eyes to find his dark emerald gaze smiling at her. "But we shall be late for Camryn's supper."

"I've postponed that affair." He held out his hand. "Tonight we dine alone."

She moved forward to place her hand in his large warm one. "Why?"

"Because I desire to be in privacy when I play for my wife."

"You played beautifully," she said with feeling. "Just as I remember."

"If so, it was all your doing." He pulled out a chair for her to sit at the table. "Being with you makes me want to hear the music again. And to share it with you."

Cotter and the footman served their meal and then withdrew, leaving them alone to enjoy their meal. "What did you do with your day?" he asked. "I could not help but notice the continuing improvements."

"There is much work to be done." She sipped her claret, savoring its silky fruit flavor. "This house has been too long without a mistress."

"As my valet has said on many occasions. Burgess is now in raptures to have you about." He sliced his meat. "And he is not the only one."

"I also received a visitor today."

"Did you?"

"Yes. Laurie called this morning."

He looked up from his plate with wary interest. "Oh?"

"Yes. He told me you were aware of his indiscretions with Elena, yet word of it never passed your lips. Not even when you were trying to woo me away from him. Why?"

"You had been hurt enough at my hands. I had no desire to add to your pain." He gave a wry smile. "I see your day was not dull in my absence."

"No, it was not." She took a breath. "And what of yours? I worried when I awakened to find you gone."

"Did you? My apologies." He set his fork down. "I spent the better part of the day with Doctor Drummond."

She swallowed. "You discussed your…bouts with him?"

"Yes, I have met with him a few times now and I find his theories to be most interesting. I've decided to continue seeing him to determine whether he can be of assistance."

Relief flowed in her veins. "I am so pleased."

His somber dark eyes held hers. "I fear you will witness quite of a bit of unpleasantness should I experience a fit in your presence."

"I am your wife. I want to share everything with you,

the unpleasant as well as the pleasant," she said fervently. "Doctor Drummond's methods seem to be providing Toby with a measure of relief. Perhaps it will be so with you as well. What happens next?"

"Next we eat." He gestured toward the untouched food in her plate. "And then I shall play for you again — a private show during which clothing will be optional."

Later, after they'd eaten and he'd played the violin for her again, he carried his wife to bed and removed her clothing. He took his time worshipping her body with his hands and mouth, bringing her to pleasure more than once before pushing into her with full strokes. Murmuring words of love and praise, along with a few of the naughty words he'd taught her, they made love late into the evening.

Afterwards, sleepy and deliciously sated, she whispered, "What now?"

He pulled her body against the warm strong length of his and wrapped his arms around her. "Now I am going to sleep with my wife in my arms."

"Through the night?" She asked the words carefully. "You are not sending me back to my chamber so you can sleep alone?"

"Most assuredly not. You're not going anywhere." He tucked her body more firmly against his, enveloping her in his delicious masculine aura. "And neither am I."

# Acknowledgments

My gratitude goes out to Kate Fall, Alethea Spiridon Hopson, and Gwen Hayes for their editorial guidance. Editors really are the unsung heroes in publishing. Thank you for making my books so much better!

Thanks also to Megann Yaqub for talking me off the ledge when I felt this book was faltering and to Joanna Shupe for her encouragement and positive words after reading the first draft of *Engaging the Earl*.

As always, my deepest appreciation goes out to my husband and sons for being such good sports about the long hours I spend planted behind my computer. Publishing this series has been the fulfillment of a dream and it couldn't have happened without their love and support.

And finally, to my readers, thank you from the bottom of my heart for coming along on this journey with me. I can't tell you how much I enjoy hearing your thoughts and opinions about my books. I hope you'll keep those comments coming!

# Author Bio

Diana Quincy is an award-winning television journalist who decided she'd rather make up stories where a happy ending is always guaranteed.

Growing up as a foreign service brat, Diana lived in many countries and is now settled in Virginia with her husband and two sons. When not bent over her laptop or trying to keep up with laundry, she enjoys reading, spending time with her family and dreams of traveling much more than her current schedule (and budget) allows.

Diana loves to hear from readers. You can follow her on Twitter @Diana_Quincy or visit her website at www.dianaquincy.com

Printed in Great Britain
by Amazon

81478755R00154